No Regrets

Patricia Haley-Glass

www.anointedvision.com

Anointed Vision

First Printing 2002
Revised Edition 2016

ISBN 13: 978-0-9663174-0-4
ISBN 10: 0-9663174-0-8

Printed in the United States of America

Publisher: www.anointedvision.com
Email: pop@anointedvision.com

No Regrets

by

Patricia Haley-Glass

Praise for
#1 Essence® & Christian Fiction National Bestselling
Author Patricia Haley-Glass
and
Her Inspirational Novels

"A must read…highly recommend this book…promise you will
not be disappointed."
— *Urban Christian Fiction Today on* Destined

"Haley-Glass engages one with subtle intrigue and touches of comedy…
An intriguing read with a subtle inspirational message woven
into the story…Riveting."
— *Faygo's Report*

"Haley-Glass has a gold mine with this series. If I [were] a hat
wearer, it would definitely be off to her. All I can say to her
right now is, 'You go, girl!'"
— *Member of LVAAABC Book Club*

"Haley-Glass showcases how God's word can be
misinterpreted with greed, lust, and selfishness."
— *RAWSISTAZ*™ *on* Chosen

"Haley-Glass shared how God does choose the most unlikely person for
ministry when we think there is no way. A must read…
Highly recommended."
—*APOOO Book Club*

"Phenomenal ... Haley-Glass did an outstanding job on each person's
outlook and how, without forgiveness, no problem can truly be solved."
— *Urban Reviews*

"The perfect blend of faith and romance."
—*Gospel Book Review*

"I sent your [Mitchell Family] series to my grandson stationed [overseas]
as a Christmas present. He loved the book…Keep those family series
coming, your books are an inspiration to millions."
— *Carol Newman, Sorority Sister & Avid Reader*

Praise

"Haley-Glass has hit the mark yet again! I couldn't put this book down — the characters are believable and compelling."
—*Maurice M. Gray, Jr., author of* All Things Work Together

"The story grabs the reader from the beginning, drawing you in…and keeping you on the edge of your seat as the plot takes unexpected twists and turns."
—*RT Book Reviews on* Let Sleeping Dogs Lie

"Haley's writing and visualization skills are to be reckoned with…This story is full-bodied…Great prose, excellent execution!"
—*RAWSISTAZ™ on* Still Waters

"A deeply moving novel. The characters and the story line remind us that forgiveness and unconditional love are crucial to any relationship."
—*Good Girl Book Club*

"*No Regrets* offered me a different way, a healthier way based in faith and hope, to look at trying situations."
—*Montgomery Newspapers*

"Your books [have] walked me out of my depression and given me the will to be forgiving to my family member. Thank you…"
—*a Cherished Reader*

Titles by **Patricia Haley-Glass**
(as of 2016)

Mitchell Family Drama Series
(listed in chronological story line order)
Anointed
Betrayed
Chosen
Destined
Broken
Humbled
Unforgiving

Redeemed Drama Series
Relentless
Redeemed

Other Titles
Let Sleeping Dogs Lie
Still Waters
Blind Faith
Nobody's Perfect
No Regrets

✦

This book is dedicated to my husband and true love,

Jeffrey W. Glass

You have brought so much joy, laughter, and fun to my life. I've enjoyed traveling the world with you, while at the same time, I'm equally content with us sitting around the house together. I can truly say my heart explodes when I hear your voice or see you smile or watch you enter a room. Sometimes when I'm around you, I feel such an overwhelming wave of love an appreciation for you that it's hard to contain. I like how we laugh over the smallest things. How we can talk about anything, knowing there's at least one person on this earth who's willing to listen. I can't imagine living my entire life without meeting you. When we're apart, I literally countdown the hours.

You are my very best friend, my protector, my confidant, and our marriage has been a dream. I'm incredibly blessed to be your wife. You are a gift beyond imagination and a constant reminder of how gracious God has been to me. I pray that our daughter, nieces, sisters, and goddaughters marry a strong, loving, and godly man like you.

My dear Jeffrey (or as I call you, Baby), you are undoubtedly my soul mate. Thank you for sharing this beautiful journey with me. I love you deeply, now and always.

✦

My flesh and my heart may fail, but God is the
strength of my heart...

—Psalm 73:26

Chapter 1

"Home sweet home" was her unspoken motto, and Karen took pride in creating a haven for her family at any cost. She steadied herself against the mahogany fireplace mantel lined with family photos. Smiling faces captured at proms, birthday parties, graduations, and other special moments created a storybook. Among the memories was also a dusty Bible that had been received as a wedding gift eighteen years ago and a few other favorite trinkets collected from countless vacations, including annual trip to Martha's Vineyard. The Clarks had worked hard to get a slice of the American dream. One glance around the room showed their efforts were paying off.

Head tilted down and eyes closed, she started from the center of her forehead and repeatedly spread her thumb and index finger forcefully slow across her brow like a butterfly struggling to stay in flight.

"Oh, God. Please help me."

Feeling a moment of relief, she meandered to the window, which was squeaky clean as far up as a stepladder-assisted arm could reach. Beyond the beds of spring tulips, Karen could see their collie running around and around the sprawling well-manicured backyard. Going in circles wasn't a question of if, only a matter of when. She envied that the only dilemma their dog had was whether to chase his tail now or later. She stared into the evening wondering where the week had gone and if her husband was coming home on time.

"Mom, Dr. Costas is on the phone."

Karen heard the teen yelling from upstairs. It was occasions like this when she regretted forgoing the intercom package eight years ago when they had the home built. She made her way back across the family room to take the call. She slipped into her favorite chaise longue and picked up the phone that was resting on the marble end table. She didn't bother to return the scream with a thank you. "I got it, Chelle-baby. You can put the phone down now. Thank you."

"Karen, this is Dr. Costas. I got a message that you called. What's going on?"

"I've had a throbbing headache for the past few days. Nothing major."

"Hmmm."

"I didn't want to take any medication without checking with you first."

"Good. Under normal conditions, it would be fine, but we've come a long way. It's been a tough fight and we don't want any setbacks in your remission."

"I know."

"Do you have any nausea or any problems with your bowels?"

"No. No fever, no fatigue, no chills either."

Karen knew the routine list of questions Dr. Costas asked whenever there was potential trouble brewing. Each time Karen got sick, she didn't find it any easier. She wanted to be brave in facing her health challenges but found herself more often afraid. She couldn't decide which was worse, knowing or not knowing.

"Good. There doesn't seem to be any need for alarm. Let's start with a simple over-the-counter pain reliever, something like Extra Strength Tylenol or Advil? Let's try that first. If the headache persists, give me another call in a few days, and we'll get you in for a look. Karen, it's also going to be important that you keep your stress level down. Remember pressure really seems to take a toll on you and we don't want to wear your immune system down. So, take some time to relax over the weekend. That's the best medicine I can prescribe for you right now. Okay?"

"That's fine. Thanks, doctor."

The phone rang as Karen put it down. Caught off guard by

the incoming call, she put the phone up to her ear to see who was on the line.

"Hey, Karen," a deep voice bellowed.

"Oh, Johnny, it's you."

"Why you say it like that? Were you expecting somebody else?"

Karen knew he wasn't really looking for an answer. She kept quiet.

"What a way to answer the phone. You answer it like one of the kids."

Early in his career he'd spent seven years as a production line supervisor before getting promoted to senior management. Barking out orders at work carried over into his personal life.

Karen heard Johnny loud and clear, internalized his comment, and opted to say nothing in her own defense. She'd learned that his personality didn't accommodate timidity or shortcomings in others.

"I just got off the phone with Dr. Costas. She told me to take some Tylenol for my headache."

"Tylenol? That's it? See you should have taken the pain pills like I suggested a few days ago. You would have been over it by now."

"I didn't want to take anything without talking to the doctor, Johnny."

"No, you'd rather sit around and whine."

"The doctor's job is to give me medical advice. It's not like either of us went to medical school," Karen snapped.

"You don't have to go to med school to know you should take a painkiller when you have a headache. That's basic common sense. Not everything has to be dramatic, Karen."

She cut in and tried to change the subject. "Well, could you stop by the pharmacy on your way home and pick up some Extra Strength Tylenol for me?"

"I wasn't planning to come straight home. I'm going to

make a quick stop, and I'll be in later."

"Later." Karen sighed. She hesitated before voicing her frustration.

"What's the big deal, Karen? I asked Tyrone to meet me at Floods for a hot minute."

Silence fell over the line.

Years ago, Karen hadn't been fond of Tyrone, back when she saw him as a partying bachelor who had been married and divorced several times with no intention of settling down. Those were the times when she had viewed him as a bad influence on her husband. That was long before she was willing to accept the truth. Johnny's strong personality didn't allow anyone too much influence in his life. He made up his own mind. Yet she found it more comfortable to blame her marital issues on outside factors. So long as nothing was her fault, she didn't have to take responsibility for fixing it.

"What about the card game?" Karen asked.

"What card game?"

"The one the Burks are having."

Karen knew she didn't feel up to going, but if dragging to their friends' place was what it took to get Johnny's attention, she was willing to go.

"Oh, yeah, okay, the couple from your church. You didn't tell me anything about a card game."

Karen knew that telling him in advance would not have made a difference. Friday was turning out to be his night, and nothing interfered.

"I already have plans. Why don't you go on without me?"

"Why do I always have to go without you? Why can't you just come home after work on Friday, for a change?"

"There you go. I try to be considerate and let you know where I'm going. This is the thanks I get. You make a big deal out of my taking a few hours every now and then to stop by the club and wind down."

"You've been doing this every Friday night for three solid

months."

"See, you're exaggerating. It hasn't been that long."

"Oh, yes, it has. It started right after New Year's, right after I closed the business."

She realized that her unemployment was a sore topic with Johnny and didn't expect him to acknowledge the truth, but his silence was confirmation enough. He hadn't agreed with her decision to quit. Her interior decorating business was doing well, but she felt it had become too much trying to manage a household, children, her health, and a career. Despite his disapproval, she closed her business in hopes of finding something less demanding. So far nothing promising had come along.

"Before, you only went out once every couple of months. That was fine," she said.

"No, it wasn't. You complained about that too."

"It was better than this. I'm here alone every single Friday night."

"You're not alone. The girls are there."

"You know what I mean. You're hanging out every Friday night is not fair to me."

"You're talking about fair. I work hard all week in order to take care of the bills, you and the kids? Remember, I don't have all week to relax like you. Somebody has to work." He took a deep breath. "I can't believe you won't allow me to have a few hours to hang out without breathing down my neck with this guilt trip. I mean, it's not like I'm doing anything out here. I don't press you about going to church so much. Why do you always have something to say about the little bit of time I take for myself?"

"I'm sorry, but I wanted us to do something together." A whisper was the most she could handle. Eyes closed tightly, she pressed her forefinger against one temple to alleviate the pain.

"If you're really serious about doing something together, I

have a few ideas."

Karen suspected Johnny was talking about sex, and she wanted to avoid his hint. "Well, I'm tired and I don't feel up to doing too much."

"That's what I thought." Johnny grunted heavily. "Look, I've already made a commitment for this evening, but we can do something tomorrow. I might even go to church Sunday."

"Fine, Johnny."

Yet again, Karen had stirred the pot of emotions. She tried to perk up and get past her disappointment. She was feeling less and less guilty about questioning his time out. She wanted to trust Johnny but didn't know how. Doubting had become a natural state of being. He hadn't made it any easier.

Karen rested her eyes, pulled her knees into a tight fetal position, and allowed her thoughts, fears, and insecurities to drift away. For a fleeting moment, she was free.

Chapter 2

Johnny could still turn the heads of women when he walked into a room. His six-foot-two silhouette stood in the arched doorway of the large banquet room. He kept his slightly graying hair short to draw attention away from the fact that he was balding. He no longer had the trim body he sported in college. Over the years, extra pounds had taken up residency on his physique. His age had started showing, but his handsome demeanor was still winning out.

Dim lighting, stimulating music, a few appetizers, and a stiff drink provided just the right mix to set Johnny's evening into motion. Floods was known for attracting a professionally dressed and diverse after work crowd.

Self-confidence, sometimes mistaken for arrogance, often oozed out of Johnny whenever he entered a room. Tonight was no different. His camel-colored tailored suit rounded out any rough edges in his appearance. Friday was usually casual day at Tenner Automotive, where Johnny was executive vice president of manufacturing and plant manager of the metal products division. No casual clothes for him. Although he had neglected to share his plans with Karen, Johnny knew early in the morning he was stopping by his favorite hangout after work and opted to dress the part.

He eased into the room like a warm knife slicing butter. There was the usual happy hour crowd in the place. Johnny had been coming to this club for over eleven years, with more frequency in recent months. He knew the regulars and was on automatic alert for the newbies, which was his term for new faces in the place.

Floods was one place Johnny was glad Karen chose not to frequent. Her presence at his favorite nightspot would cripple his ability to flirt with the women the way he enjoyed.

Standing near the bar was Johnny's close friend Tyrone. Johnny slinked through the crowded room and approached him.

"Hey, what's up, buddy?"

The two clasped hands, pulled toward their chests, and did their brotherly greeting.

"You got it, chief," Tyrone responded between cigarette drags.

Tyrone kept using the nickname he'd given Johnny at the onset of their friendship twenty-two years ago to reflect his take charge attitude. They had initially met in college, pledged the same fraternity, and ended up in the same city ten years later. IBM had relocated Tyrone many times. The two had lost contact during Tyrone's frequent moves. But they both ended up in Detroit and had unexpectedly run into one another at Floods nearly a decade.

Both leaned on the bar and Johnny scoped the room.

"It's crowded in here." Tyrone took another drag on his cigarette.

Johnny spotted two empty seats amid the crowd. 'There are a couple of seats over there, right next to those honeys."

Tyrone hadn't noticed and said to Johnny, "I don't mind sitting here at the bar." The club scene wasn't Tyrone's thing any more. There was a time in his past when he could have settled in comfortably during an evening out. He'd matured beyond his rambunctious twenties and thirties and had stopped chasing women after marrying Connie.

"Nah, come on, man," Johnny said. "Let's ease on over. It won't hurt anything. It's light conversation with a couple of nice looking ladies. It's not like we're trying to start a serious relationship with them. Come on, man."

Tyrone sighed and followed his friend toward a table in the middle of the room without further resistance.

The two men casually strolled toward the young women

with Johnny taking the lead. "Good evening, ladies."

The women acknowledged them with a simple greeting.

"We noticed the empty seats. Do you mind if we sit with you?" Johnny asked.

While waiting for the okay to join the women, Johnny checked their ring fingers. He knew married men like him didn't always wear wedding bands, but women were more likely to wear theirs.

"Not at all."

"I'm Johnny, and this is Tyrone." Johnny patted his friend on the back. Noticing the women's empty glasses, Johnny asked, "Can we get you another drink?"

The two ladies declined.

Unlike Johnny, Tyrone wasn't interested in sitting down for a warm and fuzzy, get to know you conversation with the two ladies. He wanted to keep the encounter impersonal.

"Hey, I'm heading back to the bar to pick up my pack of cigarettes that I left over there. Can I get anyone anything?" Tyrone asked.

One of the young ladies said, "I could use a cigarette. I'll walk over with you."

Tyrone wasn't expecting any company on his short trip to the bar. He was willing to let Johnny entertain both women. Uneasy, he politely led the way through the crowd to the bar, unable to make a clean break.

Johnny eyed the woman as she left the table. Her switching hips moved like sand being sifted from one hand to the other. He recalled how much of a hip man his friend used to be. Johnny found full-busted women a bit more attractive, which was why his acceptance of Karen's mastectomy two years ago had been such a surprise.

Johnny was left at the table with the other lady. He was not shy about starting up a conversation.

"You work around here, uh...?" He waited for her to give a name.

"Isabelle."

"What did you say?" Johnny wasn't sure if he heard her correctly.

"My name is Isabelle."

Johnny leaned back in his seat and exhibited quite a bit of discomfort. He picked up the book of matches from the center of the small table and twirled them between his fingers.

Isabelle noticed his behavior and asked, "What's wrong?"

He placed his elbow on the arm of the chair and covered his mouth for a moment.

"Oh, nothing really." He chuckled. "It's just your name, Isabelle. I had a close friend once named Isabelle. It's not a very common name. As a matter of fact, you're only the second person I've met named Isabelle."

"I hope that's good."

"Could be," Johnny flirted. "So, do you?"

"Do I what?"

"Do you work around here?"

"Not too far away."

Johnny stirred the small red straw in his drink, and said, "I haven't seen you here before."

"That's because I don't come here often."

And there it was. He'd found a newby. They were his preference, the ones who presented a lower probability of knowing his routine flirtatious behavior. He was hoping Isabelle wasn't going to ask about his marital status too early in the conversation. If necessary, he was ready with his standard line. "I'm just looking for a friend and this doesn't have anything to do with my marriage" spiel.

"Can I get you another drink?" he offered.

"Sure."

Johnny motioned for the cocktail waitress who came over right away to take their order. He placed his hand lightly on Isabelle's hand. "What are you drinking?"

"Strawberry daiquiri."

"And I'll take a shot of Hennessy, straight up."

The waitress scribbled the order on a napkin and left.

Johnny leaned back in the chair, rested his wrist on the table, and gazed into Isabelle's eyes. She looked away before her smile completely manifested.

"So, if you don't come here much, what does a beautiful woman like you do for fun?"

Isabelle blushed from the compliment, giving Johnny the impression that she was easily flattered. That was when Johnny knew he had her. He felt safe with Isabelle, figuring that it was highly unlikely that she knew his wife. It would be easy to work his magic. Since Isabelle struck him as someone who didn't get out much.

Every indicator pointed to an easy rendezvous without fear of being caught cheating, but he was on alert. His game seemed to work best with a married woman or a party girl who was looking for fun without commitment. The sheltered good girl type was too dangerous. Johnny didn't want to kick off a fatal attraction with a single, available, and searching woman. He wanted companionship without any strings attached.

A shred of a good time away from his problems was what he needed. He wasn't looking for a wife, seeing he already had one of those at home. Isabelle was a red flag, but something about the game drew him in. There remained the possibility that she was married. He had to find out.

"Do you and your husband come here a lot?"

"Not now, but we used to come here."

Ah, Johnny thought, *she is married.* The hot and heavy pursuit was back on.

The waitress placed a small napkin in front of Johnny and Isabelle. She plopped their drinks onto the table and asked for ten dollars. He plucked a fifty-dollar bill from his pocket and placed it on the small round tray. Tipping and spending were key parts of the player's MO. Johnny had to look good from every angle: clean-cut, fine suit, sharp car, and fat, dollar-filled pockets.

"Keep five for yourself."

"Thanks," the waitress said and whisked away.

Charm had top billing in his deliberate approach. Johnny took time to lay his trap. Now it was time to go in for the thrill.

"How can your husband let someone as beautiful as you come out by yourself?"

Johnny relied on his standard line since it had proven repeatedly effective in determining the condition of a potential candidate's marital relationship.

"My husband and I are separated."

Jackpot. Johnny was pleased. Years of experience led him to believe 'separated' generally meant "unavailable for a long-term relationship but suitable for a short-term rendezvous." It was easy to take the game home from here.

"Ah, that's too bad," Johnny said. "I know how that goes."

"Why, are you separated, too?"

"I guess you could say so. My wife and I have some major differences that we can't fix. We mostly stay together for the kids. I do my thing, and she does hers."

He had already tested Isabelle's morality by exposing his marriage and letting the chips fall as they might. Even though he was married, she hadn't left. Just the kind Johnny liked. The kind who knew he was unfaithful and liked him anyway.

"How many kids do you have?" she asked.

"Three."

He held his head down and stirred his drink again. As much of a ladies' man as he professed to be, questions about his children often penetrated his steel exterior. He was uninhibited when talking about Karen, but discussing his kids with another woman somehow felt wrong.

Tyrone had given the other woman no cause to hang around. He was sitting at the bar alone. He glanced at his watch and realized it was already a quarter to eight. He made eye contact with Johnny, who was knee-deep into flirting. Tyrone held up his wrist and pointed to his watch several times. He didn't mind meeting Johnny for a drink from time to time but always knew when it was time to go home.

Johnny got the message. "It's getting late, I'm going to head home," he told Isabelle. Can I give you a ride?" He stood up and buttoned his double-breasted jacket.

"If you don't mind. I live off the Lodge Expressway," she responded as they approached the bar.

"No problem. I'm going that way. Tyrone, I'm heading out, man. I'm giving Isabelle a ride."

"All right, chief. I'll catch you later."

Tyrone gave Johnny a look that said, "Yeah, partner, you'd better be careful."

Heading for the door, Johnny helped Isabelle put on her jacket.

Outside, he pulled a parking ticket from his pants pocket and handed it to the valet.

Johnny saw Isabelle's eyelids widen as the car approached.

He peeled a ten-dollar bill from his pocket as the valet attendant drove the new Cadillac up to the curb.

He walked around to the passenger's side of the car and opened the door for Isabelle. He hadn't opened the door for Karen in ten years, but then she wasn't someone he had to impress.

Johnny and Karen's sexual connection had repeatedly deteriorated after her cancer recoveries. Her doctors had confirmed there was no physical limitation, but it hadn't improved their intimacy drought. Johnny chalked it up to lack of interest on her part. Instead of figuring out how to rekindle eighteen years of marriage, he found ways to survive.

Turning forty had been traumatic, although he wouldn't openly admit it. He'd purchased a Porsche to stroke his aging ego which hadn't gone over too well given that he was an executive working for an American auto supplier. Even though he could barely fit, Johnny hoped the car would restore his youth. It hadn't. None of his material purchases filled the void. Feeling wanted and admired by other women seemed to be the only vice that worked.

He wasn't seeking a serious relationship with someone else. The women he pursued at the club were mostly for the thrill of the hunt, and on occasion went further during times when Karen had unofficially declared a sexual sabbatical. He liked playing the player's game from time to time. It did wonders for his ego.

"Johnny, Johnny," a sultry voice echoed over his shoulder.

He turned to see who it was.

"Tina!" He went cold on the inside, but struggled to maintain his composure. Of all the people he could have run into, Johnny was wondering why it had to be her, Ms. Motor mouth. Karen's nosy friend was the last person he wanted to see.

Tina flashed a cunning grin, knowing Johnny was caught in the act. She had him right where she wanted—squirming.

"How's Karen?" Tina asked while getting a good look at the lady sitting in her girlfriend's car.

He closed the door and walked toward the driver's side of the car. "She's fine."

"Tell my friend I said hello." Tina walked past the car and without looking back said, "No, better yet, I'll just call her myself."

"Will do." Johnny echoed as he jumped into his car. He was hoping to drive away as quickly as possible and avoid any undesired drama.

The twenty-minute drive was filled with small talk and moments of complete silence. The unexpected run-in with Tina had put a damper on Johnny's playboy routine.

He cruised to Isabelle's house without much enthusiasm.

"I'll give you my number," Isabelle offered.

She took a small piece of paper from her purse and wrote her home number on it.

Johnny took it, glanced at the writing, and shoved it into his pocket. Glancing away from her eyes, he said, "It's been nice meeting you."

He didn't want to give Isabelle his work number, but any other number was out of the question. He rattled off his number with the last two digits transposed. If he ever ran into her again, he could claim she wrote the number down incorrectly. For now, it was better to minimize contact.

As soon as Isabelle got out of the car, he pulled off without extending any extra courtesies. Three blocks down the road, he was back in husband mode.

"Ooh," he blurted. He'd neglected to schedule their home appraisal. His palm covered his mouth as his fingers scraped his chin. How could he forgot something so important? Finding a way to relieve the financial pressure was crucial with Karen out of work. Most of their emergency money was gone, and his retirement plan was not an option. They had already tapped that too many times. Refinancing seemed to be the only answer.

A few other homes in their suburban neighborhood had sold for well over four hundred thousand. He was hoping there was some equity left from the previous refinancing. They got fifty thousand out four years ago when Karen first got sick and was off work for months without warning. Two years ago the most they could get was another forty to help out while she was laid up. He needed enough to cover the next three to six months, plenty of time for Karen to get back on her feet.

Johnny sat at the stop sign, turned on his cell phone, and dialed home to see if Karen still needed him to stop by the pharmacy and pick up anything. His best hope was that Tina hadn't told Karen about his escapade at Floods.

Karen answered the phone to hear Johnny on the other end.

"Hey, I'm on my way home," he said.

"It's about time."

"I told you I was going to be out."

"If I'd known you were going to take this long, I would have gotten the Tylenol myself."

"Look, I'm tired and your nagging is really starting to get on my nerves."

"Well, I'm sorry, but I deserve a more consideration."

"I'll be there when I get there. "Bye." *Beep* went the sound of the disconnecting cell phone.

Johnny was feeling the weight of running a plant and taking care of a family. He was doing the best he could, but the only gratitude he got from Karen was suspicions and constant badgering. He thought more and more about what he'd been working for. He didn't want to give up living the American dream, but Johnny felt the installments were becoming too difficult to keep up. Something was going to have to give—and soon.

Karen heard the dial tone and put the receiver on the hook. When the phone rang again, she grabbed it.

"Johnny?"

"No, it's not Johnny. This is Tina, Karen. How are you?"

Chapter 3

The morning light poked through the loosely closed window blinds. Karen wanted to talk. She rolled over next to her snoring husband. Whatever drinks he'd consumed the night before had ushered him into a deep sleep. Since he wasn't awake, she decided to get up and start the Saturday morning chores.

For a while, a maid service had done the major cleaning. It had been a godsend during her mastectomy and chemo over two years ago, when she was too weak to do anything.

Johnny cut out the hundred and fifty dollar weekly maid service. With a three thousand dollar monthly mortgage and one paycheck coming in, it was an easy decision for him. His perspective was, "You're at home. You should have plenty of time to clean."

Cleaning the huge house was too much for Karen to do single-handedly. Saturday morning was the only block of time when the children could help. So, it was officially deemed the Clark's housecleaning time.

Karen entered the walk-in closet, which was equivalent in size to a small bedroom. An array of clothes filled the automated circular spindle, which resembled the kind found in dry cleaners. She pulled the dirty clothes from the hamper and quietly pushed them down the chute. It was a modern convenience, which eliminated her need to lug baskets of clothes from the master bedroom to the basement.

With an empty basket in hand, she headed down the long hallway lined with photos. The first room she passed on the left was the guest room. The next sparsely decorated room on the left belonged to her eldest child, John Erick. Erick, as the family called him, had graduated high school one year early and was now completing a foreign exchange program during his second year at Stanford. She stuck her head into the room directly across the hall from his room.

"Chelle, are you up?"

"I'm getting up," the teenager responded.

The fifth bedroom belonged to eight-year-old Elizabeth, the baby of the family.

"Bethy," Karen affectionately called. She'd created play names for her daughters, often saying, "It's just an extra dose of motherly love."

Karen's gentle approach this morning didn't net more than a muffled groan coming from her daughter who was covered up in the middle of the bed.

"Get up, sweetie."

"Already?"

"I told you about staying up so late. See, now you're tired. Get up before your father goes downstairs and sees a messy kitchen. Get your dirty clothes together, too."

Although Elizabeth was the youngest, she was given household responsibilities like the other kids. Johnny thought it was important for them to carry their own weight from an early age.

Karen didn't stop until she got to the laundry room downstairs. She dumped the basket of clothes sitting under the chute and separated the laundry from those items needing dry cleaning. Routinely, she checked the pockets on garments before shipping them off to the cleaners. It was common for her to find money and other miscellaneous items in the pockets of her family's clothes. She reached into Johnny's shirt and pulled out a piece of paper with the name Isabelle. On the note was scribbled, *Home phone.*

"What's this?" she uttered.

The phone number threw her for a loop. Karen stood in the laundry room completely spellbound. Her heart raced, and she took a step back to maintain balance.

"Isabelle!"

The memories of six years ago flooded Karen's thoughts as though it were only yesterday. That was when she had found out about Johnny and Isabelle's affair. It had taken every bit of strength she could muster to get past that dark point in their marriage. Karen thought the thing with Isabelle was over and had been for years.

Why would Johnny have her number in his pocket?

"Here are my clothes," Chelle said, startling her mom back into consciousness.

"Separate the rest of these clothes and start the wash," Karen mumbled in her distracted state.

"Mom, I have to finish my essay."

"That's because you were on that phone last night. All right, young lady, go finish the essay and then get right back down here and do this laundry."

"Thanks, Mom." Chelle gave her mother a quick peck on the cheek. "I'm sure glad we have two washing machines. Otherwise this would take forever."

Johnny crept down the long corridor, noticing lights on in the bathroom and in the bedrooms. He headed down the back staircase, which deposited him between the family room and kitchen.

He yelled coming down the stairs, "Who has so many lights on?"

The Hennessy shots which had helped Johnny wind down at Floods the night before had him in a foul mood. Anyone crossing his path this morning was bound to get their feelings hurt.

Elizabeth and Karen were coming up the basement stairs as Johnny was walking by.

"Elizabeth, get upstairs and turn off some of those lights," he demanded. "Where's yesterday's mail?"

"Johnny, it's on the dining room table." Karen pointed. Her nerves were in full bloom. She had many questions for Johnny, but didn't want to broach the subject with the girls present.

He poured a cup of coffee and glanced out the kitchen window.

"Has anyone fed the dog?"

Apparently, neither Karen nor the two girls responded quickly enough.

He slammed the coffee mug down on the counter and belted out, "I said, did anyone feed the dog?"

His stern, commanding tone got the attention of everyone in the room.

"Did you guys feed the dog?" Karen asked Chelle and Elizabeth before Johnny blew a gasket.

She didn't normally interfere when he disciplined the kids. Johnny was a good provider who wanted the best for his children. Both her and Johnny were proud to have three smart, honor roll children who were most likely headed for prestigious careers. However, there were occasions, like this morning, when she thought he was being a little too hard with the girls.

"I didn't," Chelle answered.

"It's Chelle's week," Elizabeth interjected.

"How many times do I have to tell you to feed the dog? Get out there right now," Johnny bellowed.

Chelle didn't budge. She fully intended to carry out her father's order, like a good soldier, just as soon as she finished writing a paragraph in her English essay.

Johnny tolerated no hesitation. "Didn't you hear me? Do it now."

"Chelle, just go feed the dog," Karen calmly reinforced. "Johnny, yelling at the kids doesn't help."

"Look, don't tell me how to handle the kids." He turned to Chelle, who was scooping the dry food into a bucket. "Next time, young lady, don't make me have to remind you. And when I say do something, I mean right away, not when you get ready. Got that?"

"Yes, Daddy." She sniffed.

Sipping his coffee, Johnny picked up the stack of mail lying on the dining room table.

"I need help around here," Johnny said. "Everyone knows what they're supposed to be doing."

"Elizabeth, honey, go out there and help your sister feed the dog. When you finish, both of you go back downstairs and finish washing the clothes, okay?"

"Yes, Mom."

Elizabeth gave her mom a hug and headed outside.

Karen and Johnny were left alone in their large, eat-in kitchen.

"You seem to be in a bad mood this morning."

Johnny continued opening the mail without response.

Before blurting out her question about why Isabelle's number was in his pocket, Karen wanted to let him calm down.

"Tina called me last night."

That got his attention. He didn't know how much she had told Karen about his choice of companionship at the club last night. "Ooh, boy. Here we go. What did that meddling witch want?" Before Karen could respond, an irritated Johnny spoke again. "Nah, nah. Don't tell me." He slammed the cup down on the table and the warm coffee spurted onto the table. "Miss Meddling makes one call and next you'll be accusing me of cheating."

"Why, have you been?"

"You tell me. You're the one doing the talking." Feeling uncomfortable and cornered, Johnny got up to get another cup of hot coffee.

"I'm not accusing you of anything, yet. I'm simply asking you a question."

"Karen, how can you listen to Tina after what we've been through? Why are you so determined to let your friend drive us to divorce court? You saw how she drove her man away, and she probably wants you to be in the same position." He pulled a clump of napkins from the table holder and plopped them on top of the coffee mess. "Don't you know, misery loves company."

"Johnny, why are you so worked up? Tina called about dinner next Saturday."

"Then why did you ask me if I was cheating? Where did that come from?"

"You brought it up, not me. But since you did, maybe I can ask you about the phone number I found in your pocket this morning?"

Through several bad encounters, he had learned not to keep loose numbers in his pockets. It was an open invitation for Karen to find the number and create a less than pleasant marital scene. The run-in with Tina threw him out of sync. Now he was paying for his carelessness.

"So now you're snooping around in my pockets? The number you found belongs to a coworker who was nice enough to help me put together the business plan for my marketing idea."

Johnny knew every strategic maneuver in the book of *Get Out of Trouble If Caught*. His tactic was to use the simple reverse psychology strategy for the awkward predicament.

"Think about it. If it were someone I was seeing, do you think I would have left her number in a place so easy for you to find? She was kind enough to offer her services. It's not like you're offering to help me put the plan together."

"Johnny, I'm not letting you put me down. Just because I'm not working doesn't mean I don't want to help." Karen's voice escalated, even though it increased the throbbing pain in her head. "Why was Isabelle's phone number in your pocket? Are you seeing her again?"

"Isabelle? Come on, Karen."

"Come on, Karen, what?"

"You think I'm seeing Isabelle? Give me some credit." He

stood up in a cloud of fury. "Huh, Isabelle, of all people." He smirked. His reaction was as if the mere thought of Karen's suggestion was ridiculous and without any merit. He wanted Karen to let it go, but he knew she wasn't ready.

"When was the last time you talked with her?"

Johnny turned in Karen's direction and forcefully said, "How many times do I have to go through this, Karen? I said, this Isabelle is a coworker. She's not the one you're thinking about."

"How do I know for sure?"

"Boy, I don't need this. I need some peace around here. I work hard all week. I want some peace on my weekends. You have the whole week to sit around here and worry about stuff that isn't even happening. I have apologized over and over. I have all but kissed your behind, and it's not good enough for you, is it? It's been six years and you refuse to let it go."

Johnny pushed his chair back with full force, screeching along the way.

"Johnny, I'm trying to talk to you."

"No, I'm through talking. Since you have so much time to focus on what I'm doing, why don't you spend some time trying to help me out? If you would help a little, maybe I would be able to get home earlier. I work too hard to stand around here and let you accuse me of something stupid like seeing Isabelle again. Better yet, let's put it this way. Since you don't care enough to help me take care of this place, you shouldn't care about whatever else I do."

"How long am I supposed to put up with you?"

"Put up with me?" Johnny chuckled. "Maybe that's something I should be asking you."

"I don't know what you mean. I've been a good wife to you."

"Good wife, huh. Would that be before or after you quit having sex with me? Before or after you decided to close up shop when you know that we have a child in college and an extravagant lifestyle? Huh, what about that? When you can come up with those answers, then we have something to talk about."

"You're just letting the devil corrupt you. You're not even trying to hear God."

"No, you didn't. You need to lay off your religious crap, Karen. God, God, God, holy, holy, holy. I am sick of your self-righteous holier than thou attitude. Trust me. You have some issues too, sweetheart."

Johnny and Karen both knew how to push each other's hot buttons. Karen felt a sense of power when she exposed his lagging religious convictions. Johnny would get the upper hand in the argument when he harped on her limited professional achievements. It was a weapon that both kept fully loaded and ready to fire off on short notice.

Karen ignored his implication and continued to speak her mind.

"What do you expect me to do, Johnny? Do you expect me to find a woman's home number in your pocket and just let it go without saying anything?"

"Honestly, I can't tell you what to do. You're good about making decisions on your own. You don't need my input. The best decision you can make at this moment is to leave me alone."

Karen and Johnny had been there many times before with the speculations, put downs and accusations. Like clock-work, this was the point in the argument when he would feel guilty and walk away. She'd buckle under pressure and cry. He didn't budge. Her eyelids were swollen but not a tear fell. This time was different.

Chapter 4

The atmosphere was thick and jaws were tight around the Clarks. Karen was stirring around the kitchen, making her usual full course Sunday morning breakfast. She seemed to garner a special bit of joy when cooking for her family and bringing them together, if only for one morning each week. Grits were simmering, pancakes browning, sausage sizzling, bacon frying, hash browns sautéing, fruit sliced, and strong coffee brewing. The blended aromas drew in anyone who was within a whiff of the kitchen.

There was the appearance of normalcy, but in actuality, it wasn't status quo around the house for Karen. Yesterday had not been such a good day for her and Johnny. *How could he do this again? Why?* She put the fork down and stared out the window for a moment, as if the answers were scribbled across the lawn.

I know that's got to be Isabelle. Does he really think I'm that stupid? I just can't believe he would hurt me like this, not again, she thought repeatedly.

The percolating anger gave her chopping fingers extra zeal. A pile of diced vegetables cut in record time was the evidence. Karen scooped the onions and green peppers up and slammed them into the skillet. Her hands were saturated with onion juice. She lifted her shoulder to brush a tear falling from the corner of her left eye. She sighed and let her head droop in discontent.

Usually it was one of the kids who reached the kitchen first on Sunday. Today it was Mr. Clark. He entered, knowing Karen was mad. She had avoided him Saturday afternoon and had gone to bed exceptionally early. He figured she intended to be asleep well before he got in the bed. Johnny picked up the newspaper Karen had laid on the table as tension loomed. He didn't care for the silent treatment. He could dish it out frequently but couldn't take rejection being tossed at him.

"So, what's the deal? Are you going the entire day without saying anything?" Karen continued ignoring Johnny for fear of getting into an unpleasant conversation in the presence of the girls.

"Karen, I know you hear me. How long are you going to keep up the silent treatment?"

"Johnny, I'm not giving you the silent treatment. I'm just cooking breakfast."

"Yeah, right. You think I can't tell you're mad? What else do you want me to do? I told you that number belongs to a business colleague. Why can't you just believe me for once and let it go?"

"Humph. You know why I can't let it go."

"No, I don't."

Karen firmly put down the carton of juice and turned to Johnny with more conviction and guts than she was accustomed to showing.

"Johnny, you may think I'm stupid and naive because I let you run around, hang out, and do what you want to do. Oh, but trust me, I'm far from being stupid. I let things go because I love what we have. But that doesn't mean you can treat me like I'm a fool. You know the number belongs to Isabelle Jones. And here I am—after all this time, thinking she was long gone and you were over her."

"She is, and I am. I keep telling you, this isn't Isabelle Jones." Johnny chuckled because this time he was actually telling the truth and Karen didn't believe him. He sensed that no matter what the story was, when it came to Isabelle, Karen wasn't buying it.

"If you want, I will even introduce you to her."

"Okay, introduce me."

Johnny offered the introduction as a good faith gesture to

ease Karen's discomfort. He took great effort in concealing his extracurricular activities. Under no circumstances did he plan on introducing his wife to a woman he was flirting with in the club. At least for now, it looked like Karen was softening.

Karen looked right through Johnny and knew he was lying. Yet it didn't sting as much as it did six years ago, when she had caught him cheating. The affair with Isabelle nearly cost them their marriage. It had taken every bit of the past years to recover from Johnny's ultimate betrayal of getting another woman pregnant. She had worked hard to hold the family and its image together. Although spiritually she didn't believe it was right to rejoice in someone else's misery, she was relieved when Isabelle miscarried Johnny's illegitimate baby. Somehow the unfortunate event enabled Karen to stay in the marriage. Whatever peace she felt during the agonizing period was short-lived with the cancer coming a few years later.

Sensing Karen's return to serenity, Johnny relaxed a bit. "Don't forget that we have the executive banquet." Karen closed her eyes and let her three middle fingers press into her forehead. Up and down, up and down. Any gesture that could help relieve the mounting anxiety was welcomed.

"Is that today?" she asked.

"Yes, and the CEO is coming which means I have to be there."

Karen had attended numerous black-tie affairs. It was the kind of life she'd grown accustomed to in Johnny's climb to the executive VP and plant manager positions. She enjoyed the various social events. But today wasn't one of her best, and she was not thrilled about going. "What time do I need to be dressed?"

"The program begins at three and the reception starts at two."

"Where is it?"

"In Detroit, at the Renaissance Center. So we should leave

here by one in order to get downtown and get parked."

"One? Johnny, you know I don't get out of church until one."

"I know, but what's more important, Karen? Let's face it. I haven't seen Greater Faith Chapel on any paychecks around here. The only employer I see is Tenner Automotive. That ought to give you some hint of where our priorities should be."

Johnny attempted to soften his appeal, realizing he was coming across in a condescending way. "Can't you miss one Sunday, or at least leave early?"

"You don't miss Floods on Friday, no matter what. Why do I always have to miss church because you have planned something else for me to do?"

"This isn't some trivial event, Karen. This banquet is important for my career. It should be important to you."

"Church is important to me, too."

"Come on, Karen. One Sunday won't kill you. Besides, you're so holy and perfect anyway," Johnny said in a semi joking fashion.

"According to you, it's only the heathens like me who need to be up in the church every time the door flies open."

"Yeah, you do. So why don't you?"

"Look, let's not get too serious. I'm not getting into a heavy argument about the church and the God thing, Karen. This is not the time. Even God had a day of rest. Can't you give me one?"

"Whether you go to church or not is up to you, Johnny."

"That's right. It's up to me, and your pushing won't get me there any faster. Tell you what," he said, nuzzling up to her, "I'll go with you Mother's Day. How's that? Won't that be nice for us to go as a family?"

She had managed to get through much of the morning without a headache. It was the first time in a long while. The last thing she wanted to do was get one started by arguing with Johnny. Agreeing and keeping quiet seemed to be the path of least resistance and, ultimately, less pain.

"Sure, Johnny, whatever," Karen said, and pushed away from his affectionate gesture.

"In the meantime, I need you with me this afternoon." Without any zeal, Karen looked at Johnny and said, "I'll be ready by one."

"Oh, yeah, I forgot to tell you. I looked over the budget for the next six months. We'll need to take out another equity loan for about eighty thousand dollars in order to make ends meet while you're off. The extra will give us enough to cover Erick's tuition for two quarters, plus be able to pay off one of the vehicles," he said.

"We have to do that again? We've been taking out a loan every couple of years. We'll never get the mortgage paid off like that."

"That's because you're off work every couple of years."

"Like I can help it."

"I'm not saying that you can. I'm only stating the facts."

"We don't have to get the loan. We can make adjustments in our budget," she stated.

"Really? I don't see you rushing to move out of this house or offering to give up one of our cars for a clunker. I don't see you tossing in any of your furs. You can't have it both ways. You can't quit work and want to keep living in the lap of luxury. Something has to give."

The alluring smell of breakfast traveled through the main floor. Chelle hustled into the kitchen. "I'm hungry," she said, causing her parents to terminate their discussion.

"It's ready. Go get Elizabeth."

"She's on her way down. Oh, yeah, Mom, can I stay after church for the teen meeting?"

"Not today, Chelle." Karen rolled her eyes at Johnny. "We can't stay for service."

"Why not?" the disappointed youth asked.

"Because, honey, we're only going to Sunday school and coming straight back afterward. Daddy and I have an important function to attend this afternoon." She added, "It's for Daddy's job, and that's more important than anything else around here."

Chapter 5

Karen's bubbly personality was a perfect fit with the warm hospitality exuding from Greater Faith Chapel. She seemed to be happiest in an extended family kind of environment, being an only child. Regardless of what she was going through, the church always seemed to lift her spirits.

The thousand member congregation was a far cry from the fifty original members who were in attendance six years ago, when Karen and Johnny attended in hopes of saving their marriage. At that time, Karen knew it was critical to find a spiritual support group to help them survive her husband's infidelity. She had looked in the yellow pages and found the church.

The young minister and his wife had received the Clark couple with open arms. They went to counseling for a month. When the discussions got too personal, Johnny pulled back. It wasn't long before he stopped going to counseling and church altogether, both to Karen's dissatisfaction.

Whenever Karen tried talking him into more counseling, his standard reply was, "I don't need some man digging into my personal business. How is he going to tell me what it takes to be a husband? You might be surprised to find that he's no better a husband than I am."

Johnny figured Reverend Lane knew of his indiscretions, and a part of him was too guarded to let someone other than Karen know certain details about his life.

Karen stopped asking, figuring that if Johnny went back, it would be his own choice.

"Morning, Mrs. Clark," a young lady greeted, standing in the church entrance.

"Ooh, you're back. So how is married life, Mrs. Newly-wed?" Karen replied and gave the young lady a hug.

"Wonderful. I want it to be as perfect as your marriage."

There were times when such a compliment would have generated a radiant smile from Mrs. Clark. Today wasn't one of those times.

Karen glanced at her watch and realized her Sunday school class would be starting in less than five minutes.

"Oh, my lesson." In her distraction over the weekend, she'd forgotten to prepare for her married women's Sunday school class. "Oh, phooey."

Karen dug around in her tote bag to see if there was anything else she could use for the discussion. Striking out, she opened the door and saw forty or so women milling around the room.

Wouldn't you know it, she thought, *of course it's a full class. Oh, well; God, you have to get me through this one.* At church, Karen was in her element. She was charming, knowledgeable, and most, confident in her abilities. It was the one place she felt respected.

"Good morning, ladies."

"Good morning."

After endless digging, Karen finally stumbled upon her lesson planner and turned it to the current lesson, titled, "When Is Enough Enough?" The words seemed to radiate off the page.

Karen inhaled. Any other lesson would have been better today. She didn't feel like dealing with any deep relationship issues. Karen was barely getting by with the everything is happy at home image, knowing how fed up she was with Johnny's mess. She had survived the first time around when Isabelle got a foothold in their marriage. A second encounter would be fatal. Perhaps she could find a way to get around the lesson, at least for today.

"How many people are prepared for today's lesson?" She hoped a few show of hands would warrant postponing the discussion. Almost every hand in the room went up. With no other way out, she said, "Okay, let's open with prayer and get started."

Karen was going to have to dig way down inside and pull out the strength needed to discuss and advise women on issues she was struggling with herself. She wanted to be honest and let the chips fall where they would, but decided that even though she and Johnny were going through a bad situation, the less outsiders knew, the better. Besides, what would people say?

Chapter 6

Fancy dresses, tailored suits, and linen and silk garments comprised her wardrobe. Whatever the function, from casual to formal, she was covered.

"I do not feel like going to this banquet," she mumbled with a groan. "What can I throw on in a hurry?"

She pushed the button on the rotating closet rack and thumbed through some of the two-piece suits as they came around, looking for the peach one.

Karen was self-conscious about the few extra pounds she'd picked up while being off work for the past four months. Her well-proportioned five-foot-seven frame accentuated her golden brown skin and engaging smile. It was something that initially attracted Johnny to her. After the mastectomy, she struggled with her appearance, and her self-esteem ended up taking a beating.

She stopped the rack and pulled out the plastic covered silk tea length dress with a matching short waist sequined jacket. She was hoping it fit. She laid her outfit on the bed, removed her blazer, and began hurriedly unbuttoning her blouse. The dress was complete by itself, but Karen opted to wear a jacket to give her breast area extra coverage.

She wondered if there was time to take another hot shower. Karen glanced at her watch. It was already after twelve. Running the risk of hearing Johnny's mouth was not worth an extra moment of solitude in the hot, soothing water. She decided not to chance it. She laid the blouse on the bed and unsnapped her bra.

Johnny eased into the bedroom like an uninvited guest who walked into the middle of a lover's quarrel and was plotting on how to retreat unnoticed.

Karen stopped at the full-length mirror with her loosely

draped robe dangling open. Covered in protective emotional armor, she dodged the image that came hurling back at her. It was an ongoing battle. Her adversary had been put on the canvas time after time and wouldn't stay down. Her trembling hands glided over the leveled mounds and lingered at the jagged scar lines of where both of her breasts had once resided. She flicked a tear from her cheek before it made its way to the trail that had been carved from earlier downpours.

The cracking sound of the settling floorboard startled Karen back into the confines of the bedroom. Her stare focused in on Johnny, and she instantly protected her body by clasping the robe tightly across her chest.

"Johnny, I didn't hear you come in."

The bout with breast cancer had tested her faith in both God and Johnny's commitment. She was having difficulty applying her beliefs, religious pursuits, and godly conversations to her real world situations. Fear had so often gotten the best of her over the past four years. She tortured herself with the same questions. Why hadn't she done self-exams sooner? What could she have done differently? What would have happened to her children if she'd died? Why did this happen to her? Before the cancer, it was easy for her to talk about faith and hope. Now that she yearned for heavy doses of both just to stay encouraged, it's wasn't so easy to believe in either. Walking the walk proved to be much tougher than she'd dreamed.

If he could, Johnny would have eased back out of the room before Karen saw him. It was too late for a quick exit. He came in trying to pretend he hadn't noticed anything.

"So, you just about ready?" he asked, avoiding eye contact.

Karen was determined to believe he had a problem with her deformed breasts, despite his reassurances. She did everything to avoid the subject. Johnny just wanted to return to a normal level of intimacy.

"Why are you looking at me like that?" she asked.

"Like what?"

"You know, like that."

"Oh, boy," Johnny mumbled.

This was a time he hated. He knew Karen was feeling sorry for herself and there was no way out for him. Regardless of what he said or did to make her feel more comfortable, she wasn't likely to accept it.

"Karen," he relented, "I'm not looking at you in any particular way."

"Yeah, that's the problem."

Johnny tossed his arms loosely into the air and shook his head. "What's the problem now, Karen?"

"Like I have to tell you." Her anger trickled out like small bursts of steam being released from a pressure cooker.

"Yes, you do. You need to tell me. What is your problem?" His words were guarded but deliberate.

With her back to him, Karen saw Johnny in the large full-length mirror. "What happened to us?"

She remembered how wonderful their connection was in the beginning. She chose to blame their latest round of sexual and marital problems on his inability to deal with her mastectomy, ignoring other looming issues.

"What do you mean, what happened?" he asked.

"I mean, what happened to love and affection?" Pausing, she turned away before continuing. "Do you even remember how much we enjoyed being together when we got married?"

Johnny scratched his head. "We've gone through a lot since those school days."

Their gazes met, and a flicker of passion quickly escaped.

"But I still care about you."

"Really, Johnny? Is that the best you can do?"

"What else do you want from me."

"How about love and maybe I'd like to hear you say that you find me attractive."

It was her constant allegations, and not the mastectomy, which forced Johnny to detest being near Karen when she was nude. It was as if the more she falsely accused him of having a problem, the more he felt it becoming one.

"Geez, I honestly don't understand you. I've always found you attractive, which is why I'm constantly reaching out to you for sex. That hasn't changed."

She smirked in disbelief. "Then why?"

"Why what?"

"Why did you start seeing Isabelle?"

Johnny sighed. "Ah, is that what this bickering is really about?" With his voice raised, he said, "When are you going to let it go?"

"When you let her go."

"I let Isabelle go years ago, and you know is."

"Do I? Do I really, Johnny? Maybe I just wanted to believe what you told me."

"Karen, you need to stop this."

Johnny sat on the corner of the sofa closest to the vanity table. "Look, Karen, you either have to forgive me and let it go or let me go, because I can't continue to put up with you always holding the past over my head." He paced the room in a slow, tormented stroll. "You either need to step up to the plate or step off."

"I forgave you a long time ago." She turned to face him. "I did forgive you. It wasn't easy, but I did. I had to forgive you in order for God to continue forgiving me." Karen could feel the words on her lips but not in her heart. She turned back to the mirror and gently applied color to her lips.

Johnny whispered under his breath, "So you say."

Karen didn't hear him and so continued to express her feelings. "But don't think I've forgotten the pain. With your cheating, I can't trust you."

"With my cheating, huh. Karen, it doesn't matter whether I cheat or not. You're going to accuse me regardless. When I go out you automatically assume I'm cheating. When I used to come home right after work every night, you still thought that I was cheating. I'm starting to wonder if this is more about you feeling guilty for not having sex with me over the last seven months. You claim that marriage is what you, but you don't act like a wife."

"I'm doing the best I can. I'm trying."

"How? It happens over and over, every time you get sick. We have sex for a while, until you choose to cut it off. It's not your illness. It's you."

Karen let her gaze float up to Johnny without response.

"Uh-huh, that's what I thought," Johnny said. "Well, I can't continue living like this. It's not working for me. Maybe it's time for a change."

"What do you mean?"

"I mean something like a separation. I think that's where we are," he stated.

"So that's where you think we are," Karen said, retracting the tube of lipstick.

Johnny stood up and headed for the door.

"Yeah, that's where we are." Leaning against the doorframe with his back to Karen, he said, "See you downstairs."

Chapter 7

The ride downtown was solemn. Neither had gotten past the flurry of strained weekend conversations. Regardless of what was going on behind closed doors, they both knew how to pull it together and put on a happy face for the public. It was a skill the couple had developed, refined, and executed to perfection.

Cadillacs, Lincolns, and limos lined the Renaissance's circular drive. Johnny wheeled the Caddy into the valet line. Karen straightened his bow tie and brushed a piece of lint off his tuxedo.

"Karen, can you grab the valet key from the glove compartment?"

The valet attendants opened both doors for the couple.

"Good afternoon, sir."

Johnny handed the man his valet key and a ten-dollar bill that he'd pulled from his pocket.

Glass elevators rose high above the ostentatious crystal chandelier and ushered them into the banquet room filled with corporate bigwigs. It was show time for the Clarks.

"John and Karen," a tall, middle-aged man greeted them as they entered the room. "Glad you could make it."

"Good afternoon, Al," Johnny greeted his mentor, who was also the CEO, with a firm handshake.

Johnny was in his element. "To get where you want to be, you have to hobnob with the big boys," was his favorite saying. If moving to the top of the company required mingling and working a crowd, then Johnny was surely headed for the top position. No one did it better.

He was excellent at charming the ladies and equally effective at dazzling the executives.

Turning to another gentleman standing nearby, the CEO continued with his introductions.

"John, this is Fred Suthers, the new VP of marketing. Fred, this is John Clark, the EVP of manufacturing and Plant Manager over our Metals Division."

The two men exchanged a handshake.

"And this is his lovely wife Karen." Al hugged her loosely. "Karen, you always look stunning."

Her charming smile had not been hindered by the grim ride from home. Karen wasn't in full bloom, but knew how to play the executive wife routine down to a tee.

"John, you are a heck of a lucky man."

Johnny wouldn't normally tolerate any man randomly hugging or touching his wife, but this was one of the few exceptions. It was as though he wore his mentor's compliment as a badge of honor. He was pleased to have such a comfortable and personal rapport with the chief officer. There were times in his career when it had come in handy as evidenced by his frequent and substantial promotions.

Al's wife approached the group and the exchange of hellos continued.

"John, now that you're here, can you join Fred and I for a few moments? I want to discuss third quarter projections."

"Sure," Johnny anxiously agreed.

"Karen, would you mind if I borrowed your husband for a moment?"

"Absolutely not."

"Great."

"Excuse us, ladies. We'll only be a few minutes," the CEO told Karen and his wife, Susan.

"Al, honey," Susan said and gently interlocked her arm with his, "you said no business today."

"I know, dear, I know. Just a few minutes." He kissed her on the forehead. "I promise."

With the men gone, the two women were left to carry on

the conversation, as usual.

"So, Susan, how are the kids?"

"Great."

Susan spewed out a report card on her children's progress with unprecedented glee.

"Well, you know Constance is in medical school, Larry is completing his junior year at Harvard, and it looks like Angeline's high school gymnastics team is headed for national competition. So I have a full calendar keeping up with the children. How about your children? How's Erick's sophomore year going at Stanford?"

"He's doing well." With pride, Karen added, "You know he's spending this quarter studying abroad in Europe."

"Ah, how intriguing. How about the girls? How are they?"

"Of course, Chelle is on the honor roll. She decided not to follow in her big brother's footsteps and graduate from high school early. Instead, she's going to use the time to brush up on her creative writing and take a few more advanced math and science classes."

"Really. I know a great creative writing tutor. It's the one Larry used."

Karen wasn't the least bit interested in a tutor. Swapping success stories about their children was one thing; adding another bill to the household budget was something else.

"How's that adorable little Elizabeth?"

"Fine." Karen smiled.

"You should bring her to our gym sometime. I'm sure Angeline wouldn't mind working with her."

"How generous. We'll try to work it into our schedule."

"Oh, boy, do I know how challenging a schedule can be. By the way, John mentioned that you are no longer doing the interior decorating."

"Yes, that's right. I stopped about four months ago."

"Well, good for you. Isn't it great?"

"What?"

"You know"—Susan leaned in toward Karen and whispered as though her upcoming revelation was top secret—"not having to work. I don't know how you managed to take care of your children, plan parties for your husband, do volunteer work, and also hold down a job."

"Umm," was the most Karen offered.

"We are so fortunate to be out of the workforce, don't you think?"

"Yeah, very fortunate," Karen pretended, knowing that a little extra income would come in handy around 712 Morning Glory Circle.

Karen enjoyed hobnobbing with the elite when things were good between her and Johnny. The social events were grueling otherwise and each word took effort.

"By the way, thanks for inviting us to your party next weekend," Susan said.

"Hope you can make it."

"Al and I wouldn't miss it. We are thrilled to be included."

Susan twirled the olive in her martini. Social drinking was an acceptable component of such gatherings. Even so, Karen never indulged.

"Tell me, it's your, what, twentieth anniversary?"

"No, our nineteenth." Karen engaged in a brief moment of reflection. "My, how fast the years have flown by for me and Johnny."

"Wonderful. We're celebrating our twenty-fifth this year."

"Congratulations. "

"Thank you. It's been a wonderful twenty-five years for us."

Susan was image-conscious and, much like Karen, the ideal executive wife, flattering, tolerant, and nonthreatening. Although she was painting the storybook twenty-five year marriage, Karen knew better. She'd heard how Al cheated on Susan. Karen also knew no matter how many skeletons were in the closet, wives in the executive circle were not about to give up the good life just because their husbands had a few marital indiscretions. Doubt, deny, and deal with it was the coping recipe.

Karen figured an afternoon of pretending was one thing, so long as it didn't continue to replace reality. Her headache was resurfacing. She'd had enough for one afternoon.

Johnny returned in time to rescue Karen as they headed for the hors d'oeuvres.

Chapter 8

Karen was submerged under the down-filled comforter when Johnny came from the master bathroom.

"Are you taking me to the airport?"

The lump on the bed showed minimal sign of movement.

"Karen." Johnny spoke sternly. "Are you taking me to the airport or not? You said you wanted to talk."

"I forgot. Where are you going again?"

"Tennessee for a production meeting. It'll be quick. I plan on getting back late tonight."

"Oh," Karen responded, with little confidence he'd adhere to his proposed time of return.

"Look, it's almost seven-thirty. I have to get out of here in order to make the air shuttle. Are you getting up or not?"

"I don't feel well." Karen poked her head from under the warm covers.

"What's wrong now?"

"I'm feeling extremely tired," she replied.

"So what's new?"

"Johnny, why can't you be more supportive and not make me feel bad about being sick?"

"I'm sorry, Karen. I'm not trying to make you feel bad. It's just that..." Johnny looked at Karen and hesitated before saying anything else.

"It's what?" Karen insisted.

"Nothing."

"What?"

"Nothing."

"It is something." She sat straight up in the bed and put some bass into her voice. "What were you going to say?"

"You're always sick with something. Always complaining

about something. If it's not me and some woman, it's your health."

Johnny sat down on the corner of the bed and used a shoehorn to slip his shoe on.

"You think I enjoyed having cancer and who knows what else?"

"No, I don't think you're happy about being sick, but I do think you enjoy using anything you can to get my attention." Johnny stood up facing Karen and adjusted his waistband.

"There's got to be a better way, Karen. This whining and manipulating can wear a person down after a while."

"It sure can." she agreed ferociously.

Johnny straightened his tie in the full-length mirror and made eye contact with Karen in the background.

"So I guess you changed your mind about taking me to the airport?"

"Yeah, I don't feel like going now." She laid back down on the bed.

"No problem. I'll get the shuttle service. I'll call you later."

Johnny's departure wasn't filled with smooches and I love you type of innuendoes. The couple had long since passed the touchy feely phase. The sporadic display of affection was an attempt to cover up Karen's distrust and Johnny's frustration.

Johnny left, and Karen climbed back under her fortress of pillows and bedcovers.

"Mommy, are you up?" Elizabeth poked her head into Karen's room, hoping to spend time with her before school.

Karen rolled over.

"Hi, baby. Mommy's not up yet. I have a headache."

Elizabeth sat on the bed next to Karen and stroked her hair. Elizabeth was at the age where she could either be babied or given big girl responsibilities. She seemed to enjoy both sides whenever convenient.

"Do you want me to stay at home with you today?"

"No, honey. Tell Chelle to help you get ready, and remind

her to lock the door when you leave."

"Hope you feel better." Elizabeth gave her mother a gentle hug. Karen lay in the bed a few more hours before getting up. She hadn't been able to keep her stress level down, as Dr. Costas had instructed. Karen had a headache from the surge of arguments that had begun on Friday, finding the phone number on Saturday, and attempting to keep up appearances at the banquet yesterday. She was paying for it this morning.

She eased down the stairs and found her way to a warm cup of tea. Phone calls were something Karen usually readily received. This morning she was not in the mood for chitchat. When the phone rang, she looked at the caller ID box before recognizing Tina's number and answering. Good timing. She wanted someone to share in her distress. Her days of praying and seeking God were rare. It required too much energy and self-evaluation. She preferred talking to another person. It required less effort and virtually no self-development on her part.

"Hi, Tina."

"Hey, girl. I'm calling to let you know I've decided to bring this guy," Tina sniggled. "That is if he doesn't get on my nerves between now and then. Oh, and I keep forgetting to ask if you need any help."

"What are you going on about?"

"Girl, what's wrong with you? Don't tell me you forgot about our conversation last week. I told you I was considering bringing a guest with me to your anniversary dinner."

"Anniversary, oh, that. I almost forgot about the dinner."

"Forgot? That's not like you, Ms. Party Planner. Something has to be wrong if you're not knee-deep into preparing for this get-together. What's wrong?"

Karen paused before revealing her business to Tina. She knew Johnny would not like Tina having a direct view into his home life, but Karen wasn't so concerned about how he felt. This time it was about how she felt. And Tina was on the short list of individuals whom she trusted enough to divulge some of her true feelings that were usually masked behind the storybook facade.

"I think Johnny's seeing someone."

"And?"

"And..."

"And I assumed as much," Tina stated.

"Why?"

Tina hesitated before giving up the information she'd been holding back. "I ran into Johnny Friday night at Floods and there was some little floozy sitting in your car."

With no regard for her throbbing temples, Karen elevated her voice. "Are you sure?"

"Positive."

"What did she look like?" She suspected it was Isabelle Jones. "I didn't get a good look at her. She was already in the car when I came up."

"I can't believe him."

"What did you expect?"

"For my husband to act like he's married."

"Oh, come on. Don't tell me it's never crossed your mind that he was seeing someone."

"I have my suspicions but no real proof. Why didn't you tell me you saw him?"

Karen had liked Tina's feisty and outspoken personality from the moment they met four years ago at the oncologist. Tina wasn't known for being timid or subtle. The friendship grew and so did Tina's candor.

"Why should I? It wouldn't have made a difference. You see only what you want anyway. Let's be for real. It's probably not his first and won't be his last."

Tina didn't trust men. Not only had her husband refused to be supportive during her struggle with cervical cancer, he'd left before she fully recuperated. To make matters worse, she couldn't have children. The revelation had been devastating, and Tina felt robbed. The betrayal of her husband and the loss of a vital piece of her womanhood left her angry, hurt, and distrustful. It slammed the door to her heart shut for other men. She dated a few and took none seriously. A safe arm's length away was as close as she let them get.

Karen was startled by Tina's reaction. "What makes you say that?"

"Please. Your husband is out every Friday night. It had to have crossed your mind at least once."

Karen was antsy. She had dreaded the possibility too often to count.

"Girl, where have you been?"

"I don't know. I was hoping things would get better."

"I hate to say it, girlfriend, but you sure lead a sheltered life. I guess living in the backwoods of West Bloomfield has taken you out of touch with reality."

"Hmmm."

Tina considered herself to be a close friend, although her words were often piercing. She found Karen to be too naive and Johnny to be too uppity. As much as she tried to be objective, her advice was often seasoned with reality.

"What are you going to do?"

An overwhelming surge of memories flooded Karen's soul. She hated to think Johnny was cheating on her. But no matter how he would sneak around on Friday nights, he never expressed an interest in leaving the marriage—with one exception. When he'd allowed himself to get caught up with Isabelle Jones, that had been a true threat. She wasn't like the women Karen suspected Johnny had been messing around with since the cancer and their sexual problems began. Isabelle was different. From the little Karen had found out about her, it seemed that she was strong and smart, working as some kind of big shot in a company with a lot of men. Karen didn't know where to turn. The emotional hurts she had endured from the affair felt like fresh wounds. He'd put his marriage on the line for that relationship, and the mere thought of Isabelle resurfacing terrified Karen. She felt an emptiness deep inside, like a sickness she couldn't weed out. She knew from experience that the only way to get rid of a cancerous pain was to deal with it at the core.

"Karen, what are you going to do? You know men don't change."

"I'm not sure what to do. I know I have to do something."

"You're always talking about having faith in God and letting Him work things out. At least that's what you're always telling me to do. But when push comes to shove, you can't follow your own advice."

"I'm tired of praying for the same old, same old. I know God can work things out, but I don't know what exactly it is I want him to work out."

"What exactly are you saying, Karen?"

"I'm saying I'm tired."

"Ump, you should have been tired a long time ago. Don't be nobody's fool."

"Tina, this doesn't have anything to do with being a fool."

"Why not?"

"Believing things are going to work out and being a fool are two different things."

"If you say so. You're my girl and I'm not calling you a fool. What I'm saying is that you can't let Johnny get away with this. You need to leave him before he tries to leave you for one of those trifling hookers he hangs out with."

"I don't know. I just might leave him. Wouldn't he be surprised?"

"Yeah, right, okay. That means about as much as when a man says he's leaving his wife. How many times have you threatened to leave?" Karen threatened to leave several times. Each had amounted to an empty emotional ploy.

Tina laughed. "If you told Johnny you were leaving he'd act like most men. He'd get mad, yell and scream, feel guilty, buy flowers, jewelry, or fur or something expensive. Knowing you, humph, you'll soften, accept his apology, and believe him when he says it won't happen again."

Karen was silent.

"I gotta admit, for a couple with so much going on, you two sure do well."

"All that glitters isn't gold," Karen uttered.

"Got that right." As much material success as the Clarks appeared to have, it gave Tina a bit of comfort to know their lives had as much struggle as her own.

Talking with Tina wore Karen down. In the end, it wasn't exactly the pep talk she was seeking. Then again, she wasn't exactly sure what she was seeking. Whatever it was, she didn't find it with Tina.

"Hey girl, I'm getting off this phone so I can get myself together for the day," Karen stated.

"Yeah, I better get going too. I'm sitting on this phone like I don't have any work to do around here. I'll catch up with you later. Be sure and let me know what you decide to do about Johnny. Inquiring minds want to know."

The wall clock displayed 9:45 A.M. as the call ended.

Karen shuffled around the kitchen in her robe with no intention of doing much of anything. She thought about her other friend Connie and decided to give her a call.

Karen's two friends were quite different. When Karen wanted a reality check, she went to Tina. If it was compassion she was seeking, that required a chat with Connie. Her warm spirit resonated with Karen the moment Tyrone introduced them eight years ago. It had been hard for Karen to believe he was attracted to such a soft-spoken and conservative woman. His type was more on the rambunctious side. It was even more shocking when Tyrone announced the marriage and exhibited signs of commitment and content. It was easy to see he was hooked, and Connie adored him. Tina was not in the same place romantically. She wasn't interested in catering to a man. She was fine alone. Regardless of their idiosyncrasies, each of their individual bouts with life-threatening illnesses created an undeniable bond among the three women.

Karen was glad Connie answered right away. Her anxiety began to ease.

"Hey, lady. Where have you been? I didn't hear from you at all last week," Connie said.

"I know, and I'm sorry. I had a headache most of the week, so I tried to take it easy," Karen answered.

"I know how a splitting headache can be. I had too many of those before I started taking some new herbs and vitamins. Thank goodness those excruciating headaches are gone."

"The headache is bearable. Mostly I'm concerned about being tired."

"You know, you should have called me. I could have come over and helped you out. Even though Tyrone tries to keep me from doing anything around here, I know how to cook and clean." She laughed.

"Girl, please, you have it made. You haven't had to work, let alone cook or clean, in who knows how long." Karen laughed too. "Anyway, how are you feeling these days? I know you weren't doing too well the week before last."

"All is well," Connie replied.

It was often amazing and at times eerie. Karen couldn't fathom that even in the advanced stages, Connie was in such denial about her inoperable brain tumor. The diagnosis was at least two years old. Karen had thought Connie was home free after the initial tumor was successfully removed during a sixteen-hour surgery and subsequent radiation. But she didn't understand why Connie refused to acknowledge her tumor had grown back. Even more astonishing was Connie's ability to completely block it out.

"I know you probably don't want to go to the doctor," Connie stated.

"Well, I did talk to Dr. Costas before the weekend."

"At least you didn't have to go in. I get tired of going to the doctor. Every time I get a toenail ache, that husband of mine is rushing me off to the doctor or the hospital. Oh, my goodness, that man is too paranoid."

"He loves you. Can't complain about that." Karen longed for the kind of devotion and unwavering support that Tyrone gave his ailing wife. Doctors had strongly recommended that Tyrone place Connie in a nursing home because she needed constant care. He had consistently refused for the past six months. Instead, he hired a full-time nurse to stay with Connie during the day and a part-time one to help out in the evenings and on weekends.

"No, I sure can't. I'm very blessed. By the way, maybe you can get the kind of vitamins I'm using for my headaches. They definitely work."

"I took some Tylenol for the headache and it seemed to help a little," Karen said.

Karen downplayed the vitamin suggestion. She was into more traditional approaches to medicine and not the holistic one Connie embraced. After the treatments, surgeries, and countless medications Connie had endured from the onset of her diagnosis, Karen understood why her friend had grown tired and wanted to try a more natural approach. Medicine that was meant to fix one problem in the body generally had a side effect that broke down something else. Karen figured whatever juices and herbs Connie had were intended to do more than calm a simple headache.

"What did your doctor say about your fatigue?"

"I didn't tell her."

"Why not, Karen? I thought that was something you were always supposed to report?"

"I'm just a little tired. I probably need to get more rest. That's it. I figure rest and leafy greens will get my energy level back up."

"You won't get an argument from me. Whatever works for

you is fine by me," Connie said. "Changing the subject, have you heard from Tina?"

"I just got off the phone with her."

"I have to give her a call. We should get together over the next week or two."

"Will you be able to come to our anniversary party?"

"Of course."

"Well, she's coming too. So we'll be together then."

"I know, but I want us to get together by ourselves for some old-fashioned girl talk." Connie giggled.

Karen giggled too. When she was feeling low, things were always better after she talked to Connie.

"Well, then, lady, I'm getting tired myself. It's time for a nap. I'll catch up with you later this week."

"Okay, Connie. I'll call you later."

Karen set the cordless phone on the counter and took a moment to reflect on her friend. She shook her head in disbelief, perplexed at how Connie dealt with her tumor. Karen understood constant pain and fear of the unknown. There were times when she felt like sticking her head in the sand too, but it wasn't the answer. If nothing else, she remembered how early detection was a key survival factor. She hadn't begun the self-exams in time, but Karen knew it wasn't too late to be observant of the signals in her body now.

Without hesitation, she picked up the phone and dialed Dr. Costas for an appointment. "Better safe than sorry" was a her newfound perspective.

Chapter 9

Karen flipped through a magazine to pass the time. The sparsely colored waiting room was intimidating. Any doctor's office was a place she had to be only when necessary and not a minute more.

The door leading to the examination rooms opened.

"Karen," the nurse called, standing behind the door, "you can come on back."

Karen put on a brave face and took gingerly steps.

The nurse closed the door behind them.

"Let's get your weight."

Karen slipped off her shoes, determined not to add extra pounds. "I've gained quite a bit since my last visit," she said timidly stepping onto the scale.

The nurse didn't reply until after the digital screen settled on 146. "Let me see where were you before. One thirty-five."

"I've gone from a four to an eight in four months."

"Don't worry. For your height at five-seven, one forty-six is well within in range."

"I just don't want to blow up while I'm off work."

The nurse jotted down the weight. Karen followed her to the door marked 3. White walls framed the room. Karen briskly rubbed her hands against her arms to generate a quick jolt of warmth. She took a deep breath as the nauseating smell of lanolin and medicated soap clogged her nostrils.

"Let me get your blood pressure."

Karen pushed her blouse sleeve above her elbow. It never failed. Every time she came to see Dr. Costas, her nerves would bounce out of whack. Her blood pressure would shoot up at the beginning of the appointment and drop back to normal by the end of the session.

The nurse wrapped the band around Karen's arm and put the cold metal end of the stethoscope in place.

Karen attempted to remain calm, but a thousand visits with a good report on each trip couldn't pacify her escalating fear. She focused on puffy cotton balls located a few inches past the tray of hypodermic needles.

"Done," the nurse said, and removed the band from Karen's arm. "Is my pressure normal?"

"One forty-six over ninety-five; it's a little high." After Dr. Costas finishes up, I'll come back and retake your pressure."

"Yep, I know the routine."

Karen undressed, wrapped herself in the paper robe, and sat on the examination table. She hummed, twitched her toes, and did anything she could to pass the time.

The door opened and a little lady with a headful of braids entered with a metal chart in her hand.

"Hello, Dr. Costas."

"So how are we doing?" She set the chart on the counter. "How's the headache?"

"I haven't gotten rid of it."

"Did you take the Tylenol?"

"The whole weekend."

"And it didn't help?"

"Some, but not entirely."

"Lie back, please."

Dr. Costas opened the robe and placed her stethoscope in the center of Karen's chest.

"Are you doing self-exams for your armpits?"

"Yes, practically every day when I'm showering."

"Glad to hear it. It's a good habit to have. You can sit up."

Karen sat up and covered herself with the paper-thin wrinkled robe.

Dr. Costas sat on the tiny stool and wheeled it up to the counter. She made a few notes in the chart.

"Any other concerns, besides the headache?"

"Actually, I do have one," Karen reluctantly admitted. The longer she kept secrets from the doctor, the more time her symptoms had to intensify.

"What?" Dr. Costas asked.

"I've been exhausted. It's probably from having so much to do around the house with my girls. Figured I'd mention it, since I'm here."

Dr. Costas didn't show any alarm. She knew from years of treating Karen that it was best to minimize her concerns whenever possible. She pulled a penlight from her pocket and a tongue depressor from the glass jar.

"Say 'aah' and open wide."

Karen did as requested.

"You may be right about the stress. Let's order some blood work while you're here. I also want to make sure you're not suffering from anemia."

"Anemia. I haven't been anemic before."

Dr. Costas wanted to put Karen at ease. She elected not to get into the medical aspects of anemia and how it tied in with her condition. There was no reason to worry Karen without more insight into what was going on. If it turned out that she was anemic, they could deal with the how and why then.

"It's nothing to worry about. Between supplements and leafy green vegetables, that's pretty much all the remedy you need."

"I can handle that."

That was Karen's hope, something simple. She felt relieved about the examination. More medicine and treatment was the last thing she wanted.

"What about the headache?"

"I need to see the blood work first, and we'll go from there. If I don't get any hints from the lab work, I might have to schedule an MRI to get a look at what's happening."

Panic showed in Karen's eyes. The MRI was a test she would avoid if possible.

"An MRI, do I really need one?"

The hair on her arms stood up. Claustrophobia was what she remembered about being in the confined space. Karen had freaked out four years ago when she needed it for the breast cancer.

Dr. Costas tried to ease her mind, sensing Karen's concern. "Karen, let's not focus on the MRI yet. Let me get the blood work back. I will call you tomorrow, and we'll go from there."

"Okay."

"In the meantime, keep that blood pressure down." She stood up and rubbed Karen's shoulder for reassurance. 'Try not to worry. It never helps anyway."

"Thanks, Dr. Costas."

"I'll send the nurse back in to draw the blood."

Chapter 10

Karen was jittery about the news she'd received from Dr. Costas earlier in the day. She milled around the big house, feeling its emptiness. This was one evening she was looking forward to having Johnny around, even if she was upset with him. When the phone rang, she grabbed it and found him on the other end.

"Karen, the production tests ran overtime. I wasn't able to catch the corporate jet. I'm going to stay overnight and take the shuttle home in the morning."

"What a surprise."

"Come on, Karen. Let's not go there."

"Why not, Johnny? Why can't we talk about your job? It seems to be the only important thing to you."

"Look, you know how demanding this job can be. We've been over this a thousand times. When will you accept it?"

"When you show a little more interest in me and our family."

"Family?" His voice rose. "Family. Why do you think I work so hard? It's so that you and the kids can have it better than I did growing up. I bust my chops to give you everything you want and need. Don't I?" he yelled. "Don't I?"

"Yes," she muttered.

"I'm the only one working, and it takes a lot to keep what we have."

"I'm not trying to put extra pressure on you," Karen said.

"Oh, no? I haven't seen you cut down on your spending. You're signing the kids up for every afterschool program that you can find. I don't see you making any changes to help out. The only thing you were willing to give up easily was your job."

"What do you want me to say?"

"What I'm asking you for is a little support. I'm staying overnight," he bellowed.

Karen was out of sorts about her visit to the doctor. Although she didn't want to feel overly alarmed, she also didn't want to be unprepared.

"Fine, whatever." He wasn't up for another blowout about where the marriage was going. Johnny made an effort to smooth the waters and find a less volatile subject. "So what did the doctor say?"

Karen sighed. "Dr. Costas did some blood work."

Having been with Karen during the cancer years, he'd learned those two words were an automatic barometer for trouble. "What does blood work have to do with a headache?"

"I don't know. The only thing she said about the headaches was that I might have to get another MRI."

"MRI?" Although it was painless, he knew how much Karen dreaded the procedure. "Is it that serious?"

"Don't know yet. Dr. Costas didn't say I needed one for sure. We'll see what's going on after the test results come back."

"Hopefully it's nothing."

"Well, I've been exhausted lately. I mentioned it to Dr. Costas, and I could tell she was concerned."

'You didn't tell me anything about being exhausted."

"I told you before you left."

"Yeah, but I assumed you were...well..." He hesitated and didn't finish.

"Uh-huh. I told you I wasn't feeling well, but you didn't believe me. You thought I was begging for attention."

Johnny sensed her edginess. "Stop it. I don't want to hear anymore. We'll talk about it when I get back."

"That's it? That's the extent of your concern?"

"I'll be here if you need me," he replied.

'Thanks a lot for the support."

"What else can I do from here? I'm not a doctor." Johnny attempted to restrain his irritation with her attitude when he was trying to be helpful. "I'm only your husband, and that doesn't seem to be enough for you."

"I wonder why."

"That's it. I'll talk to you later."

Karen didn't feel up to carrying the conversation on either and chose to let it end on a sour note. She terminated the call and wondered how she was going to spend the rest of the evening alone and disillusioned. Of all nights, the kids were going to be out late at the church's afterschool spring event.

Karen realized the marriage was in trouble, but talking about leaving and actually doing it were worlds apart. She didn't know what to do. She tried to lift her spirits by reminiscing about the good years. Maybe going back to the beginning could erase some of the damage. She made her way downstairs to the media room. Among the stack of videos, Karen could pick out the wedding one in a few seconds. The smudged, barely legible label read, Wedding—March. The year had rubbed off long ago.

She sought out a few more sentimental videos for her pick me up party. She fumbled through the stacks and retrieved several labeled Children's birthdays. Back upstairs she went with an armful of memories. She inserted the wedding video and pushed play after she settled back against the headboard. The first image on the screen was the smiling young couple in their simple living room ceremony accented by inexpensive daisy bouquets. She had been thrilled to find a dress big enough to cover her seven months pregnant stomach. Bliss abounded in the young couple.

The video reminded Karen of how wide-eyed and in love they were in the beginning. They had met in their junior year of high school, become inseparable friends, and both ended up going to Wayne State. Johnny's pursuit of a law degree was cut short when Karen became pregnant their junior year in college. What they lacked in money, they made up for in romance.

The joy she had experienced in the marriage for many years was fading away. She pushed away the tears. The hopes, dreams, love, and experiences she and Johnny had once shared got sucked into a sea of distance and bitterness. It seemed that the possessions they once talked about having had become more important than one another.

The years hadn't been kind to her marriage or her spiritual stability. There was a time in the past when God had played a significant role in her life, and she would pray about everything. In the early years of the marriage, she grew in her faith and felt good about having a one-on-one relationship with the Lord. Twenty years ago she confidently believed in her heart that God knew her personally and made everything right.

Johnny never did get into the religious arena. His position used to be, "If it makes Karen happy, then I have no problem with it, so long as she doesn't push it on me."

Her religious pursuit slackened as their socioeconomic status grew. At times she felt guilty about putting God in the backseat. It was as if she had abandoned him during the surplus years.

Karen watched the videos until she finally drifted into a deep sleep. She didn't budge when the girls poked their heads into her room around nine o'clock to let her know they were home.

A ringing phone startled Karen from her sleep the next morning. Half awake and with no concept of time, she aimlessly stretched out her arm and grabbed the phone without uncovering her head.

In a groggy, semiconscious voice, she answered the call, Hello— umm."

"Karen Clark, please."

"This is Karen."

"Mrs. Clark, I'm calling from Dr. Costas's office."

That instantly got her attention. Wide awake, she popped up in the bed.

"Dr. Costas wanted me to call you first thing this morning about your test results."

"Yes," Karen anxiously egged the nurse on for information.

"Your white blood cell count is high and the doctor wants some additional tests run."

Karen knew her white blood cell count was high whenever the cancer was active. Her heart was racing and anxiety meter was in overdrive. "What do you mean, high?"

"There's no need to be overly concerned."

"Why shouldn't I be? I know that means my cancer might be back." Karen raised her voice. "How can you tell me not to be concerned?"

"Mrs. Clark, please calm down. Dr. Costas is having the lab do some additional tests today."

"Do I need more blood tests?"

"No. She ordered the test yesterday from the sample we'd already drawn. Some tests take longer than others. She didn't want to wait for all the results before contacting you."

Karen tried to calm herself. She closed her eyes and rubbed her hand across the right side of her head.

"We will need you to have an MRI done for the headaches."

"When?"

"If possible, we'd like you to go early tomorrow morning. The doctor wants to get the tests and lab work done as soon as possible in order to get to the bottom of your discomfort. Do you think you'll be able to go?"

Karen wasn't up to the MRI or any other test. She had been through plenty. It was the last bit of information she wanted to get after such a strained weekend. A part of Karen wanted to stick her head back under the covers and sleep off the nightmare, to wake up and be back in the ideal household that she'd known years ago.

"I'll need to call you back after I check my schedule."

Karen covered her head and tried going back to sleep. Eleven-fifteen, read the digital alarm clock on the nightstand sitting next to the bed. Karen hadn't realized it was that late but wasn't ready to get up. It required too much energy, both physically and emotionally. She was hoping that a few more minutes underneath the warm confines of her blanketed fortress was going to do a world of good. Suddenly she thought about the girls and popped up in the bed. Karen felt bad about not getting up in time to see them off. Thank goodness Chelle got herself and Elizabeth off to school, especially on days like today.

The bumping, thumping and running water coming from the bathroom woke her. She hadn't been out of bed the entire morning and didn't seem to care.

He was out of eye's view, but she knew that it must be Johnny and called out to him.

'Yeah," he yelled back.

"I didn't know you were here. When did you get in?"

Johnny emerged from the bathroom and hustled into the closet.

"I took an early flight and got in about an hour ago."

Karen got up to go to the bathroom. Too much sleep was as tiring as too little. She was drowsy and tired from sleeping nearly five hours beyond her norm.

"You're not going to work today?"

Johnny left the closet as Karen closed the bathroom door. He buttoned his starched white shirt.

"I'm on my way in now. I had to come home to get some clothes. I hadn't planned on spending last night in Cookeville, so I didn't take anything with me."

She ran her fingers through her hair. After going bald the first two times with chemo and radiation, she opted to leave it short. Karen walked past Johnny and grabbed her robe off the sofa. Under her breath, she whispered, "At least something brought you home."

"Why aren't you dressed? What's wrong?" Johnny asked.

"The blood tests didn't come back with good news."

It wasn't news he wanted to hear. He definitely knew it wasn't news Karen wanted to hear. Yet he didn't know how to react. As tense as their relationship had been over the past week, he was reluctant to step into a bigger can of worms. He decided, uncharacteristically, to let Karen lead the dialogue. The best he could hope for was to get his tie on and get out before another verbal explosion occurred.

"I also need an MRI."

She hung her head and twiddled her fingers. She rolled her head back, bit her lip, and stared at the ceiling in an effort to suppress the swelling tears.

Johnny knew how uncomfortable Karen was with tests. He couldn't figure out what was the big deal when she'd done so many times.

"I don't want to do the MRI."

"Well, I mean, Karen, if it's something you have to do to get better, you just have to do it."

"I'm not trying to get out of it, Johnny. I just wish I didn't have to do any more tests."

"Yeah, but you do. So there's no point stressing yourself out about it."

She was ready to cry.

"You don't understand. No matter how I try to share my feelings with you, you just don't get it."

"Ha, ha, ha, ha," Johnny belted out cynically. "I don't get it, huh? What exactly is it, Karen, that I don't get?" He let out another laugh.

"It's not fun going through illnesses, tests, pains, and—"

"And what, Karen? I am here for you. I've been here for you. I didn't leave you like Tina's husband did. So tell me, what is it that I don't understand?"

"I need you to show me more compassion and support, you know, like Tyrone does for Connie."

"Tyrone and Connie? They don't have anything to do with this. Please. I give up." Johnny threw his hands up in frustration. "Fine, Karen. I'm not getting into a deep discussion about my insensitivity. You've already told me enough times about that. Let's get back to the doctor. When is your test? I'll go with you."

"It's tomorrow morning." She perked up.

"Wednesday, aah." Johnny sighed. "I can't go tomorrow morning. I have an executive staff meeting."

"Can't you skip part of the meeting and go with me? You are the boss."

"Karen, this is a big meeting. The chief operating officer is coming down to go over the third quarter projections. I have to be there."

"You can't miss one meeting?"

"Karen, come on. It's only a test. Don't try to make me feel guilty. If it were a life-threatening procedure, you know I'd be there."

"Really? I guess it's not enough for me just to want you there."

"Karen, my job is not easy. Not very many people work their way up from the factory line to senior management like I have. I've worked hard to get us where we are. So I'd appreciate it if you didn't try to make me feel guilty about doing what I have to do to take care of this family."

"I'm not talking about the family. I'm talking about me. You seem to be more committed to Tenner Automotive than you are to me."

"What's wrong with loving my job?"

"What's wrong with loving me?"

"I can't win with you. If I don't get out there and work to take care of my family, it means I don't care about you. If I show commitment to my job, it means I don't care about you. You're never happy, no matter what I do."

"Your career seems to be your one true love."

"I don't expect you to understand where I'm coming from. When you got pregnant—"

Karen interrupted. "What do you mean I got pregnant?"

"I'm sorry," he said letting his gaze drop. "I meant to say when we got pregnant, you were in a position to graduate early, before Erick was born. I wasn't as fortunate as you were. I had to drop out and take a factory job." His voice elevated. "Did I complain? No. I did what I had to do. Every time I tried to go back to school, you know something came up. Between the children, our responsibilities, and you getting sick, it took me fifteen years after we got married to finish my degree."

"So why do you make it seem like it's my fault?"

"I'm not saying it's your fault. I'm not blaming you either. I'm only asking you to understand where I'm coming from as a man. You always talk about my showing you some support. What about showing me some?"

Johnny grabbed his keys and left the room, leaving Karen to sort out her raging emotions. In response, she returned to her safe haven underneath the bedcovers.

Before backing out the driveway, Johnny placed a call on his cell phone.

"Hey, Tyrone. What's going on?"

"Not much happening. Trying to keep it together. What's going on with you?"

"I got a lot on my mind. I was wondering if we could hook up for a drink after work?"

"On a weeknight? What's up? What's going on?"

"I need to talk," Johnny said.

"Okay. Let me check on Connie first."

"I'm sorry, buddy. I didn't even ask. How's she doing?"

'This has been a good week for her."

"I don't know how you do it. Your wife has been sick straight through the past couple of years. I have to give it to you, man. You got that."

"Karen has her share too and you've been there for her. It's what husbands do."

"Nah, I haven't been able to stand as strong as you have."

"I'm only doing what I can. I love her, and that's all there is to it," Tyrone stated. "I'll have to get back with you about tonight."

Tyrone hadn't forgotten the years he'd played around. His world had changed when he met Connie. He couldn't explain what it was that drew him to her. Her big round eyes set against her honey-colored skin often caught the attention of men. But it wasn't her looks that drew Tyrone. He had met plenty of appealing women in his day. There was more to Connie. Something about her connected below the surface. Tyrone was proud to admit how she had managed to convert a player into a dedicated and faithful husband. He placed a call home.

"Hey, how you doing, babe?"

"I'm fine, same as I was when you called an hour ago. You worry about me too much. "

"If I don't, who will? I love you, girl." Tyrone cleared his throat. "By the way, Johnny gave me a call. He wants to get together after work. If it's okay with you, I'm going to grab a drink with him right after work and then come on home."

"Is anything wrong?"

"I don't know. He seemed like there was something heavy on his mind."

"Go on with him. I'll be fine."

"Are you sure? Johnny is my buddy. I want to be there for him. But you are my first priority, no exceptions."

"I'm sure. Go on out and have a good time."

"I'll be in soon as I can."

"Take your time. I might invite the girls over for dinner,

since both the cook and the housekeeper are here today."

"If you feel up to it. Don't overdo it, babe."

"I don't know what I'd do without you," Connie said.

"That's something you don't have to worry about."

Chapter 11

Karen was spraying water on the leaves of the nine-foot tree towering in the foyer. The housewarming gift had only been a few feet tall when they received it eight years ago. Thanks to Karen's nurturing touch, the plant matured into full bloom like other things in her care. She heard the familiar sound of Chelle yelling for her to get the phone.

"It's Aunt Connie."

Karen walked down the hallway past Johnny's office and the back staircase into the family room. There she could relax in peace. She got situated on her chaise lounge and excused Chelle from the phone.

"What are you doing tonight?" Connie asked.

"No plans."

"Good. You have to come over for dinner. I won't take no for an answer."

"I don't know, Connie. Johnny's out."

"I know. Tyrone told me they were going out for a drink."

"He did, huh?"

Karen didn't know and was mortified that Connie had a better handle on Johnny's whereabouts.

'There won't be anyone here with the girls."

"What about the sitter down the street? Come on, Karen, no excuses. We haven't gotten together in quite a while. I had the cook put together a nice dinner."

"I'll see what I can do. I'll check on the sitter. If she's available, I'll be over around seven."

"Great. I'm calling Tina, too. I haven't seen her in a while either. It will be nice to have the three of us together."

Connie and Karen had been friends first. Tina came into

the fold four years later. Karen was the linchpin in the trio, but Connie and Tina had managed to develop their own solid connection.

Maybe getting out for some fresh air was exactly what Karen needed to shake the funk she was in.

"Mommy, what happened to you and Daddy last night?" Chelle asked, since no one had been up when she had gotten home last night.

"I was tired, sweetie. I went to bed early, and your dad had to stay overnight in Tennessee. I checked on you around ten-thirty and you were both knocked out."

"Oh," Chelle muttered.

"Did you get your homework done last night?"

"Yes, and I got an A on my spelling test." Elizabeth was eager to share the good news with her mom.

"You did? Well, I am very proud of you little lady," Karen said rubbing her daughter's back.

Elizabeth beamed from ear to ear.

"Chelle made me study the words over and over."

Karen was pleased with her girls and particularly grateful that Chelle was responsible and mature. She had been a vital component in the family's livelihood while Karen was sick. Many people helped, but Chelle prepared most of the meals, did the laundry, and personally watched out for Elizabeth. Her grades never dropped below her standard As and Bs.

"Chelle, did you decide whether or not you are going to the Teen Redeem in D.C. next month? We have to turn in the enrollment form at church Sunday."

"I don't know if I want to go. It's right before finals. What do you think?"

"Well, it's only one weekend, and you deserve a break. I think you should go." Karen hugged her daughter. "It's not every day you get to meet other Christian teens from around the world."

"Will you get the deposit money from Daddy for me? I'll

turn it in when we go to church." Chelle kissed her mom on the cheek. 'Thanks, and I love you."

Karen had a strong bond with each of her three children. Witnessing the joy in her two beautiful girls gave her reason to stay in the marriage. She couldn't dare traumatize the children by taking on the role of a struggling single parent. Over the past nineteen years, the family had endured plenty of tough financial times with both her and Johnny contributing to the household. Karen couldn't imagine doing it alone.

Chapter 12

Karen second-guessed herself during the twenty-minute drive to Connie's house. Did she feel up to being around others or not? Maybe she would go back home and nestle under her warm bedcovers and feel better in the morning. She slowly turned into the subdivision off the main road, accepting that her opportunity to leave was escaping. She was startled by a horn blowing. Karen looked into the rearview mirror to see Tina waving. Too late to turn around; she had been spotted. She pulled the Lincoln SUV into the circular driveway.

Tina pulled her five-year-old economy car into the driveway behind Karen. The two ladies gathered their belongings and got out. "I wasn't sure if you were coming," Karen commented.

The women embraced.

"Why not? A single woman like me is always looking for a home cooked meal. It's nice having rich friends like you all."

"There you go with that rich stuff." It was a comment Tina often made in jest, but Karen chose to take it as a compliment. "We're struggling just like you and a whole lot of other people."

Connie came to the door with a walking cane. She didn't look as tired to Karen as she had the last time they were together. She was swollen but visibly doing better. Karen recalled how Connie's weight had shot up seventy pounds from the steroids last year. The rashes were another side effect she suffered from her barrage of medication. It was the final factor in Connie's decision to switch from traditional to holistic medicine. Her skin had smoothed out around her cheeks and neck. Her hair was short and slicked back. Despite her cropped cut and heavy frame, Connie's warm personality overshadowed any shortcomings in her appearance.

"Well, well, if it isn't two strangers."

Both Tina and Karen hugged Connie on the way in.

"I'm so glad you both came."

"Something smells good," Tina said.

"Dinner is ready. Let's eat," Connie replied.

Being in the midst of her two closest friends was rejuvenating to Karen. The trio had weathered physical battles, with each challenge weaving them a bit closer.

"I'm so glad you talked me into coming. I really needed to get out," Karen admitted.

"Why, what's up?" Connie asked.

"Oh, nothing."

"Come on, Karen. It's just us girls," Connie reassured her.

"Speak up, girl. What's on your mind?" Tina added.

At first Karen was reluctant to open up about the issues going on in her marriage. But after giving it some thought, she decided to go ahead. She needed a listening ear.

"Johnny and I are going through some issues."

"That's all? Oh, girl, please. You already went through that stuff. I thought you were leaving him?" Tina sighed.

"Maybe I will. I don't know."

"I knew that wasn't going to happen."

"It's not so easy to walk out after nineteen years, three kids, and a boatload of memories and bills. You're so eager for me to leave—are you willing to pay my bills?" Karen's voice was raised. "I'm not willing to just disrupt my children's lifestyle because Johnny and I can't get it together."

"Leave him for what? What's going on?" Connie asked. She was trying to jump into the heated discussion, but no one was letting her get a word in edgewise.

"I don't want to get into it. It's a long story."

"I have nothing but time to listen," Connie offered compassionately.

"Humph. It's not a long story. It's the same one women hear all the time," Tina contended.

"Tina, stop. You always have something to say. You are so quick to tell everyone else what they're doing wrong in their relationships," Karen yelled. "Where's yours?"

"I'm only being honest."

"Oh, please," Karen snapped. "You aren't even being honest with yourself."

"What does that mean?"

"You always have something to say with that smart mouth of yours. Big Tina, the one who always has to set us straight, the one to tell it like it is. I am so sick of you always being so pushy. You want honesty?" She'd never spoken to Tina with such boldness. Her nostrils were pulsating and ready to spew fire. Her head was bobbing and weaving like a duck dunking for food. "How about this, Tina: you're a big hypocrite. You're a mean woman who needs to deal with the fact that your husband left you." Karen didn't know much about Tina's ex, but what she did know was that he'd bolted.

"That wasn't my fault."

"It might not have been his fault either. Not everybody deals with illness the same way. Maybe he wasn't able to take it," Connie jumped in.

"It doesn't matter why he left. The bottom line is, he's gone. Because he left, it doesn't mean every man out there is a dog," Karen suggested.

"Most are," Tina responded.

"See, that's what I'm talking about. You're an angry, bitter woman, and if you don't watch it, you'll be old and alone without any man, any children, and maybe any friends."

"Ooooh, aren't you in a tizzy. Just because you're mad at Johnny, don't take it out on me."

"I'm not taking out anything on you. I'm giving you back a dose of your own medicine. People like you have no problem dishing it out but don't do too well taking it." Karen glanced at the wall, as if that's were her retort was directed. "And you have the nerve to talk about Johnny."

"That's right. I can talk about him. He's not my husband. It's easy for me to see the dirt he does."

"How? You don't sleep in his face every night. How do you know what my husband's doing other than what I've told you, and I regret that."

"I don't have to sleep with him to know men are trifling, can't be trusted, self-centered, and uncaring."

"See what I mean? You need help," Karen reaffirmed.

"Me? I don't have a cheating man living under my roof."

"Who's talking about cheating? Is that what this is about? Is Johnny cheating on you?" Connie was looking for a point to enter the heated dialogue.

"I didn't say he was cheating. Tina is the one who says he's cheating. I really don't know if he is or isn't."

"There you go making excuses. When are we as women going to stop making excuses for these dogs?" Tina asked.

"When we become perfect enough to judge somebody else," Connie said.

"I'm not judging anyone. I'm merely telling the truth as I see it."

"It's not your place to judge her man. We feel awful about what happened to you. But Tina, not every woman has gone through the same thing you did with your husband. Some husbands are very supportive to their women through sickness and in health," Connie calmly interjected.

"I'd expect you to say something like that." Without thinking about the ramifications, Tina blurted, "You live in denial about your own health."

"Tina," Karen shouted. She jumped up and pointed her finger in Tina's direction but not right in her face. "You have some nerve. That's cruel and cold, even for you. You're selfish and hardhearted. You're really a trip."

As cutthroat as Tina could be, even she felt awful. She'd let anger rule and as a result hurt someone she cared about.

Connie had always been the most timid among the three friends. Karen knew she'd be hurt by the piercing comment and went to comfort her. Connie sat up on the edge of the chair and pushed Karen away.

"I'm sorry. I shouldn't have said that," Tina admitted.

"You're right. You shouldn't have," Connie told her.

"Connie, you can talk, since you have a good man. Most women don't. I didn't."

"So what are you going to do about it?" Karen asked.

"What do you mean?"

"Are you going to keep walking around spitting venom or are you going to learn how to forgive?" Connie asked.

"I don't have anybody to forgive. Bobby is long gone and my cancer is over. That chapter is closed and behind me."

"The cervical cancer might be gone, but the cancer in your heart isn't. With the bitterness and hurt you're carrying, you'll be forced to forgive somebody before it eats you up. You're unhappy and hard to be around," Connie told Tina.

Tina kept unusually quiet. She had already overstepped her bounds and said more than was necessary.

"You need to find the Lord," Karen suggested.

"Yeah, I see what a great job He's done for you; a cheating husband, and you live in fear every day that your cancer is coming back."

"God didn't give me cancer, and He certainly didn't make Johnny go out and see other women."

"He didn't stop it either," Tina fired back. "I believe in God like everybody else. But if I'm going to end up like the two of you, no thank you when it comes to living on that faith stuff. I don't see anything between the two of you that would make me want to hang out there on a wing and a prayer."

"That's close to blasphemy," Karen uttered.

"You can say what you want. The doctors and medicine

have done just fine by me. I'm in full remission, and I don't have relationship issues. I'm doing pretty good right now, if you ask me."

"So you don't think God has control over medicine and doctors? Do you truly think you're alive and well because of some hospital and some doctor?" Connie asked.

"Yes," Tina confidently acknowledged. "Yes, I do. I know that sounds terrible to two Bible-thumpers, but God wasn't around for me. I was sick and alone and scared. I prayed night after night for God to let Bobby keep it together. I wanted children. I wanted the storybook family like everybody else. I begged God to let me have a child. I didn't feel God's presence when the doctor told me I had to choose between living with a hysterectomy or dying with my uterus. What I felt was depression."

Karen and Connie didn't utter a word. Both must have known nothing they said was reaching Tina in her current emotional state. The best thing was to let her get it out. It was the first time she'd expressed to them some of her deep-seated feelings about her past medical challenges.

"I know Bobby wanted children. It was the one thing we talked about for years before getting married. He left. There was nothing I could do, nothing I could say—nothing. He never admitted it, but I know he blamed me for letting myself get the cancer. Once he found out it could have been detected much sooner from my annual Pap smears, he freaked out. I trusted my doctor like everybody else. How was I supposed to know he didn't read the results? I had no idea that I needed to call the doctor to make sure he read my results. I bet most people don't." Refusing to be overcome by emotion, she cleared her throat and sat up in the chair. She flicked a tear from her eye as if to say, "Don't come back."

"It wasn't your fault. You can't blame yourself," Karen told her.

Tina was on a roll. She continued reliving memories of

her painful cancer bout without hearing a word from Karen.

"Every year my doctor said he'd call me if there was a problem with my Pap smear. I didn't hear from him. No news was good news. I assumed everything was fine."

Both Karen and Connie knew Tina needed to vent and didn't interrupt any more.

Tina wiped her eyes and nose again.

"I didn't know Pap smears were that important. I relied on my doctor. I was young and dumb. The farthest thing from my mind was getting cancer of my cervix."

Tina gritted her teeth and held her head back.

"Where was God when my world was falling apart? There weren't any angels camped around my bed singing praises and hymns. I was alone, deciding if I wanted to live or die."

"But you chose to live. That's the bottom line. You're here. Whether you acknowledge God or not, He let you live."

Tina sobbed softly.

Karen pulled a tissue from her purse and moved next to Tina. She took the tissue and wiped her tears.

"You are alive," Connie said.

"You got past that time in your life," Karen added.

"Everybody has challenges, some more than others. You just have to deal with it the best you can, without hurting others along the way."

Chapter 13

The crowd at Floods was thin on weeknights. There wasn't the usual flow of attractive, unescorted women being admired by a slew of flirtatious men. A few isolated conversations, soft piped in easy listening music, and sparse lighting set the ambiance.

The men arrived about the same time and took a small table near the bar. The mood was different but the drinks were the same. Johnny had his usual Hennessy straight up, and Tyrone had a gin and tonic.

Johnny propped one elbow on top of the table, and covered his mouth with his open palm.

"You look stressed. What's up?" Tyrone asked.

"I don't know where this is going," Johnny said, shaking his head.

Tyrone was confused. He wasn't accustomed to seeing his friend in such a worried state. Johnny exuded confidence and control in his walk and in his talk. That was his trademark. Johnny's attitude was new for Tyrone. It bothered him.

"Where is what going?"

"Me and Karen."

"What?" was the best Tyrone could say in utter surprise. He was expecting Johnny to open up about something job related, not about his marriage. Tyrone figured every couple had their moment, but overall, he believed Johnny and Karen had what it took to go the distance.

"We're struggling. No, I'm struggling." Johnny believed he still loved Karen on some level, but he couldn't deal with the physical and emotional void in their relationship. Love didn't seem to be enough to get through the rough spots.

"I'm not getting what I need physically or emotionally."

Johnny saw himself as being strong-willed and confident in business. At home he wanted unwavering admiration and constant appreciation. That was how his previous affair came into play. It gave him the ego boost he desired, without pressure. It was as close to free love as he could get.

"I wonder what Isabelle is up to these days?"

"Isabelle? Man, you can't even think like that."

"Why not? Those were some good times. With Karen and I...well, you know."

Tyrone shook his head and tapped a cigarette out the pack. "Johnny, man, you just can't go there."

"Why not?"

"Because, it's one thing to go out for a drink. It's a whole different ball game getting involved in a relationship. I'll tell you, that can lead to a lot of problems." Tyrone paused and reflected on his past mistakes. "The sacrifice might be too much."

"I know, I know. I'm not serious about Isabelle, or anyone else for that matter. But I might as well be, if you ask Karen. She won't stop dogging me about it. What happened with Isabelle was six years ago. I admit what I did was wrong. I made a mistake. I've tried patching things up, I really have, but it's not totally on me. No matter what I say or do she thinks I'm cheating."

"Are you?"

"I'm at that point," Johnny replied.

"Shoot, you have it made. You have a wife, a great job, smart kids, and a nice home. Most men only dream about having it as good as you."

"Tyrone, everything isn't always what it seems."

"Like what?"

As close as they were, Johnny was self-conscious about exposing certain aspects of his private life.

"I'm just saying we have some real issues."

"Who doesn't?"

"I mean real problems. Karen hasn't given it up in seven months, and it wasn't steady about a year before that. We were cool for about six months after she got out the hospital the last time."

"Wasn't that a couple of years ago?"

"You got it."

"Do you know what the problem is?"

"I wish I did. What I do know is that she started losing interest little by little. Seven months ago it dropped to none at all. At first I thought it had something to do with the chemo treatments, but the doctor says she's fine physically. I don't know what it is. What am I supposed to do? I'm sick of begging. I can't let things go on like this. It's not easy holding back. I have needs. I want some sex. No, I need some sex."

"Wow," Tyrone said a took a gulp of his drink. "I had no idea, but you have to think this thing through. You don't want to get into a situation that could damage your marriage."

"I'm not sure we have a marriage. There's a lot of water under the bridge."

"Well, if you're not sure, take time to work it out."

"Time, that's the problem. It's been a long time since we both felt good about being together. I honestly don't know what happened. I can't forget those big, beautiful eyes, her smile," Johnny said seeming to light up briefly before continuing. "And who could forget that knockout body. She was the full package, plus Karen was easy to talk to and fun to be around back then." He tapped against his glass and said sullenly, "I guess we're not a couple of young crazy in love kids anymore."

He sat in silence for a few moments.

"We were so in love. We had the world by the tail twenty years ago. Everything was at our fingertips," Johnny lowered his gaze and stared at the tabletop, lost in his reminiscing. "I thought everything would be wonderful for us after the baby came. Man, I have worked my butt off for Karen and the kids.

That doesn't seem to be enough for her anymore." He took a swig of his cocktail. "Heck, it's not enough for me anymore."

Johnny sighed and leaned back in his chair, fumbling with the napkin. He gave a slight grin, remembering how intelligent she was. It was what had initially attracted him to her. At the time, he had thought she was the smartest, most attractive girl in high school.

"She used to be," he paused, searching for the right word, "sharp. I mean, man, she was on the ball."

"Karen is a sharp lady," Tyrone agreed.

"No, man." Johnny shook his head. "She's changed. She's comfortable doing nothing. She sits around the house every single day, and it seems to be good enough for her."

"I can't say anything. Connie stays at home."

"That's different; you can afford it. Don't get me wrong; it's all right to be at home. But I can't imagine that's what Karen really wants. She was headed to graduate school after college. Now she doesn't even bring it up anymore."

"It's hard to go back to school after you've been out for a while and have gotten into a routine," Tyrone said.

"I did it, but it takes some motivation. She doesn't have it. I want someone more aggressive. I want to toss ideas around with her about work and career stuff. I need that." Johnny reared back in his chair. "I hate admitting it, but that's how I got caught up with Isabelle. You don't run into too many women in manufacturing. She was sharp as a tack and ran a mean operation. I've never met a woman who was such a strong business match for me."

"I don't know what to tell you, Johnny. What are you going to do?"

"I have no idea. Right now, I just want some peace in my house. Karen and I have been bickering ever since she found Isabelle's phone number in my shirt pocket Saturday."

"Jones?"

"No, not that one. I'm talking about the young lady we

met at Floods the other night. You remember the one I gave a ride home? Well, turns out her name is Isabelle too."

"Really. How weird is that? I didn't realize the two of you had gotten into anything Friday."

"We didn't. I ran into Tina right outside the club. After that, I dropped Isabelle off and went straight home. You know what a big mouth that cobra has."

Tyrone had seen Tina in action and didn't want to feel the wrath she'd put on Johnny. He laughed at the predicament his buddy was in.

"That woman is evil. It's no wonder she got cancer. She hates men, all of us. I'm surprised it hasn't eaten out more of her insides." Johnny spared no harshness when describing Tina.

Still laughing, Tyrone interjected, "So you ran up on the player-hater." He shook his head in amusement.

"Man, that stuff isn't funny. By the time Karen let me know she'd found the number, she was ready to blow a gasket. She accused me of cheating, and who knows what else she's thinking."

"You know how women stick together." Tyrone chuckled.

"Get this—Karen swears I'm seeing Isabelle Jones again. No matter what I say, she believes I'm lying."

"Are you?"

"No." Johnny was somewhat insulted by the implication and let his tone show it. "I honestly haven't talked to her since I broke it off six years ago."

"Don't get upset with me. You're the one who brought her name up half an hour ago."

"You're right. I guess I did."

"I'm telling you, Johnny, don't entertain the thought of another woman unless you're prepared to lay a lot on the line." Tyrone settled back in his seat. "Be careful, player. So what are you going to do about Karen's suspicions?"

"I offered to introduce her to the Isabelle I met Friday to

prove it's not Ms. Jones."

Tyrone started laughing again. "You must be kidding. This is going from bad to worse."

"Now, come on. You know I'm not introducing them, but I had to give Karen something. Otherwise, man, she wasn't easing up. She was going for the jugular, and I had to toss her a bone."

"You need to settle down like me and stick with your girl. Back in the day, messing around was fun. Now I'm too old for that lying and cheating. Too much drama for me."

"Look at you, Mr. Henpecked."

"Whatever. It's all good, because every night I go home to a woman who not only loves me, but also likes my company after eight years of marriage. I don't have any complaints. I'm telling you, Johnny, there is nothing like going home to a woman who you know loves you."

"What are you talking about? You hang out with me from time to time."

"True, every now and then for a few drinks—that's it. But you better believe no one is with me when I leave Floods."

"Who would have thought it? Big, bad Tyrone has gone soft."

"Hey, call it what you will. I'm not messing this up."

Johnny knew his friend was sincere and truly did love his wife.

"Is Connie getting any better?"

"She's hanging in there. I wish there was more I could do to make things easier for her."

"Let Karen tell it, you are the star husband."

"Oh, yeah."

"Yeah, today she asked me why I'm not more supportive, like you are with Connie. She thinks you are the example to follow."

"Nah, not me, man. I just do what I can. You know I've done enough dirt in the past to last me a lifetime."

"So what changed you?"

"I can't explain it, man. I got sick of playing around and never having anybody who was really in my corner. Then Connie came along. She was something special." His countenance lit up as he talked about her. "Finding the right woman to love will change a man."

Johnny leaned in sporting a smug grin. "Yeah, right. You sure your urge to settle down didn't have any connection with that woman who claimed you got her pregnant?"

Tyrone chuckled. "I can't believe you remember that."

"Yeah, I remember. Man, that kind of stuff will put fear into any man," Johnny said. He wouldn't forget when Isabelle got pregnant during the affair. An extramarital child would have jeopardized Johnny's reputation, his financial stability, and his family. He shrugged his shoulders and gave a sigh. "Tyrone, that's the only reason I keep out of real trouble. I'm not taking a chance on hooking up with one of those women and end up getting her pregnant."

"You can lie your way out of a few phone numbers and a boatload of late nights at Floods. You can't get away from DNA, not even someone as smooth as you, player," Tyrone stated.

Johnny sighed. "Seriously, I don't know how I feel about Karen. We're different. Of course, I care about her. You could even say I love her to some degree, but I can admit that I'm not in love with her."

"Ah, that's too bad, partner. I hate to hear this." Tyrone trimmed the rim of his glass with his finger.

"I'll always take care of her financially, but my heart isn't there anymore. Man, it's gone. I see her as a social partner and the mother of my children. I see her as everything but my lover."

"I don't know what you're going to do, if you don't love your wife anymore. That's what will keep you going during the rough patches. I guess that's where the new, or is it the old, Isabelle comes in?" Tyrone was being facetious.

"The new Isabelle is not an issue. Now, the old Isabelle, that's different. After all these years, I have to admit she was quite a package. It's hard to find a woman who has beauty, brains, and is bold enough to stand up to me. She was something special. Honestly, that was the first time I stepped out on the marriage. If I'd met her at a different time in my life...well, you never know how it might have turned out." Johnny gawked at his glass. "Maybe it wasn't the right time six years ago. Maybe this is the right time."

"You need to keep yourself together, Johnny. Don't do something you might regret."

"You're right. I'm not looking for anything serious. A little conversation and maybe...well, you know." Johnny pressed his lips together to restrain the grin. "A brother has needs."

"The grass is always greener," Tyrone pointed out.

"Right now, green grass sounds good to me. I'm tired of playing in the same spot where the grass has worn down."

"Sure, you say that now. Let someone else get interested in Karen and see how you feel about her. Your feelings will sober up quickly. "

"Think so, huh?"

Tyrone had known his friend for enough years to speak candidly. "Sure. As much as you don't think you want her, I know you don't want anyone else to have her either. That's the way it is, bro."

Johnny was humored at Tyrone's implication that the old cliché had any merit with him. "Nope, that's not me."

"Okay, if you say so. Just don't do anything you might regret later," Tyrone reiterated. He looked directly into Johnny's eyes and spoke from his heartfelt experience. 'You know, it can be hard to clean up certain kinds of messes." Tyrone sipped his drink. "Hey, partner, you know whatever you decide, I'm here for you."

"Thanks, man."

Tyrone patted Johnny on the back, intending to lighten the atmosphere. "Just don't do anything crazy, if you know what I mean."

It was eight o'clock. Johnny raised his hand to beckon the waitress.

"Yes, I do know what you mean. I'm heading out. I'll catch you tomorrow."

Johnny wasn't ready to go home. Instead, he went to the company's executive suite located on the mezzanine level of the Renaissance Center. He plopped down on the chair facing the ceiling-high windows. He was considering the warning Tyrone had given. Should he or shouldn't he? His thoughts volleyed back and forth. At the end of the match, his desire for companionship had the stronger serve.

He turned on his cell phone and punched in a four-digit code to access the private directory. Names and numbers appeared. He hadn't used any of the seven phone numbers he'd collected in the past three months, and couldn't place faces with each. He continued scrolling through the list until the name Annette appeared. He remembered her from the club—funny, sexy, and separated. He hesitated for a moment and then let the number dial.

She answered.

"Annette this is Johnny Clark. We met at Floods a few weeks ago and, well, I enjoyed our conversation. So I was wondering if you'd be interested in joining me for a drink at the lounge in the Pontchartrain?"

He stared at the glimmering lights lining the Canadian side of the river. He was pleased when Annette accepted his offer and asked what time.

"Forty-five minutes sounds good to me. See you then," Johnny said.

He looked down at the floor while tapping on the cell phone in his hand. It was going to take more than one evening to sort out his problems. Tonight he was comfortable settling for an intoxicating drink, a relaxing view, and the friendly conversation of an attractive woman to whom he had no commitment.

Chapter 14

After the executive staff meeting ended, Johnny returned to his office and listened to messages on his company cell phone. It would be a short task, given that only his family, Tyrone, his secretary Sonja, and a few designated business representatives had the number.

"You have one new message to review. Please press two now." Johnny pressed the button and heard, "Hello, Mr. Clark. This is Mr. Lewis with E-Finance. Based on a rough approximation we can give you a new equity loan with sixty thousand dollars back at eight percent. I know you asked for eighty thousand dollars, but you need to maintain at least twenty percent of the appraised value of your house in order to avoid PMI. Let me know if you want to proceed. Thanks, Mr. Clark. Look forward to hearing from you."

Sixty thousand—that's it, Johnny repeated to himself. It would be tight, but what choice did he have? He shoved the dilemma into the back of his mind and shifted to an area where he had more success, his work.

Johnny was on top of his game at the office regardless of the shambles his life was in at home. His career aspirations wouldn't allow him to settle for less than an office large enough to tastefully house an eight-foot-long cherry wood desk, a ten-seat conference table, and a sofa and matching wingback chairs.

He twirled a pen in his hand while thinking about last night. He and Annette had left the Renaissance Center before ten-thirty and went for a bite to eat. He took her up on the offer to grab a nightcap at her place. When they arrived at her house just before midnight, she was in the mood. He wasn't relaxed because it had been a while for him. He didn't want to seem overanxious and unable to control himself. Her kisses and caresses had worn him down. Protection, coupled with the admission that her tubes were tied enabled him to relax into the moment.

Thinking back on it, Johnny didn't know if he felt more relieved or guilty that the encounter had taken place. He wanted to satisfy his physical needs, but it didn't make him feel good about cheating. At least he'd kept the six-year-old promise he'd made to himself, which was never to have sex with another woman while he and Karen were intimate. The only time he'd ever had sex with two women concurrently was with Karen and Isabelle. After the fallout from the affair, the promise was a commitment he had to maintain.

"Mr. Clark, I have the production manager on the line. He says it's urgent."

"Okay, Sonja, put him through on the speakerphone."

"Deon, hey, buddy. What's going on out there?"

"We have a problem."

Johnny prided himself on running a tight, award winning operation.

"What kind of problem?" He sat up tall with anticipation. "We have a set of bad blocks. We're having difficulty running them through without the line repeatedly crashing."

"Have you requested a new shipment of blocks?"

"I have, but there's a backlog of about six weeks."

Johnny jumped up. "That won't do."

"I know."

"This is one of our biggest orders. We have got to get this shipment out by next week, no exceptions. The third quarter numbers are in jeopardy if we don't," Johnny spouted.

"I don't know what else to do."

"I can't go to Al with bad news." Johnny was adamant about finding a solution before accepting failure and telling the chief officer.

"Well, I'll do whatever you want me to. I just wanted to keep you in the loop. I already put in a call to your assistant. I know he's supposed to start traveling down here for situations like this."

Normally Johnny would defer a production problem to his assistant VP. But he saw this as a prime opportunity to personally handle a critical problem while also being able to take a break from the home front.

"Yeah, thanks for filling me in, Deon. This is critical. I'll handle this one myself. I'll be there late this afternoon. In the meantime, get on the phone with the backup supplier and see what we can get. I also need you to check and double check that line. Make sure it is fully functioning and that it is not the source of our problem."

"Will do, boss. I'm on top of it. I'll see you when you get here."

Johnny buzzed his secretary.

"Sonja, can you please see if the corporate plane is going to Tennessee this afternoon? If it is, get me on the list. If not, book me on a commercial flight."

"Okay, sir. I'll do it right away."

"Also, get me the most recent problem reports for the block lines. Yes, and, uh, get DeWayne on the line. I need to give him the update and to let him know I'm going down in his place."

"Anything else, sir?"

"Yes, hold my calls. I need to run home and grab a few clothes before the flight leaves. Call me on my cell phone and let me know which flight I'm taking."

Johnny had pressing issues at the top of his priority list. Smoothing the waters with Karen wasn't one of them.

Chapter 15

Karen would have given anything to have Johnny walk in. She sat in the waiting room building up assurance before the MRI.

The nurse eased the door open leading to dressing rooms.

"Mrs. Clark, you can come on back."

Karen quickly gathered her belongings. She was anxious to get the procedure over but in no hurry to get started.

"Take off your jewelry and clothes and put them in one of the dressing room lockers. You can leave on your underpants and shoes." The nurse rattled off instructions like a computerized recording.

"When you're ready, come on out with the surgical gown on."

Karen followed orders. She found herself fidgeting in the dressing room.

"I'm ready," Karen told the nurse.

"Okay, I'll take you into the examination room."

The chilly, dimly lit hallway seemed endless. Karen would have been relieved with Johnny as close as the waiting room, since visitors weren't allowed in the actual imaging room.

She hated using the MRI machine but couldn't deny the value it had in helping to pinpoint her diagnosis. Yet, it didn't give her much ease in going through the process. Her body froze when she saw the white, tubular, coffin like apparatus. Being submerged in the confined space gave Karen an eerie feeling of being buried alive.

"Let me hook up the IV."

The table slid Karen inside the tube. There wasn't any physical pain associated with the exam, other than the momentary prick that came from having the IV needle inserted into her arm. She tried closing her eyelids to block out the surroundings, to no avail. Her vital signs were too elevated for her to fall asleep. It was if the tight space was cutting off her air. Screaming wouldn't help. She had to endure the next sixty minutes any way she could.

It was bad enough having the MRI done on her breasts. Having her head done was worse. The procedure required whatever part of the body being examined to be placed in the center of the machine. That meant her head had to go completely inside the tube. Once inside the machine, Karen couldn't move, but it didn't stop her from weeping.

God, please be with me. Tears rolled down her face and wet her ear. *Help me to get through this.* The table slid in a bit farther. *Why do I have to go through this alone, again?* Without explanation, a sudden burst of calmness consumed Karen. Her mind was clear. The hour passed and not even Johnny dominated her thoughts.

Karen was happy to have the exam over. Driving home, she was feeling better than she had in the past few days. The headache had subsided to a faint discomfort. Saturday was rapidly approaching. She was ready to start preparing for the party. She made a mental note to stop by the caterer and finalize the menu. She also needed to order champagne and balloons. There was so much to do.

She pulled out a small piece of notepad paper from her purse and commenced to jot down a long list of to-do items. Planning and organizing. She was beginning to feel a little like her old self. It was a lifestyle she'd come to enjoy.

Karen pulled into the driveway and wheeled to the three-car garage after a full morning of running around. She was humming and singing a few tunes from her contemporary gospel music. The day out had done her good. It was as if the weight had fallen away, giving her a brief reprieve. She pushed the automatic garage door opener. While the door was opening, she began gathering her items together. Like a ton of bricks, it hit her. *What am I doing?*

Her marriage was struggling dangerously near separation. She didn't know where they were headed. Where did an anniversary party fit? She shook her head in dismay and went inside the house.

She looked around the oversize kitchen as though the answer was magically written on the wall. She picked up the note left on the counter and immediately recognized it as Johnny's handwriting. She was eager to read it, since they hadn't spoken after the dispute yesterday afternoon.

Karen was expecting to see him when she arrived home from Connie's last night, but Johnny hadn't gotten in before her. She felt him crawl into bed sometime in the wee hours of the morning, and he was up and gone before she woke up.

Perhaps it was a note of apology. She quickly read it in hopes that it was.

Karen,
I have a major production problem in Tennessee. I'm heading back down there this afternoon. I expect to be gone several days. I'll give you a call when I get to the plant.
Johnny

"What? That's it?"

Karen was filled with anger and slammed the note onto the countertop.

"That's it? I can't believe he left again."

Karen grabbed the phone and dialed Johnny's cell phone with her heart pounding. She didn't know what she was going to say, but that didn't stop her.

She heard, "Welcome to the voicemail system."

She hung up and frantically dialed his office.

"Good afternoon, Mr. Clark's office."

"Sonja, this is Karen. I'm trying to catch up with Johnny."

"Oh, his flight left about ten minutes ago. I thought he'd

stopped by home before catching the flight," Sonja said with a tinge of uncertainty.

"I barely missed him," Karen quickly suggested, to eliminate any perception that she didn't know where her husband was. "I was out running errands this morning. When I got back, I got his note." She was determined not to reveal the depth of her embarrassment. "Oh, well, I guess I missed him. I'll wait for him to give me a call from the plane."

Karen ended the call, fuming.

Chapter 16

A succulent smell of hazelnut and vanilla engulfed the kitchen. Karen stirred a teaspoon of honey into her cup of hot tea. She had longed for a relaxing moment after the hectic morning of errands and the MRI. She slid onto the chaise longue in the family room, careful not to spill a drop of tea. Party plans were underway and the tests were done. The day was looking up. Johnny was the only remaining element driving her blood pressure up.

When the phone rang, Karen was ready to give Johnny a piece of her mind.

"This is Dr. Costas's office. The doctor would like to see you."

"Can you please tell me why she wants to see me?" Karen was worried. Every time the doctor asked her to come into the office after a series of tests, it wasn't good news.

"To go over your MRI results."

"When?"

"This afternoon, let's say around two-thirty?"

Karen glanced at her watch.

"It's almost two o'clock now."

"I know this is short notice, but I know she would like to see you today. Her schedule is packed the rest of this week."

"Fine," Karen conceded. "I'm on my way."

Ten minutes wouldn't make a difference. Karen decided to clutch this rare bit of peace before facing the doctor. She sipped the tea and savored the warm feeling that it provided. She took her time, got dressed, and headed toward whatever news there was.

Dr. Costas kept pretty close to her schedule. It was no surprise for Karen when the nurse took her into the doctor's office right away. Karen made herself as comfortable as she could while waiting.

She couldn't help but notice the brightly colored poster that said, *Prescreening can save your life—how much do you really know about cancer?* Karen went on to read the bold highlights.

- Over 95 percent of individuals diagnosed with breast cancer in the earliest stage live beyond five years
- 70 percent of lumps found in breasts are benign
- More white women get breast cancer, but more black women die from late diagnosis
- Men and women are subject to both breast and colon cancer
- 9 out of 10 incidents of colon cancer could be prevented if polyps are detected and removed in the early stage
- Ovarian cancer is not easily detected
- Cervical cancer of the uterus is detectable through a routine Pap smear
- Twice as many black men die from prostate cancer than white men
- Lung cancer kills more women yearly than breast cancer
- 1/3 of all cancers could be eliminated with changes in lifestyle and diet, not even counting smoking

Karen realized how much she didn't know about the other forms of cancer. She made a mental note to talk to Johnny about getting prescreened for colon and prostate cancers. She wouldn't bother asking him to check for breast cancer. He was too macho to consider the notion of getting a "woman's disease." It would be hard enough to talk him into getting his prostate and colon checked, seeing that the screening had to be done through the rectum.

The physician entered the room dressed in a white lab coat.

"Doctor, I didn't expect to hear from you this fast."

"I wanted to get back with you as soon as possible, so I put a rush on the tests."

Karen was both reluctant and, at the same time, eager to get the results. She could finally put her fears to rest. A clean bill of health was what she hoped for. "Remember Tina?" she asked Dr. Costas.

"Of course. How is she doing?"

"She's fine. We were together last night for dinner."

"Glad to hear that's she's doing well. We were fortunate with her case."

"That's what I want. The same results she had."

"That's what I'd like for you too, Karen. About your test, I've reviewed the results of your MRI. It looks like you still have the same small tumor lodged near your brain."

"What! "

"Karen, calm down. Did you hear what I said?"

"What?"

"I said that it's the small tumor. It doesn't appear to have grown or moved any. That's good news. So long as it hasn't changed, it's best for us to leave it alone."

Dr. Costas's diagnosis didn't comfort Karen. Connie's struggle heightened Karen's fear about tumors. Doing nothing left Karen troubled. She already felt horrible about not identifying her breast cancer earlier with self-exams. The concept of early detection and treatment was ingrained in her mind after battling cancer for four years. She didn't see the tumor as an exception.

"So what does that mean for my headaches?"

"It means I need to do some other tests."

"More tests. Why? What else can we test?"

"The MRI results are good news. However, the blood tests didn't come back as well as I would have liked."

"What do you mean?"

"Your white counts are definitely up."

Karen slumped in her chair and braced for what Dr. Costas was about to say.

"I'm concerned that your cancer might be back."

Karen let Dr. Costas's words saturate her inner soul. Her body was numb. Getting the bad news wasn't an unfamiliar pill but was no easier to swallow this time around. She knew how often breast cancer recurred in women. Her prayer was not to be one of those patients who yo-yoed in and out of remission.

"Karen, are you okay?"

"Um-hmmm."

She couldn't speak. It required too much energy and would be just the impetus needed to convert the lump in her throat to a stream of tears. Crying wasn't what she wanted to do with Dr. Costas in the room.

The doctor rolled the stool over to Karen and took her hand. "I know this is difficult."

Karen remained quiet. She was in shock.

Dr. Costas could tell Karen was struggling with the news. She wanted to encourage her as best she could under the circumstances. "We need to jump on this right away. We have been successful with your treatment in the past. Timing is key."

"What do I have to do?"

"I have made arrangements for you to be admitted to Wayne State University this afternoon."

"That soon?"

"We can't waste any time in getting a clear diagnosis. You will feel better when some of the uncertainty is addressed. If it turns out that we're dealing with the cancer again, I want to know. You know our best weapon against this cancer is early detection and aggressive treatment."

Karen was fidgeting in her seat. She jumped up and paced

the room.

"Not the hospital, not today. I can't go today," she stammered. "What about my children?" she blurted desperately struggling to contain her emotions. "I need enough time to make arrangements for them."

She was becoming more frantic.

"I don't have anyone to take care of them. Johnny's out of town. I have to find out when he's coming back."

"All right, but we can't wait too long to get the additional tests done. It may come back negative, but with your history, well, I..."

"What?"

"Like I said, I prefer to get a jump on the rest of the tests and treatment, if necessary."

"This is too fast. I need time."

"When can you check in to the hospital?"

Karen wrung her sweaty palms together and rubbed them on her paper-covered knees. "I promise, I'll go tomorrow."

"Good. I will make the necessary arrangements. I'll also update your general practitioner on what's happening."

"How long will I have to stay in the hospital?"

"I can't say for sure, but prepare to be there at least several nights."

The ride home was long and slow. The route that Karen had taken so many times to get home from the doctor's office seemed foreign today. A million thoughts and fears flooded her mind. It was a place she had hoped to never visit again. God hadn't been at the forefront of her most recent thoughts, but it looked like that would be changing.

Chapter 17

Johnny hadn't gotten the production problem at the plant under control, but his little trip away from home was turning out to be the space he needed to gain perspective.

He wasn't sure what was going on with him and Karen. One issue was certain--he was fed up with bickering. What would it take to leave? When he'd mentioned separation the other day she hadn't responded. Johnny leaned back in his seat in search of a relaxing position. In his gut, he didn't see her leaving regardless of how bad it got between them. It didn't surprise him. She enjoyed the accolades that came with being the Clarks. They were the jet setting couple living in a big house situated on a couple of acres, with three adorable children to boot.

He hated how difficult it was for her to make tough decisions. Make a decision and deal with the consequences was his philosophy. Her uncertainty was expected. His wasn't. On this rare occasion, Johnny wasn't sure what he wanted. Separation seemed like an option; then again, was it? Maybe it was time to make a move.

Leaving the kids would be hard. Abandoning his children was the act of a coward, but he would still provide for them. Yet, taking care of the finances for two households would require planning. There was so much that would have to be worked out. Perhaps staying was easier. He wondered if it was possible to hang in there at least until Elizabeth went to college.

Before he got too far down that road, he revisited his immediate needs. Karen hadn't given any indication that she wanted to stay in the marriage, but she wasn't doing what it took to keep it together. He was tired of waiting around. If she didn't want him in her bed, there were others who did.

Memories of Ms. Jones brought a certain warmth. Time they spent together had been memorable, both positively and negatively for him. But, he couldn't ignore how painful it had been for his family. Curiosity, a couple shots of Hennessy, and an empty bed got the best of him.

Johnny went back and forth about dialing the old number he had for Isabelle. The set of digits had both comforted and haunted him for several years. Johnny ripped a corner of the notepad and scribbled the phone number as he recalled it. After a bit more volleying, he finally gave in.

Tyrone's advice was tossed aside as Johnny barreled into dangerous territory. He picked up the receiver and attempted to dial the number three times, never completing the call. The fourth time he let it go through. Suddenly it dawned on him that he didn't know what to say. He searched for words but none came. It had been a long time since he and Isabelle had spoken. The phone rang four times and went into a voice message.

A familiar soft and sultry voice instructed him to leave a message.

Johnny hadn't been sure if the number was any good after losing contact for several years. Hearing the voice on the message left no doubt.

He paused, searching for a suitable message to leave. "Hi, uhm." It was difficult pulling out words. Perhaps if she'd answered in person, it would have been easier. Tipsy or not, Johnny knew Ms. Jones was not a situation to be toyed with. Making one call could start an avalanche of events he might not be able to handle. With the exception of a few grunts, he hung up without saying anything and wondered if caller ID would give him away.

He pulled out his cell phone without hesitation. It was early in the evening which meant there was a good chance Annette was already home from work. He closed his eyes and pressed his thumb against his forehead. He was involved with Annette for one purpose. Calling her on a business trip could send the wrong message. It would be better to call her when he got back to Detroit. Perhaps he could make a quick stop at her place on his way home.

Chapter 18

"**M**ommy," Chelle whispered, wanting to wake Karen but not startle her.

"Hmmm," she responded, semi awake. Karen recognized the voices of her little ones, regardless of how groggy she was.

"We're getting ready to go to school."

Karen prided herself on being a mother. Lately she had been distracted and had left the girls to be more self-reliant than usual. Thank goodness Chelle was able to help out and give her mother a little time to deal with her dilemmas.

"Did you eat something for breakfast?"

"Yes," Chelle responded.

Elizabeth wasn't going to be left out of whatever conversation was going on with her mom. She loved the doses of attention Karen dished out. She spoke up before Chelle could finish. "We ate cereal again."

Elizabeth jumped on Johnny's side of the bed for a closer connection with her mom. Whenever her daddy was gone, she saw it as a license to fill the empty spot.

"Chelle wouldn't let me have any more juice."

"You had two glasses. That's enough for one morning," Chelle firmly instructed.

Elizabeth was hoping Karen might override the older sister's restrictions.

"Two whole glasses?" Karen tickled Elizabeth's tummy and her daughter let out a giggle. 'You're going to float away. Don't you think two glasses is probably enough, Bethy?"

The child continued to giggle. "Okay, okay, yes."

"Elizabeth, let's go. Let Mommy sleep."

"But I didn't see you after dinner last night," Elizabeth reminded her mom.

"I know, sweetie. Mommy was tired."

"Oh, yeah, Mommy, I forgot to tell you Daddy called."

"When?"

"Right after you fell asleep. He told me not to wake you up."

"Convenient," Karen said under her breath.

"What did you say, Mom?"

"Nothing."

She sat up and opened her arms for both kids to embrace her. Elizabeth didn't hesitate for a minute.

"I'm driving you to school today."

"Yeaaaaa," Elizabeth screamed.

"Mom, you don't have to."

"I want to, honey. I need to talk to you both." She paused to get herself together and to hide her fear.

"I'm not feeling well."

"You want me to stay home with you?" Chelle offered.

"Me too?" Elizabeth jumped in.

"No, no, my sweethearts. I have to go to the hospital."

"Oh, Mommy, not the hospital." Chelle was saddened in remembrance of how afraid she was four years ago when her mother went to the hospital.

Elizabeth was unusually quiet.

Karen pulled her daughters tight to her chest, squeezing them unrelentingly. She kissed the girls on their foreheads and whispered, "Shhhhh. It's going to be okay, babies."

"How long do you have to be there?" Chelle asked choking out her question.

"I'll only be gone a few days. Nothing major."

"Can I come and see you this time? I'm old enough now," Elizabeth said.

She hadn't understood the severity of her mother's illness four years ago. She was barely four years old at the time. All Elizabeth knew was that she couldn't visit her mom in the hospital like Erick and Chelle. Everyone said she was too little. She remembered how much she missed her mom.

Karen tried to console her worried daughters but wasn't able to abate their tears.

"When do you have to go?"

"Today."

Karen wanted to shield the girls from as much fear and worry as she could. At the same time, she reveled in seeing how responsible and mature Chelle was. Karen opted to be honest and trust her daughter with difficult news.

"I'm going right after I take you to school. Don't worry. Daddy's coming home." Karen feathered Chelle's hair back from her face. "He'll probably pick you up and let you come visit me this evening. Would that be okay?"

Chelle nodded with tears slowly rolling down her cheeks.

"Okay, let's get ready to go, young ladies."

Karen tried to get up from the bed. Neither girl would let her move.

"Sweethearts, it's going to be all right."

Karen cupped her hands around Chelle's face and peered at her daughter.

"I love you, Chelle, baby."

Elizabeth wrapped her arms around Karen's waist, not quite able to reach all the way around. The three huddled together for several more moments before making a move.

Karen finally managed to tear herself away from the girls long enough to get dressed and get them to school. Normally only one of the girls would sit in the front seat, but today was different. Both slid into the long front seat and gave Karen minimal breathing space. Each of the girls savored every inch of the ride to school with their mom.

The car eventually pulled up to the private school. Karen put the car in park and turned to look at her daughters. Her eyes were watery but her voice was clear. Karen knew the girls needed to sense she wasn't afraid and everything was going to be fine. She embraced the two girls, with Elizabeth getting securely squished in the middle.

"Aunt Tina will probably pick you up after school."

"Are we going to stay with her while you're in the hospital?" Elizabeth asked.

"No, baby. Daddy should be home this evening. In case he can't get back right away, you might have to stay overnight with Aunt Tina. We'll see. Either way, I will call the school and let them know who's picking you up. Okay, sweethearts?" She kissed both girls on the cheek. "I'll be back home before you know it. Now go on. Don't be late for class."

Karen couldn't hold her tears back much longer. She hurried her girls from the car and on their way. "I'll call you this evening."

"Bye, Mommy. I love you," Elizabeth blurted.

"I love you too," Chelle somberly echoed, and closed the door. Karen watched the girls walk toward the school. Leaving them was painful. Thank goodness she only had to say goodbye once. She drove two blocks from the school and had to pull over. Tears were clouding her vision.

After she got herself together, Karen pulled away. There were quite a few things she needed to do before heading to the hospital. She needed to get groceries, a few toiletries, and most important, get the girls' care squared away. She would have liked to do a couple loads of laundry but knew there wasn't going to be time. The girls would have to handle that alone this week.

She was at least going to cook a decent meal for the family before leaving. She made enough for several days, figuring the leftovers would last until she got back home.

Time quickly ticked away as Karen completed her errands and packed a bag for the hospital. She was thankful Tina had agreed to take care of Chelle and Elizabeth until Johnny got back in town. Once Karen canceled the anniversary party and got in touch with Johnny, she'd be ready to go. According to the secretary, his schedule included a closed-door session for the entire morning. There was no way to reach him.

Karen glanced at the time on the kitchen clock. "I should be out of here by one."

She set a pan of meatballs in the refrigerator. The phone rang just as she was tossing the salad. She wiped the residual dressing from her fingers and hurried to the phone, relieved.

"Johnny, thank goodness."

"I got a message that you called."

"I have several times. It's been difficult to get a hold of you today." After letting the words loose, Karen cringed.

"That's because I'm working." Johnny was taken aback by her attitude. Somebody had to work. She should understand that without a reminder. He didn't have time for this. "There's a big problem I'm handling down here. We've been meeting all morning."

"I know. Sonja told me."

"So why are you giving me grief?" There was silence. They weren't getting anywhere, and Johnny was short on time. He decided to change his tone and come at the situation differently. "Karen, I called you last night, but you were asleep."

"I know. Chelle told me."

Johnny was unprepared for Karen's calmness. He fully expected her to be ranting and raving about his being out of town for several nights without much prior notice. It was usually a no-win situation. When he neglected to forewarn her about quick trips, she would make a fuss about it. When he did tell her, she made a fuss. It was an argument regardless. He waited for her to strike.

"Johnny..." She paused and took a deep breath. "Dr. Costas wants me to check into the hospital this afternoon, and I need you to come home for the girls."

"The hospital? For what?"

"To see what's causing my headaches. And there's also the chance that the cancer might be back. She wants to run more tests."

"Back again! Is that possible, even though your breasts are already gone?"

"I don't know. I guess."

"How do you feel?" he asked, stunned.

"How do you think I feel? I'm scared to death. I can't go through it all over again. I don't know if I can take it."

Johnny wouldn't say it, but he felt the exact same way. The possibility of replaying her cancer treatment over again was a devastating blow.

Karen felt emotionally vulnerable but refused to break down on the phone with Johnny. His lack of compassion was a pill she didn't feel like swallowing.

"Do you know how long you'll be in the hospital?"

"Not really. Maybe a couple of days, depending on the test results."

Johnny sighed and offered nothing else.

"When can you come home? The girls need you."

"I'll have to wind things up here and come back tonight."

"Will you be finished with whatever you're working on down there?"

"I don't know."

"What are you going to do if you're not finished?"

"It's not an option. I have to come back. Somebody has to be there with the girls. I'll do what I have to do."

"Thank you. I feel much better knowing you will be here. They were upset this morning when I took them to school."

"You don't have to thank me for taking care of my kids. You make it seem like I'm doing you a favor. I'm not. Those are my children too, and regardless of what happens with us, I will always love them and take care of them."

"I'm not worried about you taking care of them. I've always said you're a good father. I can't deny that."

"Anyway, I won't get in until late tonight. Is there any way Connie can keep them until I get home?"

"I don't think so. You know she isn't driving anymore."

"No, I didn't know, but okay. I would ask Tyrone to pick the girls up, but I know he's downtown today. There's no way he'll get back out to the burbs in time to get them." Johnny seemed to be at a loss for options.

"Don't worry. I already have Tina onboard."

"Tina--" He didn't elaborate.

"She'll keep them until you get home." Karen knew he wasn't thrilled with the arrangement, but what else could she do?

"I'll pick them up when I get in," he conceded. "Just make sure she doesn't have a lot of mouth when I get there. I won't be in any mood to hear it." Johnny had enough on his mind to keep his own blood pressure up without any help from Tina. "I don't need to hear what that hypocritical witch has to say."

"Well, I'm just glad she's able to get the girls for us. She'll probably bring them to the hospital after school."

"I'd rather pick them up there, but..." he paused, "there's no guarantee I'll be back before visiting time is over."

"I'm sure you'll work it out with Tina."

"Yeah, right."

Karen was tired of being the go-between for Johnny and Tina's spats. She wasn't going to waste her energy smoothing the tension between them. She decided to let it be their problem and no longer hers. She had plenty of her own issues to handle. "Oh, and I'm not expecting to hear from Erick since he called last week. But if he does, don't tell him what's going on. I'd rather be back at home before telling him anything."

"I guess you're right. Don't make sense to raise an alarm with him before we find out more. He can't do anything from Europe anyway," Johnny said.

"I agree." She checked her watch. Time was ticking away. "I'd better go. I should be checking in before two."

"Well, I'll let you know when I get into town tonight."

It wasn't the best of times for the couple. Karen was not comfortable going into the hospital on such shaky ground with Johnny. "I love you," she told him.

"You take care of yourself, and I'll see you soon," was the Johnny could muster.

Karen felt rejection from Johnny's response, but not total shock. "Fine. I'll see you soon."

Chapter 19

Karen survived the boatload of paperwork and the relentless poking and prodding associated with her preadmission process. She dreaded her stays in the hospital. It hadn't become comfortable yet and probably never would.

"All done, Mrs. Clark. Let me find out your room number and order a wheelchair. We'll have you on your way in a few minutes."

The nurse was full of pleasantries. It wasn't adequate to convert the grim look on Karen's face. Her established routine was to come into the hospital, get the treatment over and get back home. She felt strange this time.

Maybe the rest will do me some good, she thought. Johnny would have to keep up with his job, the house, and the girls. It would be good for him. It was something Karen had done for years with little to no appreciation from her husband.

"Am I going to the cancer wing?"

The nurse flipped through the chart looking for indication of where the doctor wanted Karen.

"You know, I'm not sure. It looks like Dr. Costas has you here for some tests. Looks like you're going to the fourth floor B wing."

Karen squinted. Her frequent visits to the hospital made her familiar with the cancer sections. B wing wasn't one of her usual stops. "Which tests am I having?"

The nurse was careful not to exceed her authority and give Karen answers that conflicted with the doctor.

"Did you have a biopsy or a CAT scan already?"

"No."

"I imagine that's what the doctor will order, but I'm not

sure. You'll have to confirm that yourself,"

The nurse perused the chart again before sending Karen on her way with the orderly.

Karen sat limp and quiet on the wheelchair powered ride. It was bad enough struggling with the cancer she knew about. Now there was the added threat of more unknowns. What more?

The orderly wheeled in and out of elevators, up and down corridors, making his way to fourth floor B wing. He pulled up to a room across from the nurse's station and stopped. He double checked the chart to make sure it was the right room.

"Yep, this is it, room 407."

He wheeled the chair into the room. The curtain was partially drawn, making it difficult to see the other patient.

"This isn't the right room. I'm supposed to be in a single."

The confused orderly gleaned the chart again.

"No, this is the room they have down for you."

"Can't be. I asked for a single."

"I don't know what to say. This is what they have down."

The happy-go-lucky orderly didn't know what to do. "They probably put you in here because the single rooms are filled. Matter of fact, this whole wing is full. This is the only bed left." The orderly sensed Karen's discontent. "If you want, I can check with admissions to see what they can do."

"No, that's all right."

"Karen Clark, what are you doing here?" a voice echoed from the other side of the hospital room.

She stretched her neck from the wheelchair to see who could possibly know her in such an inopportune place.

"Reverend Lane, what a surprise. What are you doing here?" The curtain was blocking Karen's view.

"I'm visiting with Mother Walker."

"Ms. Emma Walker from church?" Karen asked.

"Pull the curtain back so I can see you," a strong voice piped up. The orderly honored the elderly lady's request.

"Now, that's a heap better." The older woman adjusted the pearl colored glasses on her nose. "Karen Clark, is that you?"

'Yes, ma'am. It's me."

"Well, I'm glad and not so glad to see you." She laughed at her own humor. "I'm glad to see you, but not in this hospital."

"Yes, Ms. Walker. Likewise."

"Now, you know better than to call me Ms. Walker. Big Mama, Mother Walker, or even Ms. Emma will do fine."

"Okay, Ms. Emma." The lighthearted dialogue brought a smile to Karen.

"Excuse me, Mrs. Clark, I need to get back downstairs. Is there anything you need before I leave?" the young orderly asked.

"No, I'm set. Thanks."

"Push the nurse's call button if you need anything." Karen sat on the side of her bed facing Mother Walker.

"How are you doing, Ms. Emma?"

"I'm fine as can be. I'm going home in a few days."

"Good for you."

"We're happy to have her going home," Reverend Lane added.

Mother Walker was known in the church as a mighty prayer warrior. She didn't have much in the way of formal education. Her wisdom came from seventy years of living. After her husband died, she dedicated her life to serving the Lord and helping his people. It was often said that her hotline rang directly with God. She was able to give support without judgment, and it drew individuals to her. Mother Walker was the one called on day and night whenever there was someone in the church who had problems and needed prayer.

Karen wasn't expecting help in the form of Ms. Emma, but there she was.

Chapter 20

Tina wanted to tell Connie about Karen. The three had their differences, but when the situation got serious, pettiness got shoved aside.

Tyrone had recently bought Connie a telephone headset so she wouldn't have to rush around. Relaxed, Connie answered the ringing phone to find Tina on the other end. "What a surprise to hear from you this early in the afternoon. Aren't you working today?"

"Yes, I am. I'm calling to see if you talked to Karen today."

"No, not today. Why?"

"Well, she called me a little while ago and asked if I could pick the girls up from school. She's going to the hospital."

"For what?"

"Her cancer might be out of remission."

"Oh, no. When is she going to the hospital?"

"I think she left a little while ago."

"I wonder why she didn't call me?"

Tina had her speculations about why Karen hadn't told Connie. She knew Karen shielded their friend from bad news in case she was too emotionally fragile to handle it. Tina didn't share the same sentiment. From her perspective, Karen and Tyrone were doing Connie a disservice by constantly protecting her from certain situations. Tina believed they were enabling her to continuously live in denial, even about her own medical condition.

"She probably didn't want you to make yourself sicker by worrying."

"She's always worrying about me. I keep telling her I'm fine except for a few headaches here and there. It's not like I'm an invalid or anything."

Tina shook her head. Why Connie's denial bothered her

so much was unclear, but it was evident she had no intentions of being an enabler like Tyrone and Karen.

"I can see how she'd be worried about you. You've had those little headaches for quite a while—quite a long while."

Connie didn't respond to what Tina was insinuating. She blocked the negativity that often came from Tina without letting it impact their friendship.

"That girl, why would she be thinking about me at a time like this? She needs to be focusing on herself right now and getting better."

"Humph." Tina was in full agreement. "You know that's how she is. Worrying about everybody and everything except herself."

"Well, if there's any way I can help you with the girls, let me know."

"Thanks, but I should be fine. They're only going to be with me for a few hours until their lying and cheating daddy gets back from Tennessee tonight."

"Tina, why do you have to say that?"

"Why not? It's the truth. He's no good, and I don't know why Karen puts up with him. Do you know I caught him at the club with some woman last Friday night? What nerve? I'm sure he lied his way right out of it."

"I don't know what to say. I really hope they're able to work it out. They've been through enough, and I do believe they love each other."

"You have got to be kidding. Nobody cheating on you loves you. The only person Johnny Clark loves is Johnny Clark. Karen might tell us a lot, but you'd best believe she's not telling us everything," Tina said.

"I'm sure there's more to it than we know. We just have to be supportive. "

"Yeah, right. You go right ahead. I'm being real. Johnny doesn't deserve any support from me. What he deserves is a kick to the curb, and that's the truth. I'm through with it."

"Okay. Well, like I said, let me know if there's anything we can do. Tyrone and I will be available."

Connie was sad. She knew that Tina wouldn't have any appreciation for a long-term relationship until she dealt with her anger and feelings of rejection. Connie picked up the frame that sat next to the sofa. It held a picture of her and Tyrone embracing in front of a sidewalk cafe in Rome. She kissed her fingers and touched the framed picture. The conversation with Tina reminded her of how grateful and secure she was in her marriage. She decided to call and let Tyrone know how much he was adored. She could also tell him the news about Karen.

A few rings and he was on the phone.

"Is something wrong?" Tyrone spent his time away from Connie thinking about her.

"I'm fine, honey. I'm calling about Karen."

"Why, what's up with her?"

"She's back in the hospital."

"Oh, no. When?"

"Apparently she just went this afternoon."

"Is it serious?"

"Tina told me the cancer might be out of remission."

Tyrone sighed and slumped in his chair. Even though Karen wasn't his wife, he couldn't help but feel compassion for his best friend, Johnny. He had felt that moment of despair so many times with Connie's illness. The worst time was hearing there had been a setback. Those words had a way of penetrating his flesh and drilling right down to the inner core of his heart and painfully severing circulation to key organs in his body. That fleeting, lifeless moment had felt like an eternity to Tyrone. He was sure it would have no less impact on Johnny.

"Boy, this is tough. I'm going to check in with Johnny."

"Tina said he's coming back from Tennessee tonight."

"I'll catch up with him tonight then."

"You are a good friend. Johnny is blessed to have you and so am I."

"No, I'm the fortunate one, and I count my blessings every day." Tyrone seized every opportunity to flatter his wife. "I'm off to a meeting, if everything else is okay with you."

"Sure, go on. I'll see you when you get home."

Tyrone hung up content. Connie was an inspiration to him. She didn't wait around for a better day. She focused on making each day the best, as though it was her last. He saw her as someone who did more living while sick than most able-bodied people. Every day she found a reason to smile, and that made him happy. He would often say, "If she can find a reason to be happy every day, in spite of her pain and suffering, then who am I to feel down in the dumps?" Being around her had taught him that regardless of how bad the situation was, there was always somebody going through much worse.

This was one of the happiest times in Tyrone's life, even with Connie's illness. He understood what it meant to love unconditionally, to love so unapologetically, and it felt good.

Halfway out of the office, he turned around, went back to the phone, and placed a call.

"You have reached the voice mailbox of John Clark..."

Tyrone waited for the automated voice to spill out the rest of the greeting so he could leave a message.

"Hey man, it's Tyrone. Look here, partner, Connie told me about Karen going back into the hospital." He paused for a moment, twirling the mini pack of Post-it notes on his desk. "Call me if you want to talk. I just want you to know I'm here for you, partner. I'll catch you later."

Chapter 21

Johnny was exhausted from a long day of nonstop meetings and pressing issues at the manufacturing plant. He slung the hanging bag and his sports jacket into the backseat of the car and headed out the airport parking lot. He slid his hand down his face. Last night it had seemed like a good idea to stop by Annette's once he'd arrived back in town for a quick visit. After fourteen hours of work and travel, it was no longer a consideration. Going home and kicking off his shoes was the ticket.

He pressed the accelerator and made tracks down the Southfield Expressway. Faster he got to Tina's, the quicker his nightmare would be over. He dreaded having to pick the kids up from her. He rolled onto the street where she lived and was glad to see an empty spot. Since she rented the first floor of a duplex, he was able to see his car from her front door. He left it running as a reminder that he needed to get the kids quickly and get back on his way. He knocked on the door, hoping Chelle would be the one to answer it.

Tina pulled back the corner of the curtain, saw Johnny, and cracked the door open.

"Where are the girls?"

"They're here."

"Tell them I said let's go."

Tina turned toward the living room and said in a sub-dued tone, intended to annoy Johnny. "Girls, your dad's here." She turned back to Johnny with a smirk. "So you're babysitting tonight, huh? Too bad. I know it's going to mess up your little plans. I guess the only play you'll be getting tonight is playing daddy."

"I'm not in the mood, Tina."

"Don't get all snippety and mad at me because you were

cold busted at the club last week."

"Stay out of my business. I'm not going to tell you again."

"Oh, and what are you going to do, make me? Your barking doesn't scare me. I'm not your wife."

"Oh, that's right. You're nobody's wife," he fired back.

"And you're pathetic," she lashed out as the bantering escalated.

"You're a joke. I can't believe I'm standing here wasting my time arguing with you." Johnny stuck his head in the crack and yelled for the girls to come on.

Chelle shouted toward the door that they were coming as soon as Elizabeth got out of the bathroom. Johnny and Tina continued their tiff in the meantime.

"The only person wasting time is Karen. She should have kicked you out a long time ago. Eventually she's going to get tired of you." 'Yeah, you'd like that, wouldn't you?"

"Um-hmmm."

"That's what I thought. Spoken like the jealous woman you are."

"Jealous about what?"

"Because I've never looked your way."

"You must be out of your mind. I can't stand being near you."

"That's what you say. But the truth is that I could chase women all week long and you can rest assured I will never so much as glance your way. And you can't stand that, can you?"

"You have some nerve, you lying, cheating, no-count dog. I'd rather be alone than to put up with some trifling excuse of a man who chases every skirt that comes his way."

"Whatever kind of a man I am, the fact remains that I don't want you. Then again, you're used to men not wanting you. What was your husband's name again? You know, the brother who got up and out of here like a squealing pig who'd been stuck under a fence?"

The girls were ready to go, and Tina widened the door

opening to let them out. Johnny headed them toward the car. He was two steps behind.

"You good-for-nothing," she yelled, slamming the door, not wanting the girls to overhear any of her vulgarity.

Johnny chuckled. "Have a nice day," he said, relishing the victory he had gotten over Tina with the remark about her husband.

Chapter 22

Light crept into the cold hospital room. Karen slept with the covers clutched tightly under her chin, clinging to the futile warmth. She didn't want more blankets. A little discomfort was the reminder she needed that this was not home.

The nurse's stethoscope clicked against the electronic thermometer that she had jammed into her pocket.

The noise startled Karen, and her eyes opened slowly. She scanned the room mixed-up.

"Good morning, Mrs. Clark," the nurse greeted. She read Karen's chart and pulled back the curtain separating her side of the room from the other patient.

Karen gradually got her bearings and relaxed a bit.

A nurse placed her cold hand on Karen's pulse who didn't flinch. "Your breakfast should be here in a few minutes."

The chitchat didn't ignite interest in Karen. "When is my doctor coming in?"

"I don't know. Let's see here, who is your doctor?" The nurse leafed through the clipboard of papers.

Karen could have jumped in and saved the nurse from searching, but she was quite despondent.

"Ah, there it is, Dr. Costas. She hasn't made rounds yet. I'm sure she'll be in soon."

The nurse slid the dividing curtain back. "Good morning, Ms. Walker."

"Morning. How you feeling this fine day?"

"Why, I'm just fine. But I should be asking you how you're feeling. You're the patient."

"I might be the patient, but I'm not claiming any sickness. I feel good even when I don't feel too good. It's all in what you believe."

"That's a great attitude, Ms. Walker," the nurse said. "I'll be back with your medicine."

Karen elevated her head with the bed's remote. "Good morning, Ms. Emma."

"Didn't seem like you rested too well. I heard you tossing and turning in your sleep last night."

"You're right."

"What's on your mind? What's worrying you?"

Karen knew Ms. Emma from her role as a teacher in the church. Many respected her wisdom and consistently supportive attitude. So Karen considered sharing her heart's grief.

"I have so much on my mind." She sighed. "I miss my kids."

That wasn't the only thing Karen was thinking about. She was in distress about her marriage but didn't feel right sharing something so personal and embarrassing.

"Umm. I know how it is to miss your child. My grandbaby, Rachel, lives in Chicago. Sometimes I miss her, but it don't cause me to toss and turn all night."

Ms. Emma had seen and done a lot. God had given her compassion for others that seemed to go deeper than surface chitchat. She had a way of putting people at ease, allowing them to lower their guard and open up.

"Are you sure it isn't something else on your mind?"

"Yes, there is something on my mind." Karen chose her words carefully. "It's my cancer. It might be back, and I'm scared." Karen was choked up and the words didn't glide out. She was upset and out of sorts.

Yet nothing seemed to excite Ms. Emma. Her tone stayed calm and rational.

"Cancer."

Karen was expecting some superficial words of encouragement, which was what she expected to hear once a person knew she had the big C. Not so with Ms. Emma.

"What you scared about?"

It was not a question Karen was accustomed to hearing. The answer seemed obvious.

"I'm scared of getting sicker and maybe even dying. I'm afraid my kids will be left without a mother." She sobbed softly. "I feel badly."

"About being sick?"

"No, about getting sick."

"Why do you feel badly? There's nothing you could do about it."

Ms. Emma couldn't see it, but Karen was wiping the tears away.

"I feel like I've let my children down. This is my fault."

"How?"

"Because," Karen uttered past the lump in her throat. It took a few moments before she could get more words through. "I could have prevented this." She began babbling. "I didn't think much about breast cancer, no reason to. My family didn't have a history of cancer. My mother didn't have breast cancer, and neither of my grandmothers had it before they died. I didn't do self-exams or get a mammogram. I was too young to even think about it. I was planning to get one when I turned forty but never got the chance. I ended up getting cancer at thirty-five." Karen got choked up. "If only I'd been more in tune with my body."

"You feel like you should have done more?"

"Yes, I do. I could have done self-exams. If I had checked my breasts monthly, like they recommend, I wouldn't be going through this again and again, and now again. When will it stop?"

"Karen, you can't give up on the Lord. I know you're not feeling good about the way things are going right now, but don't let that make you waiver in your faith."

Karen continued sobbing softly. She heard Ms. Emma's words of encouragement but was in no emotional condition to truly receive them.

"Ms. Emma, I'm tired. I'm just tired of suffering through this cancer. Every time I think I've licked it, it comes back. I don't think I can take any more of this. I'm worn out."

"Baby, you can't lose hope. You have to speak life into your bones. Proverbs 17:22 says a merry heart doeth good like a medicine, but a broken spirit dries the bones."

Big Mama was known for pulling a scripture from the Bible at just the right time to help someone through a tough situation.

"Ms. Emma, I've prayed about it for a long time. Sometimes it seems like God has given me all that he's going to."

"Nonsense. As much as He loves you, He won't ever get tired of you needing Him and asking for help. I'm an old lady, close to going on to glory, but I know what I'm talking about."

"I don't even know what to ask Him for anymore. I've asked for healing in my body, in my marriage, and in my heart. None of them are fixed. Actually, they've grown worse."

"Everybody's got a cross to bear. We each have dark times in our lives. We're going to have some hurt and some pain, but praise be to God that after the darkness comes the light."

"I've had more than my share of darkness. Why do I have to keep getting cancer over and over? Why me?"

"I suspect that's what Job asked. God probably answered old Job and said, why not you? We don't always know the ways of the Lord, but we read in the Bible that He has a plan for us and all things work together for good."

"What's good about dealing with an illness I can't seem to beat?"

"He won't put more on you than you can bear."

"Well, I don't even know what else I can do."

"Oh, glory," the old woman belted. "Apostle Paul said in Ephesians that when you have done all that you know how to do, then you need to just stand still." The church mother spoke with confidence and passion. "Stand and believe that God is going to move on your behalf. Nothing is too hard for

God."

"I don't know how much farther I can go living like this."

"You know, it's not always about you. Sometimes He chooses you to fill shoes no one else can."

"I don't feel like filling shoes for anybody."

"That's how you feel right now. But what if God heals you from this cancer? What if you become a witness to many, many more women who might not know about having hope in Jesus?"

"I don't know." Karen respected Mother Walker's words of wisdom. Yet nothing she said seemed to penetrate her wall of sorrow. "I feel so far from the Lord. I got so caught up in my home life and my marriage and the kids. You name it. It's funny how years ago, when we had nothing, I loved the Lord and centered my life on Him. It seemed like the more money we made, the less I talked to God." Karen teared up and took a heavy gulp fighting back her mounting emotions. Maybe this is my punishment."

"Oh, no. I can't let you believe that. No, no. God is a father who loves His children. It's not His desire to cause you hurt and pain. In the book of John, it says He wants to give you life, and more abundantly."

"The only abundant thing I have is fear and guilt."

"My dear, you need a heavy dose of God's peace and joy."

"I can't feel peace, let alone joy, in the middle of this."

"Because you can have both at the same time."

Karen's struggle with her spirituality left her unsure as to whether or not the joy and peace Mother Walker was speaking about was achievable.

"I can't even imagine feeling good right now. I don't think it's humanly possible."

"Oh, let me tell you about having peace and unspeakable joy in the midst of the storm. That's my testimony, to count it all joy. No matter what you're going through, God's mercy and grace is enough to make you want to leap up for joy way down inside."

"Maybe it's just my time, Ms. Emma."

"What do you mean by your time?"

"My time to let go. Why keep going around and around in circles like a dog chasing his tail?"

"Now I know you know better than that. Not every sickness is unto death. Beloved, you have lost your hope. The Word says that through the comfort of the scripture, you might have hope. God has set the choice of life and death before you. You're the only one who can choose which way to go. Think about those precious babies of yours. They need their mama."

A knock on the door interrupted the conversation.

A young lady entered the room with a tall, slim figured man close behind. The two appeared surprised to see another patient in the room. They said hello as they passed Karen's bed.

"Hi, Big Mama," greeted the young lady once she walked up to Ms. Emma's bed and gave her a hug.

"What are you doing out here so early?" Ms. Emma asked the two.

"We wanted to see you," the tall gentleman answered.

"Rachel, this is one of the women from my church. Karen, this is my grandbaby, and that handsome young man is just like my grandchild too. His name is Neal."

Karen greeted the couple.

"Rachel? Ah, Ms. Emma has told me about her granddaughter in Chicago. Nice to meet you."

"How are you feeling today?" Rachel asked Karen.

"I'm getting by."

"Now, what did I tell you? You're more than just getting by. You're delivered. Speak with authority and life."

Rachel jumped in, "Speak it like you mean it."

Rachel and the man chuckled.

"You know your grandmother, huh?"

Rachel leaned over and laid her head next to Big Mama. 'Yes, ma'am, I know my grandmamma. Don't I, Big Mama?"

"Umm-hmmm."

"Big Mama, we're not staying long since you're doing so much better. Neal needs to get back, and I probably should too."

"I told you to go on home. God is here with me. There's no need for you and Neal to be fretting over me. I'm well and blessed. Go on back home now, you hear. I know you have a lot of work to do with that big job of yours."

"Big Mama, the most important thing in the world to me right now is being here with you and Rachel," Neal replied.

"That's so nice to see how much you care about your grandmother. You don't see that much anymore," Karen said.

"I love my Big Mama," Rachel said.

"She's not so hot on her old grandma when I give advice about relationships."

"Big Mama, let's not go there."

"Are you two married?" Karen was confused.

"People often think that." Rachel glanced at Neal. "But we're not, just close friends."

Neal grinned. "We're connected at the hip, right, Rach?"

Big Mama didn't wait for Rachel to answer. She cut in. "That's right."

Rachel had heard that song and dance a thousand times. She pushed on to another subject.

"I'll be back next weekend, Big Mama."

"There's no need for you to be running up and down that road to see after me. I've told you I'm going to be just fine. You might as well get on the road. Don't wait for the dark to catch you still here in Michigan. Get going."

"You know Rachel isn't going to leave until she's spoken to every doctor and nurse in the hospital about you, Big Mama," Neal said.

"No doctor can tell me different once God has told me I'm

going to be all right."

"Okay, Big Mama, but Neal's right. I'm not leaving this hospital until I know for sure that you're doing as well as you say you are."

Big Mama squeezed Rachel's hand.

"I know you care, baby, but you have to take care of yourself now, you hear me? Stop worrying. It doesn't help matters anyway."

Big Mama glimpsed at Neal, who was sitting on a chair near the foot of her bed.

"I'm asking you to help look after my grandbaby once you get back to Chicago, because I know how hardheaded she can be."

Neal chuckled. "You know I will."

Rachel shook her head. It was amusing for her to hear Neal and Big Mama reference her safety as if she weren't in the room. She didn't bother to comment. It would do no good. Rachel appreciated these two people who always had her best interest at heart.

So too was it with Big Mama. She was determined to see after Karen whether she approved or not.

Chapter 23

The early part of the day had been packed with tests on Karen's breast area. She was left feeling worn out for the afternoon. She tried to shut down and feel sorry for herself, but Big Mama wouldn't allow it. She continued encouraging Karen and to boost her spirit.

"Ms. Emma, I'm sorry to see you go home. It's been such a blessing to have someone to talk to."

"I'm glad I was here with you. Don't think you were put in this room by accident."

Karen remembered how much she had complained about not having a private room when she first arrived. Thank goodness she'd ended up with Ms. Emma.

"God made a way for you to be put in here with me. Now I'm going home, but I'll be back to check on you young lady. Reckon I'll get some of the folks from church to come with me." Mother Walker slowly approached Karen and patted her hand. "I'm coming to see you, and I'll be keeping you in my prayers."

"Ms. Emma. I appreciate your kindness." Karen admired her spiritual walk. "Could you please pray for me before you go?"

"Yes, ma'am. I don't turn down a chance to go before God on behalf of somebody."

Karen wasn't feeling too good about praying, but found herself embracing the words of Ms. Emma.

When Karen was alone, time served in the hospital was slow and boring, especially with the church mother gone. Karen drifted in and out of sleep the rest of the afternoon and into the evening, allowing time for a few bites of food.

She wasn't expecting to see her family this afternoon. So, it was a special treat to wake up and see the girls coming through the door with their daddy close behind.

"Mommy," Elizabeth shouted, and anxiously ran up to Karen's bed.

Karen placed her index finger to her mouth and said, "Shhhhh."

Elizabeth had waited several days to see her mom. She'd finally arrived. Karen might get her to pipe down verbally, but her excitement was staying.

Chelle greeted her mother with a calmer, more controlled expression.

Karen spread her arms wide in a gesture for the girls to give her a hug. They responded without a spoken word and fell into their mother's arms. Having them close to her heart gave Karen comfort. It was the best medicine she'd gotten all day.

"How are you feeling?" Johnny asked. He found a chair in the corner of the room.

Karen nodded.

"What does that mean?"

"It means I'm doing okay. I'm a little tired, but I'm feeling better with my family being here." Karen brushed Elizabeth's hair back and gave her a kiss.

It was an awkward visit for the couple, since they hadn't been on the best of terms when Johnny left for the business trip a few days ago. Neither had made amends before Karen got sick and went into the hospital. Now they were stuck making small talk for the benefit of the girls.

"How are you making out at home?" Karen asked the girls.

Chelle was able to get a word in before Elizabeth. "We're doing okay."

"I've been helping out too," Elizabeth echoed.

Chelle helped her pull a chair close to the bed.

"When are you coming home?"

Johnny, flipped through the Wall Street Journal, stopping

long enough to hear her response.

"I don't know, sweetie. The doctor hasn't told me yet. I hope it's soon."

Nearly an hour passed before Karen and Johnny bothered initiating conversation with each other.

"We got the equity loan approved but it's less than we need."

"What are you going to do?" Karen asked.

"Not sure, but I have to do something to keep us above water." Karen sighed and slid the palm of her hand up her forehead with her eyes closed.

"It's getting late and we need to get on home," Johnny reminded the girls.

"No, we haven't been here that long."

"It's time to go, Elizabeth," Johnny strongly reinforced. "You have school tomorrow."

Elizabeth recognized her father's tone. It meant business. She shed a few tears, but didn't speak again in opposition to his order.

It bothered Karen to see the girls so sad about her hospital stay. "I want both of you girls to know how sorry I am."

"Sorry about what, Mommy?" Chelle asked.

Karen was emotionally choked up trying to get the words out.

"I'm sorry I got sick again on you girls." She was talking to the girls but also periodically directed her eyes and comments toward Johnny. "I know I've let my family down."

Johnny was at a loss for words, but Chelle wasn't. She was quick to comfort her mother.

"Mommy, it's not your fault that you got sick."

Elizabeth handed Karen a tissue and grabbed another for herself. "I should have taken better care of myself. I really messed up."

"No, you didn't mess up, Mom. I love you."

"Me too, Mommy," Elizabeth added.

Johnny remained silent. He wanted to reach out to Karen but didn't have a read on how receptive she would be. Most of the time he was not sure what she wanted from him. Asking him for one thing and then judging him on something else was the norm. For the time being he elected to keep quiet.

The girls pulled themselves together long enough to walk out with their father.

Chelle stopped at the doorway, turned to her mom, and said, "I almost forgot; happy anniversary, Mom. I know it's not until tomorrow, but I just wanted to say it anyway."

"Yeah, Mommy, happy anniversary. See you tomorrow."

Johnny had forgotten about their anniversary. If it hadn't been for Chelle's prompting, it would have passed without his acknowledgment.

"Thanks, my sweeties." She glared past Johnny, expecting him to interject, but he didn't. "Oh, yeah, Chelle, thanks for sending out the cards and making calls to cancel the party."

"You're welcome."

"I helped too. I put on the stamps."

"Thank you, baby." Karen blew Elizabeth a kiss.

Johnny hadn't planned on coming to the hospital until tomorrow. He was glad they'd come before the anniversary. He'd forgotten about it but had no intention of publicizing it. His oversight was one less thing he needed Karen needling him about in the future. "We'll see you tomorrow," he told Karen.

Karen wept openly when they left. It felt like her heart had been ripped out, because she saw how much fear her illness was causing the girls. She knew the emotional roller-coaster ride was hard to deal with at their age. She agonized over the ordeal being too much for them. One year she was well and everything was great. The next year she was sick and the girls were scared. She couldn't keep putting them through this. She shut her eyelids tightly, forcing away the remaining tears.

Maybe they were better off without her. Karen felt she was in a no-win situation. She either wanted to be alive or dead. There was nothing as bad as living in the middle. If she got better, the kids would have to deal with the uncertainty of not knowing how long it would last. If she didn't get better, the children would have to deal with her death. Her thoughts were scrambled. After much agonizing and unrest, she fell asleep.

Chapter 24

The morning rushed in, not that it made any difference. The drain of going in and out of remission along with her troubles at home took its toll. Karen slipped into depression. She wanted to sleep away her problem and wake up with it resolved. Yet she couldn't find enough peace to get any sleep. The very thing she needed was exactly what she wasn't able to get.

"Here's your breakfast tray, Mrs. Clark."

Karen, who was balled up in the fetal position, pulled the cover tightly around her neck.

The dietician pushed the cart closer to the bed.

Karen ate a few bites of toast and a couple spoonfuls of oatmeal. Between poor tasting food and her loss of appetite, the tray remained virtually untouched.

Morning dragged on. Karen watched a few game shows and soap operas intermixed with short naps.

Karen was in the middle of a nap but heard someone enter the room and immediately woke up. "Dr. Costas." Karen was a bit groggy, but she was eager to get the test results about the breast cancer. She wasted no time in getting to the point. "Has it spread?"

The candid question caught Dr. Costas off guard. She wanted to check Karen's emotional stability before breaking the news. The nurses had noted signs of depression in her patient's chart. Dr. Costas wasn't surprised by the discovery but was nonetheless disturbed.

"Is your husband coming out here today? I was hoping to speak with you together."

"Doctor, what did the results show?" This time her voice was stronger and louder.

Dr. Costas set the chart on the edge of Karen's bed and put both hands in her white lab coat pockets. "I did get the results." She spoke softly. "They didn't come back the way I would have liked."

Karen was speaking in a near hysterical tone. "So you're saying the results came back positive."

The doctor nodded in agreement. She knew any dialogue would only engage Karen in a more dramatic reaction.

"Oh, God, it is back." She hung her head and wept. "Why me?" she screamed so loudly that a nurse came running in from the hallway. "Can I help?" the nurse asked the doctor.

"We're fine."

'You're fine." Karen bellowed. "I'm not."

"I need you to calm down. You're going to wear yourself out. Please, take a deep breath. I'm going to order something to help you relax. Nurse, I'm putting Valium on her chart. Could you please rush it along?"

"Yes, I'll get it right away."

"I know this is a tough time for you."

Karen remained quiet. She routinely avoided stressful situations and usually settled for less than what she wanted or needed. It wasn't like her to have outbursts like the one she was currently having. A part of her was ashamed.

"I know it isn't the best time to talk about our next steps. I want you to get some rest now." The doctor clasped her hands together and drew them up to her lips like she was contemplating more to say. "Karen, there is no easy way to say this."

"What else could there be?"

"The tumor—"

Karen cut Dr. Costas off before she finished.

"You told me the tumor hadn't grown any more. That's what you said."

"That's true, but with the cancer returning, it changes our position a bit."

"How?"

"I need to do a biopsy on your tumor to confirm it's not malignant."

"What would make you think it is?"

"I can't say for sure without the biopsy, but I'm optimistic based on your MRI results. I really don't think the tumor is an issue, but I have to check in order to be certain."

"Can't we work on the breast cancer and then deal with the tumor?"

"Ideally, it would be nice to segregate the illnesses in your body and deal with them one at a time. However, we don't have that luxury. Do you recall when we talked about radiation therapy?"

"Yes."

"Well, in order to set ourselves up for the best possibility of success, we'll hit the breast cancer hard. That requires a substantial dose of radiation. So I'll need to make sure there is no other cancer in your body before we begin treatment."

"What difference does it make?"

"Each human body can safely be exposed to a certain amount of radiation in a lifetime. We will be approaching that level with your new breast cancer treatments. So you see, I need to make sure there is no other known area of cancer in your body. If there is, it can affect the amount of radiation and the treatment options I plan to use on the breast cancer."

"What you're saying is that I will basically use my lifetime allocation in one shot."

"That's one way of putting it." Dr. Costas hesitated before sharing any more information with Karen. She had known Karen long enough to anticipate her response.

"Most likely we will need to follow up with chemo."

"Chemo! Oh, God, no." She dreaded having to repeat the brutal process. Nausea and exhaustion had been unbearable for her the last two times.

"Why don't we take one step at a time. We'll begin with radiation then deal with chemo, okay?" Dr. Costas said.

"Chemo makes me too sick. I definitely don't want to do that. I don't know which makes me feel worse, the chemo or the cancer." Karen sighed in disgust at her options. "What about the radiation? If I take the treatment now, what would happen if I got cancer again down the road? What treatment options would I have left?" Karen had her suspicions about the answer.

Dr. Costas avoided giving a confirmation. She was aware of new drugs that had recently been approved by the FDA as well as some other experimental ones out there. She preferred treating Karen with familiar options like surgery, chemo, and radiation treatments. Experimental treatment was a last resort.

"Let's not worry about such a hypothetical scenario." She patted Karen's blanket-covered legs. "Right now, I want you to put your energy into fighting the cancer. You need to be as optimistic as you can. A positive attitude couldn't hurt on your road to recovery. Okay."

"Thanks for being honest with me, Dr. Costas."

"The nurse will be in with something to help you relax. We'll talk tomorrow about the treatment. In the meantime I will be ordering the biopsy."

"Will I have to get my head shaved?"

Karen was traumatized after losing her hair with the first series of treatment years ago. It was less traumatic the second time around with the help of wigs and short hairstyles.

"Because of the location, they will only need to shave a small part off the back."

"Will the radiation take out my hair?"

"Well, that I can't say. Twenty percent of patients don't lose their hair. Let's hope you're in that group."

"Humph. Hope."

"Don't worry about the hair. You look great with the short haircut."

"Yeah, but short and bald are two different things."

Karen embraced her femininity. To have no breasts and to be bald at the same time didn't make her feel good about her womanhood. She didn't think it would make Johnny too happy either. She had heard him say time and time again that her appearance didn't bother him. She didn't believe him. How could it not bother him when it bothered her so much.

Chapter 25

Dr. Costas called Johnny to update him on Karen's condition.

"This is Dr. Costas. If you have a few minutes, I'd like to speak with you about Karen."

"Why, what's going on?"

"Well, Mr. Clark, to be honest, Karen isn't doing too well. The cancer has returned. She's struggling with the news."

Thoughts and emotions swirled out of control. Johnny suspected the cancer was back but hadn't wanted to accept it. "How can she have breast cancer? Both her breasts are gone. I don't understand."

Dr. Costas sighed.

"Breast cancer is a tough cookie. You never really know if you've gotten it all. Sometimes it takes years to resurface in the other breast or in lymph nodes found in the armpits. It can also spread to a number of other areas. Unfortunately, it's very common."

Johnny couldn't grasp what was happening, not after a boatload of treatment and confirmations that the cancer was in remission.

"Her breasts are already gone. How can she have cancer? I thought the whole objective of removing her breasts was to eliminate any place for the cancer to grow?"

"Yes, to some degree, you are correct. The problem is that Karen's cancer has metastasized. That's when cancer spreads beyond the initial area. The biopsy confirms it has spread across her chest area and even into her shoulder areas. We're hoping it hasn't spread to any of her vital organs."

"How will you know if it has?"

"Well, I am waiting on the pathology report. That should shed some light on what we're working with here."

Johnny's silence was an indication that he was struggling with the diagnosis. Dr. Costas continued trying to enlighten him with as much information as she could about Karen's condition.

"As I've said, breast cancer is tough. The size of a breast doesn't increase or minimize one's chance of getting cancer. I know she wasn't predisposed to cancer through her family history. Often there is no rhyme or reason for why some people get cancer and others don't. We just treat it to the best of our ability."

Delivering the bad news to the couple touched Dr. Costas deeply. She'd developed some level of emotional connection with the Clarks having treated Karen for over four years.

"I'm disappointed too, but what Karen needs right now is a tremendous amount of support."

"I support my wife," Johnny said, sounding offended.

"Of course. I apologize. I didn't mean to imply you don't."

Johnny was embarrassed about rushing to a defensive position. It made him look guilty. "I apologize for my snappy comment."

"There is no need for apology. This is going to be an emotional time for both of you, which is the main reason for my call. She's struggling with the diagnosis, understandably."

"Ah, man."

"She is quite depressed, and that's not good for us. She has to be strong to fight this disease. I think she's giving up hope of recovering."

"What are her chances?"

Since Karen had already given the approval for Dr. Costas to share medical information with Johnny, the doctor wanted to be as completely honest with him and disclose the severity of the prognosis, while not being too pessimistic.

"I really don't know. I want to believe we have a shot at a full recovery."

"She's already had the lumpectomy and chemotherapy.

That didn't work. Then she went back into the hospital to have both breasts removed with the double mastectomy. That didn't work. The radiation and chemo combination didn't work. What else is there?" he asked.

"Well, we have her scheduled for treatment. She hasn't exceeded her lifetime intake of radiation. I recommend we use an intense radiation treatment immediately followed with chemo. Let's hit it hard. I think it's the best shot we have."

"Did you tell her about the chemo?" Johnny knew it was something Karen hated having to do.

"Yes, I did."

"I know that didn't go over too well."

"No, it didn't. She was so upset about the chemo that I wasn't able to tell her the rest of the news."

Johnny couldn't imagine what else could be left. "What's that?" he asked, although he wasn't eager to hear the answer.

"Karen has been given a significant amount of chemo and radiation."

"And...?"

The couple had already endured. Dr. Costas felt awful about pouring more salt in their wound. "The positive news is that the treatments will kill off the cancer cells. The side effect is that in the process, it also kills the bone marrow and red blood cells. It might also break down the immune system."

"What are you saying, Dr. Costas? Are you telling me the treatment is worse than the disease? Which one is going to kill her first?"

"I know it doesn't sound very good, Johnny. But I feel obligated to share each possible outcome with you. It's only fair that you know what we're dealing with. The fact is after we get past the cancer, there is a possibility that we might have to deal with leukemia if her bone marrow is severely depleted."

"Good grief. Does it ever end?"

"We'll stay hopeful and take one step at a time. We just

have to constantly evaluate our options as we go."

Johnny was filled with gloom. "Let me know if you need me to sign anything for the treatment."

"Thank you, although that shouldn't be necessary. Karen is fully coherent and has to make the final decision. However, I think it would help if you could confer with her about it. Like I said, having you and the children around her might give Karen the extra motivation she needs to fight. It's going to be key. We need her strong going into this treatment. It is quite intense and will take a great deal out of her."

"I'll see what I can do. I'll talk with her about it today."

"Good."

"Will she be able to come home during the treatment?"

"Her treatment can be done on an outpatient basis, but with her history, I'd prefer keeping her in the hospital. We're better prepared to handle complications."

"Thank you, Doctor, for calling. I appreciate it."

"There's no need to thank me, Johnny. I would say I'm just doing my job, but it goes beyond that. Karen has been such a delightful patient the entire time I've known her. She has a great deal of life in her. I'd like to see her continue to enjoy it. I honestly would."

When Johnny got off the phone, he couldn't find enough willpower to move from his seat. He was helpless. What could he do? Should he tell the kids or should he wait?

He stood and scratched his head. Being indecisive was not a position he often found himself in. He was the one in charge and calling the shots. He handled the tough decisions that others dreaded without so much as a flinch. Nothing was out of his control, except for Karen's cancer. He was at a loss.

He sat on the bedroom sofa with his head back and staring at the ceiling. He leaned over and grabbed the family's personal phone book off the end table. He thumbed through it and found Erick's number in Europe. He dialed 011 and hung up. Maybe he shouldn't call. It would probably scare him. He couldn't help her way over there anyway. Johnny shook his head. He was uncomfortable being in such an awkward situation. Was it better to tell Erick later, after they had more information? Johnny grew tired of going back and forth on whether or not to alert their son about his mother's condition. If it were Johnny, he'd want to know. He decided Erick was old enough to handle tough situations. He dialed the number.

There was no guarantee Erick would answer. He was taking full advantage of the Stanford exchange program, and often called his parents after spending a weekend travelling the countryside via train.

"Morning, Stanford University. Might I help you?" the British accent echoed.

"Yes, my name is John Clark. My son, John Erick Clark, is in the exchange program from the U.S. I need him to give me a call at home."

"Very well, sir. I will inform him straightaway."

"Thank you."

"Good day, sir."

It was already eleven o'clock at night in London. Johnny suspected Erick would return the call early tomorrow.

The girls had an afterschool program at church. Johnny decided to use the short break to take a nap before picking them up and heading to the hospital. He relaxed on the sofa for a quick snooze.

Johnny wasn't expecting any calls. He was slow to answer the ringing phone. He didn't feel like talking to anyone, but felt obligated to answer it with Karen being in the hospital.

Johnny greeted with minimal reaction.

"I have a collect call from Erick. Will you accept the charges?" the automated voice asked. "Press or say one now."

After a few moments and oceans of static, there was a human voice on the other end of Johnny's line.

"Hey, Dad."

"Boy, why are you calling collect?"

"The dorm monitor gave me a message to call home. I figured it must be important. So I called."

"This is going to cost me an arm and a leg. What's wrong with your calling card?"

"I already used up my minutes for the month."

"We're barely through half the month. How did you use it up?"

"I talked to Mom a couple times this month."

"You sure didn't talk and entire card worth with her."

"Some of it and the rest was on my friends."

"Boy, I am not spending money for you to keep in touch with your buddies. That's what a summer job is for. You are thousands of miles away. You could have any kind of emergency. You'd better start doing a better job at spreading that card across the month."

Johnny needed to conserve on all spending. The home equity loan was netting twenty thousand dollars less than he'd hoped. According to his calculations, the extra money would have provided a financial cushion. Instead, he had to tighten his financial belt.

"Look, I didn't call to get into your irresponsibility. I wanted to tell you that your mom's back in the hospital."

"For what?"

"Her cancer is back."

"How'd that happen?"

"I really couldn't tell you. We're all shocked."

Erick hadn't forgotten the first time he saw his mother so unhappy. He was eleven when he overheard her telling Aunt Connie about that woman, Isabelle. She cried and cried. He didn't understand what was wrong at the time, but figured it out later. It made him cry to see her so sad. Many times when his parents would go into their bedroom and close the door, he would sit at the top of the front staircase and doodle in his sketchpad. Muddled voices escalated to shouting and screaming, finishing off with silence sprinkled with sobs, over and over, night after night. It was easy to catch her crying after that. It wasn't long before she got the cancer. Then she really cried, kind of like she did when that Isabelle woman was around.

Erick had it rough during his teenage years. His mother was in and out of the hospital. His father was always working. There was no time to give him advice about girls or school. He was expected to be a man and take care of his sisters without any guidance. His mom would have been around to help him through the teen years, had it not been for his father. She was always there for Erick. It was his father's fault. When time came for college, he couldn't wait to go far away from home and grow up without bearing a shoulder of responsibility for the family.

"What did you do to her?"

"Boy, how are you going to ask me some crap like that?" Johnny was outraged, and his tone of voice left no room for speculation. "What the heck do you mean?"

Johnny tolerated no disrespect from his kids. How old or independent they were didn't make a difference.

"I've been reading up on cancer in my human biology class. Lifestyles, stress, pressure, and even suppressed grief, hurt, guilt, and anger may be contributing factors in getting cancer and relapses by weakening the immune system."

"So what? I don't care two nickels about what you read."

"It's obvious you don't care about Mom. If you did, you wouldn't be seeing other women right under her nose. I wonder if it has anything to do with her getting sick?"

"Son, who do you think you're talking to? Let me tell you something, young man, don't you ever disrespect me again. You'd better remember that Karen is my wife, not yours. Don't you ever tell me how to act with my wife. That is not your place. You have some nerve, boy. Don't get so high and mighty that you cross the line. Don't forget, I'm footing your bills. You're not so much of a man that you're able to take care of yourself without my help." Johnny was furious and held nothing back. "I have to go. Here's the number to the hospital and my calling card number. Call her. I know she wants to hear from you."

Erick was a perfect blend of his parents. The passive and compassionate side of him wanted to apologize to his father for stirring the waters into such a heated discussion. The other side didn't want to apologize for telling the truth.

As it turned out, he didn't have to make a decision. Johnny hung up before he had a chance to say anything.

Erick grunted while holding the receiver. He slammed the phone onto the hook. "Some things just don't change." He walked back to his room feeling the weight of the world on his undeveloped shoulders.

Johnny was furious, mainly because he was afraid there might be some truth in what his son said. He couldn't shake Erick's darts, no matter how hard he tried. Could his son be right? Could her cancer be from suppressed hurt and anger? Johnny didn't want to believe it, but if it was true, he had a great deal to think about. It was only twenty-four hours ago when he was contemplating getting back on the roller-coaster ride with Isabelle or Annette.

"I wonder if..." he questioned himself. "Nah, couldn't be."

Johnny recalled how traumatized Karen had been when his affair with Isabelle and the unexpected pregnancy were exposed. Karen suffered a sizable depression but decided to stay in the marriage. He knew staying didn't negate her hurt. He shook his head in disbelief at how the storybook relationship had gone so sour. He stayed because taking care of Karen and the kids was the right thing to do. He had to believe they had a better life as a result.

Despite his rationalization, Johnny couldn't determine if his continuing to stay in the marriage was best for the family. The couple had survived, but things had never been quite the same since. Every time the couple had a major disagreement,

Karen threw Isabelle in his face. He tried to ease her mind, with no success. She hadn't shown any indication that trust was being restored.

Johnny continued pondering. Who had actually benefited from his hanging around? Karen ended up with cancer. He was miserable in the marriage and so was she. He didn't get along with his son. Johnny twirled the pen between his fingers. His reflections were making his head pound. He could only hope the affair with Isabelle hadn't contributed to Karen's illness now or back then. He couldn't handle the idea of being a factor in her getting cancer. The guilt pricked at his peace. He felt sick. With his getting and acquiring the finer aspects of life, Johnny was losing the most important piece— his family. He couldn't help but feel like his hard work had been for naught.

His phone vibrated on the end table. Johnny picked it up and read *Jacoby Marketing*. It was Annette. The few females who were fortunate enough to have his number were assigned a fictitious company name in his directory. It minimized the chance of Karen finding another woman's number on his phone. Johnny deleted the number and set the phone back on the table. Sex was the last thing on his mind.

Chapter 26

A room opened up on the cancer wing two days after Mother Walker left the hospital. That was almost a month ago. She had been an inspiration to Karen. Now that she was gone, there was no one around to encourage Karen in a way which mattered.

Karen was tired of being poked and zapped. What had it been for? She initially came into the hospital to have some additional tests done in hopes that the cancer wasn't back. Since then she had added a brain tumor biopsy and the need for intense radiation therapy.

At least the biopsy had gone well. There was no malignancy or growth in the tumor. It provided no threat to her life.

The dietician wheeled in the lunch cart.

Karen barely lifted her gaze toward the lady.

"Lunchtime, Mrs. Clark." She rolled the tray close to the bed. "Umm. Let's see what we have. Chopped steak, green beans, and mashed potatoes. Looks good."

The doctor left strict orders with the staff that Karen had to eat. She was showing advanced signs of depression. She wasn't eating or sleeping. She picked at her food, taking only a few bites every meal. She had lost close to eighteen pounds in the last month.

As much as Karen disliked the constant nag of a needle sticking into her arm, she couldn't deny her lack of appetite and weight loss. So, she didn't resist when Dr. Costas started administering the necessary fluids and meds through an IV.

Karen's counselor came in behind the dietician.

Dr. Costas was monitoring Karen's increasing anxiety and decided it best to get a counselor involved before her patient sank deeper.

"Why don't you try to eat a little," the counselor asked.

"I'm not hungry," she responded in a groggy voice.

"Come on, you have to eat. Dr. Costas left specific instructions. You'll have to eat in order to regain your strength."

"I'm strong enough."

"Not enough to bounce back from therapy." The counselor elevated the bed slightly. She wanted to help Karen relax and get her positioned to eat.

"I don't even know if the therapy worked."

"I understand how you must feel."

"No you don't. I've had all kinds of surgeries, treatments, and medications. What did it do for me? Not a single thing. I'm right back here, sick again."

The counselor wanted to lift Karen's spirits perceiving her patient's mounting sense of hopelessness.

Karen's counselor had seen patients in this state of mind countless times. Once a person entered the downward spiral of depression, it seemed nearly impossible to break them out. Not even the love of family could fully break the hold.

"You have to keep hanging in there, Karen."

"Why?"

The question was unexpected by the counselor. "Because I'm sure your family wants you to live a long, happy, healthy life."

The children did generate some kind of a positive reaction from Karen.

"Well, I'm tired. I'm sick of being sick. I want to be done."

"Karen, you can't give up so easily. There is a very good chance the cancer is gone with the radiation."

Karen didn't have a response. She was determined to believe information was being kept from her.

"I don't feel like going through more treatment, only to end up back here a year from now. I'd rather get it over now and be done with it."

151 NO REGRETS

"How can you say that? What about your children?"

Tears formed in Karen's eyes. The thought of leaving her babies hurt deeply, but not even that could overcome Karen's depression.

"What good am I to my children lying here? I think they'll be better off without me. I know Johnny will be better off."

"Do you believe that?" Karen nodded in affirmation and the counselor continued. "I believe children always need their mother. I'm sure they miss you and hoping you'll be coming home soon."

"They do need a mother, one who is home and can take care of them." Karen blew her nose and wiped her eyes. "That's not me. I've let them down by letting myself get sick again. I'm sure Johnny has a replacement in mind. They don't need me."

*　　*　　*

The morning and early afternoon trudged along with Dr. Costas checking in by late afternoon. Reading the report set off alarms. Karen should have been strong enough to go home by now, but she wasn't. Dr. Costas was struggling with her diagnosis.

From medical accounts, the treatment was successful, yet Karen wasn't showing any improvement. There was no physical explanation for why Karen seemed to be getting sicker. Dr. Costas could only speculate the lack of physical improvement was resulting from her patient's deteriorating psychological state.

Even so, Karen had vehemently refused to take drugs for her depression and anxiety. It appeared to Dr. Costas that Karen didn't want to get better. Regardless of how much encouragement came through the door, none of it remained.

Dr. Costas was distressed about her longtime patient. She

was fully aware that no medicine was capable of restoring a person's broken will to live.

Chapter 27

Colorful cards and balloons lined the windowsill. It was Sunday afternoon and the room was crowded with well-wishers from the church. They were squeezed into the room like sardines. As the weeks passed, Karen's group of visitors got smaller and smaller. The first couple of days, her room was packed. The longer Karen was hospitalized, the less people carved time out of their schedules for a visit. The crisis in Karen's life warranted support, but not catastrophic enough for people to alter their ongoing day-to-day activities. Giving a few hours and a greeting card every so often was as good as it got for most visitors, except for today. It was a full house.

Much of her adult life, Karen had worn a smiley face for others. She tried to act upbeat, but the effort was too great. Struggling to maintain an elite lifestyle was one thing. Hiding depression required much more resilience and skill.

"How are you feeling?" a visitor asked. Most didn't know what to say. They searched for words to break the ice.

"I'm a little tired." She managed to squeak out a grin, something far short of her radiant smile. How many times had she been asked that question for which there was no answer? It was more of a substitute for "hello," seeing no one wanted to honestly hear about how sick she was.

Karen mostly kept quiet and dozed off. Occasionally she responded to something a visitor said.

"We had a guest speaker at church today. The message was truly anointed," a church member said.

"Umm, sure was," an older visitor affirmed.

"The speaker is going to be there this evening too. I don't usually go back in the evening, but I am tonight."

"He was just that good, Karen," one lady stated.

"It wasn't just him. It was the whole atmosphere," Elder Jones clarified.

"Yessss."

"God is good."

"All the time," three people synchronously chimed in.

During her confinement, Karen hadn't been able to keep up on current events or other happenings on the outside. It left a limited number of discussion topics for visitors.

"So, the weather has been nice. After the little bit of rain last week, it warmed up nicely," spouted one visitor.

"Yeah, they say March winds, April showers bring May flowers," someone added.

Elder Jones shook his head. "Spring already? The year is almost half gone. Time is just flying by. Seem like it was just Christmas."

Karen listened, but didn't join in.

"It'll be Mother's Day before we know it."

"I hope we have you home by then."

Karen gave a weak grin. None of the conversation was actually directed toward her, except for a few pointed statements here and there.

Reverend Lane, Mother Walker, and her friend sliced the crowded room. Mother Walker's yearning for righteousness commanded a high level of respect from those in the church. The group made way for her as she approached the bed, like God parting the Red Sea for Moses.

Unlike the other visitors, Mother Walker had a specific purpose. Every time she came across a sick person, her primary objective was to find out if they knew the Lord. Then she commenced to praying for their physical and spiritual healing. "Glad to see you."

Karen rallied a genuine grin. "Thank you for coming."

"Now you knew I would eventually get here." She patted Karen's hand. She scanned the room and saw many elders and sisters congregating with extra chairs squeezed in every nook. I see we have some powerful saints gathered here."

Some were checking their watches, suggesting it was time to tactfully announce their departure. Big Mama's entrance was going to be a nice, easy out for many.

"Oh, look at the time. Three-thirty. I'd better get going," a sister noted. "It'll be time for the evening service before I know it."

"Yeah, I'd better head out too. Big Mama, here, you can have my chair," Elder Jones offered.

Big Mama moved at her own pace, appearing to be in no hurry. Her philosophy was, "pace yourself. When you rush through life your just hurrying to death. Live one moment at a time."

"Before you rush out of here, I want to pray. The Bible says where there's two or three gathered together, God is in the midst."

Not a word of defiance was uttered. The crowd, both old and young, gathered around Karen's bed without hesitation.

Big Mama pulled out her small bottle of anointing oil and rubbed it on Karen's forehead.

"Lord, you know your daughter. You knew her before she was born. You knew she'd be lying in this bed on this day long before she arrived. Now we ask you to pour out your healing blood on her. You may not come when we want, but Father, you're always on time."

"Yes, Lord," Elder Jones interjected.

The circle of prayer continued for nearly a half hour, with each person joining in. Big Mama often tarried, or, as she would say, "took as much time as she needed to do God's business."

Johnny and the girls walked in near the end of prayer. He wasn't eager to join in the circle, so he opted to stand near the doorway and not interrupt. He was content waiting for them to finish until he saw the woman rub oil on Karen's forehead.

It wasn't foreign to him. Shortly after Karen joined the church years ago, she brought home a small bottle of the oil. Johnny forbade it. The oil bought no favoritism with him. Even though she explained it was used in conjunction with prayer, the oil seemed like evil voodoo. He refused to have it in the house or anywhere near him.

As a result, Karen only used the oil at church from what he knew. He didn't have any control over what was spoken and done at church, but this hospital room was well within his dominion. He burst through the crowd with the girls in tow.

"Excuse me," he interrupted with a voice of authority. "I don't mind if you want to pray for Karen, but I prefer you not use the oil stuff."

Those praying were stunned at Johnny's outburst and didn't know how to react. Everyone remained quiet. Subtle attitudes and uneasiness clogged the room.

Karen was humiliated, but too upset to cry.

Elizabeth worked her way to her mother's bed.

Reverend Lane, being one of the leaders in room, wanted to bring peace to the situation. "We apologize for upsetting you. Maybe we'll leave now and let you and your family have some quiet time with Karen."

Mother Walker slowly walked to Johnny and stood in front of him. Deep down, he didn't want to set this old lady straight, but he was poised for anything.

She asked him, "Are you getting enough to eat?"

"What?" Johnny grunted in surprise at the peculiar and seemingly random question.

"If you're not, some of us women at the church can fix you some meals and bring them to the house for you."

Her generosity caught him off guard. The only response he could give was, "Uh, no, I'm, uh, okay right now."

Big Mama knew exactly what she was doing. She had enough wisdom not to throw fuel on a fire. Where some saw a strong man in Johnny, she saw a frightened lad lashing out like a cornered bull. He needed her motherly compassion, not judgment.

Her natural reaction would be to pray for someone in his condition, but she sensed the last thing he wanted was more prayer. Big Mama wasn't one to force religion. Johnny would find his way to God without her pushing.

"Well, I'm going to keep your whole family in my prayers every day until God shows what He's going to do for you." Not a word of animosity came across her lips. Unlike some of the other churchgoers, Big Mama had learned a long time ago to accept people for where they were with the Lord. She knew Johnny wasn't a very religious man based on the information Karen had shared. Silent prayer was the only way to reach a hard-hitting man like Johnny.

"Karen, I'm glad to see you. God bless you."

"Thanks for coming by, Ms. Emma and for the prayer."

Big Mama led the way as the room emptied.

Karen had not been up for a lot of company, but was glad so many people from the church had taken time to visit. She was outraged at Johnny for being so rude. She didn't miss his thoughtless, selfish, and controlling attitude.

The way was clear for Elizabeth, who pulled a chair close to the bed.

As the visitors thinned out, Karen was glad to see her girls. Yet, she wasn't able to muster the usual level of enthusiasm. Her energy wasn't there. She was battling exhaustion on every front. She felt tired of being sick, tired of Johnny's domination and unfaithfulness, tired of being emotional, tired of being away from the kids, tired of hoping for a better day, and just tired of being tired.

She corralled enough might to give Johnny a look of frustration in her weakened condition.

There was nothing more for him to say. He'd already said too much. At the time, he was quite smug with his actions. Receiving the piercing gawk from Karen, he wasn't as haughty about it. He kept quiet.

"Did you have to stop them from praying for me?" Her words were slow and lethargic. It took the sharp bite off and made them easier for Johnny to swallow. "It's not like you're praying in their place."

Johnny didn't respond. He knew she was upset and didn't want to keep agitating her. He searched for a neutral topic. "Erick called."

Karen was curt. "I know. He called right after talking to you."

Johnny was hoping that Erick hadn't told her the details of their heated confrontation. Talking about other women wouldn't be a winning discussion.

Karen rolled her gaze from his direction and returned to her conversation with the girls.

He realized their discussion was over. It was becoming clear to him the hospital was her domain, where she was the one calling the shots, not him. Johnny planted his feet on the floor, dug his body into the wingback chair, and tilted his head back with eyelids shut. He folded his hands, intending to catch a nap until it was either time to go or Karen was ready to talk. Whichever came first.

Chapter 28

The nightstand was awkwardly placed behind Karen's head, next to the bed. She strained to reach backward for the phone. She pressed multiple numbers, having to start over repeatedly. Finally, she was able to get through to the church.

"Reverend Lane, this is Karen Clark."

"Yes, Karen." He sat up straight in his chair, bracing for the worst. "Is something wrong?"

"Nothing new." She paused. "I want to apologize to you and the other saints. I am truly sorry for the way my husband acted yesterday."

"There is no reason to apologize. You and your family are going through a very trying time. We understand the impact this kind of trial can cause. Rest assured, there are no hard feelings."

"I just wanted to let you know how I felt."

"Why, thank you, but don't you worry another moment about apologizing to us. Put your energy into getting well."

"Thank you for being so understanding. Could you please extend my apology to the others?"

"I will do just that."

"Can you especially apologize to Ms. Emma for me?"

"Like I said, Karen, it is not necessary, but I will do as you ask. Is there anything else you need me to do for you?"

"No, that's it."

Completing the one call was the only item Karen had on her to-do list for the day. Good thing, because the small task zapped her strength. Now that it was done, she recoiled back into her depressive shell and fell asleep. Hours later she woke up to Ms. Emma sitting in the chair reading the Bible. Karen focused to make sure she wasn't dreaming.

"Ms. Emma, is that you?"

"It is."

"How long have you been here?"

"Ooh, I'd say about two hours."

"That long." Karen thought she'd only been asleep a few minutes. Glancing at the clock, she realized it must have been more like four hours. She wasn't expecting Ms. Emma, but Karen was glad to see her. Being able to apologize in person was better than having Pastor Lane pass the message along.

"I didn't know you were coming out here today, especially after Johnny acted the way he did yesterday. I'm so sorry."

"You don't owe me an apology for your husband. He's doing the best he knows how to do with you being sick. I didn't pay him no mind."

"But you did stop praying when he busted in."

"Of course I did. I meant to show him respect. Praying for his wife when he didn't want me to wasn't going to be helpful for you. There would be a nasty spirit in the midst. Besides, I'm still praying for you. You don't have to pray out loud to seek the Lord. When I was speaking to your husband, I was praying. You have to pray at all times, without ceasing. Karen, he needs just as much prayer as you do. He's a strong-headed man. He's hurting and doesn't have any where or anybody to turn to. He needs the Lord, and I aim to pray until he finds Him."

"I appreciate you praying for my family. They'll need somebody to pray for them if I'm gone."

Big Mama sensed the melancholy in Karen's spirit.

"Prayer can fix a heap of trouble."

"Not for me, Ms. Emma. I'm tired of dragging my family through this agony."

Big Mama recalled the same conversation with Karen, but didn't point it out. "You're too hard on yourself, my dear."

"If I am, it's because I've caused my children a lot of pain.

They don't say it, but I see it in their eyes. Hurt isn't difficult to see if you love somebody. I've been thinking about what's better for the girls—for me to be here sick or for me to let go so they can build a new, more stable life. It'll be easy for Johnny to get a new wife." She wanted to say he'd already found a bed partner, but decided not to bring it up with Ms. Emma. She would keep it inside.

"Karen, sugar, it's not your decision to make. How long you live belongs to God and God all by Himself. Don't you be in such a hurry to die. We're going in our due time."

"How do you know this isn't my time?"

"Well, do you feel like that's what God's telling you in your spirit?"

"I don't know what I feel right now."

"Well, if you don't know, then you need to wait on the Lord until you do know. In the meantime, you must hold fast to your confession of faith. That means believe for the best no matter what things look like. After you have done everything you know to do, then the Word tells you to stand. Just stand still and wait until you hear from the Lord."

"I've gotten tired of waiting. This is the third time around with my breast cancer. I don't have any hope left."

"Then tell God you need Him to give you hope. He will give you whatever you need."

"Is he going to heal me once and for all? Will I get up and walk out of here, never having to come back again? Will I go home to a husband who loves me?"

"I don't know what's in store for you. It's according to the will of God." She paused. "What I can say is that God has placed the exact amount of faith in you to walk through your specific challenges. The portion you have is for you. The measure I have is for me. So, by faith, you are equipped to overcome every challenge in your way.

"See, that's what bothers me. We talk about prayer and faith. It's easy to preach about faith when we're doing good.

How many times have I told someone to just have faith when they were going through a tough time, never realizing how hard it is to believe when you're the one in the situation?"

"You're only human. You're going to get weak. That's why God says in second Corinthians that He is strong when we are weak."

"Why me?"

"I'm not able to tell you why God allows some to get sick and not others.

"Deep down, I know God isn't the blame for my problems," she said because it sounded right. "I have done enough in my past to bring on my own cancer. I have enough guilt to last a lifetime. Maybe I brought this all on myself. This could be my punishment."

"Don't you ever believe God let you get sick to punish you. He loves you. We all have sinned and made mistakes and fallen short of the glory of God. We don't have the answers about your sickness, and we don't need to. We're not God. Just pray and believe for your healing."

"I believe in God. I pray. So why am I not healed?"

"I don't know, beloved. No matter how close I get to the Lord, no matter how much I want to seek His face, I won't ever know all His ways."

"Maybe I'm doing something wrong. Maybe I should have just fasted and prayed and believed for a healing, instead of going through this medical stuff."

"I can't tell you how or when He's going to heal you. He can move through a miracle, a divine touch, or He might heal you with medicines and doctors. I don't know what He has for you. Just don't you put Him in a box."

"What does that mean, Ms. Emma?"

"He can touch you in more ways than you know how. So you don't want to tie His hands."

"Do you think I was always supposed to get cancer, or was it something I did to deserve it?"

"No one deserves cancer, just like no one deserves trouble with their heart or trouble in their marriage or being poor. Truth is, some things we don't have any control over. What I can tell you is that there is a plan for everyone's life and only God knows what it is. He promised to never leave you or to forsake you. In the same way, He didn't promise everything would be easy and you would escape suffering. As a matter of fact, Jesus says in John 16:33 that we will have trouble. She should expect problems, but don't be overcome by the notion that life won't be easy every second. But He's able to work it out and get you through the rough times."

"I could have done without suffering with this cancer."

Big Mama bent over to pull a tissue from her purse.

"Are you all right, Ms. Emma?"

"Yes, beloved, I'm fine. I'm just full with the Holy Spirit."

"I wish I knew God like you do and was able to have more faith. But for right now, I don't see my way getting any brighter."

"Everybody's got a cross to bear. Maybe that's why some folks get sick and some don't. Could be that the cancer is the cross you have to bear, and the old heart attack might have been mine. You cancer could be a little piece of the whole puzzle God has planned for your life. I don't rightly know. What I know for sure is how much He loves us, and that's sufficient."

"Perhaps I don't want to carry this cross far enough to see the rest of the puzzle. Because I'm mad. I'm hurt. I feel guilty, and most of all, I'm tired."

"What are you mad about?"

Karen was speaking her mind, no holds barred. "I'm mad at Johnny for putting me through so much crap. I'm mad at myself for not checking my breasts. And," she deliberated, "I'm mad at God." She waited for a reaction from Big Mama but got none. "Did you hear me, Ms. Emma? I'm mad at God too."

"Yes, I heard every word."

"Isn't that terrible? You think maybe that's why I'm not getting healed because I am so mad?"

"Well, let's see. Do you love your parents?"

"My parents died a long time ago, but I love them. They were very good to me, and I miss them."

"Did you ever get mad at them about something even if it turned out not to be their fault?"

"Yes..." Karen reluctantly answered, not knowing where Ms. Emma was headed with the question.

"And you still love them, huh?"

Karen nodded in affirmation.

"There you go. Love saw you right past the anger."

"I wish it was that easy. This guilt and anger is eating me up inside. I can't seem to let it go."

"You have to let it go. In order for you to live, you have to let some of that junk in you die. If it doesn't kill your body, it will surely kill your spirit, and it's no way to live."

"You're right; this isn't any way to live." Karen wouldn't voice any more of her inner feelings to the church mother but continued to contemplate the situation. Karen didn't want to be mad any more than she wanted to stay in a struggling marriage. What could she do? Getting well and rushing home wasn't the super cure. What she had to look forward to at home was more of the same. Staying on the endlessly running merry-go-round was a sobering image.

Chapter 29

Karen had been in the hospital a month, and Johnny was feeling the pressure. Chelle was quite the little trouper, cleaning, cooking, and getting Elizabeth off to school every day. Chelle wanted to carry the housekeeping load but she was only fifteen years old. She had her own schoolwork and teenage livelihood.

Johnny sat in the home office located near the front foyer. The junk mail and bills were scattered across the desk. He was much more organized in his personal affairs when Karen was around. He hadn't realized that she routinely sorted their mail and separated out junk from substance. Now, he had to do it without her assistance.

Chelle entered his office, not quick to interrupt. Johnny saw her standing there and signaled for her to come in.

"Daddy, the water faucet is leaking in Elizabeth's bathroom. What should we do?"

Johnny sighed from being overwhelmed.

"Did you turn the water off?"

"Yes."

"I'll take a look."

"Last year mine did the same thing and Mommy had the plumber come out and fix it. It had something to do with a washer or something like that."

Johnny hadn't known anything about it. He was amazed to know Karen handled various projects around the house without his input. He shook his head. She wasn't home to handle the day-to-day activities and it was falling in his lap.

Chelle was headed back out the room when she remembered something.

"Oh, yeah, Daddy, I need some money to pay for our field trip."

"I didn't know sophomores took field trips."

She was happy to see her father in an easygoing mood. "We've already had three trips this year. Mommy went on two of them with me."

"I didn't know that. Your Mom seems to do a lot, doesn't she?" Chelle nodded her head in agreement.

Johnny couldn't figure out how Karen used to work, take care of the house, and keep up with children.

"Daddy, don't forget that lower school is off tomorrow for parent-teacher conferences."

Johnny didn't pretend to have any clue about what that meant for him. He was quickly realizing how out of touch he was with the children's schooling. Karen took care of that business.

"Chelle, what do I have to do?"

"You have to go meet with Ms. Bartel, Elizabeth's teacher. You should have a note with the time on it. She gave it to you last week."

Johnny aimlessly flipped through papers on the desk. He scouted through mound of bills, which included the mortgage on the summer home, the boat maintenance and slip fee, an invoice from the fur storage company, a notice from the landscaper for spring cleaning, the boating membership fee, the monthly tuition bill for the girls, and the supplemental insurance for Karen, in addition to the basic utilities, phone, cable, mortgage, credit cards, car notes, and a variety of insurances. He retrieved the Stanford letter while searching through the pile. It read, *Spring Quarter—Tuition, Room & Board, Miscellaneous fees—Total: $20,000.* He ignored the total and tucked it in the top drawer. It would have to wait for the equity loan check. Johnny was expecting it any day and checked the mailbox as soon as he got home each evening.

"It's a purple envelope," Chelle eased in to bring structure to his futile search.

That little bit of information was what he needed to hone in on the document. He ripped open the envelope and glanced over it. The time read two-thirty.

"I have a meeting at two-thirty tomorrow." He rubbed his chin. Stress was kicking in, and the day was merely starting.

"We're not off in upper school tomorrow, so I won't be able to stay at home with her."

"Where does she usually go on days off?"

"She stays at home with Mommy. When Mommy was working, she just took off for the day."

The answer wasn't as simple to Johnny as it seemed for Chelle. He didn't shy away from his obligations as a father. He needed a job to provide for his kids, but without a family the job was insignificant. Which took priority? He never had to wonder when Karen was home. Her role as a mother and wife freed him to live without having to set priorities between family and career. Without her picking up the slack, he was feeling the full weight of his responsibilities.

He had blindly assumed it was his efforts that had gotten him advancements on the job. Never had it been so apparent to him that Karen's support and efforts within the home had allowed him to thrive outside their home. He was starting to appreciate Karen's worth in the relationship, whereas he used to think she was sitting at home, carefree and eating bonbons. One month of overwhelming reality had erased such thinking.

"We're heading to school, Daddy. We'll see you tonight." Johnny waved the girls off, gulped down a swig of orange juice and headed off to work later than normal and with more worries than he cared to sift.

Even the peace he expected at work didn't come. The day was hectic. It hadn't been necessary before to bring personal matters to the office. Today Johnny was doing the best he could to balance work and home.

"Sonja, can you please get Ms. Bartel on the phone at my

daughter's school?" He handed her a business card with the phone number. "See if I can reschedule the parent-teacher conference for some time tomorrow evening."

"What if she doesn't have any evening slots?"

"Anything except two-thirty. I have that meeting tomorrow with the production crew from Tennessee."

"That's right. I'll see what I can do."

Sonja made the call and went to Johnny's office to relay the message. Even though the door was open, she knocked.

"Excuse me, sir. I was able to speak with Ms. Bartel. Tomorrow evening is not going to work. I had to set you up for nine o'clock tomorrow morning. It was the only time she had that wasn't in conflict with your meeting."

"Thank you, Sonja."

The appointment meant he would have to miss part of the morning at work. Johnny wasn't thrilled with the time, but there was nothing he could do. He had to figure out what to do with Elizabeth for the day. It hadn't been a problem when Karen had gotten sick the other times. He had paid for a live-in nanny and she took care of the kids. Funds were flowing back then. He could afford the gourmet option for child care. Times had changed, and he was looking for more of a sack lunch type solution.

Off and on he contemplated what to do with Elizabeth. It was turning out that the little things Karen handled daily added up to be just as significant and time-consuming as his obligations. His appreciation for Karen's contribution as a partner and mother was rapidly growing as he stood on the front line at home. By the time Johnny got home, he was worn out. The idea of spending a couple of hours doing bills before bed wasn't a thrilling scene. It was getting tighter and tighter without Karen's financial input. Johnny thought about getting rid of the Porsche and saving the $750 monthly payment. His insurance would go down as well. He didn't want to let his toy go, but financial options were limited. A roof over their heads, food in their stomachs, working utilities, and an education were necessities. Luxuries were expendable.

Chelle helped with dinner, but there was more that had to be done around the house, like cleaning. The girls did laundry and washed dishes regularly, but that was the most they could handle. The house was not nearly as clean as the way Karen kept it. Johnny couldn't afford a service. Several women from the church had offered to come by and clean, but he didn't want strangers rooting around the house. At least that was how he felt a month ago when the place was clean. Times had changed, and so had Johnny's attitude about receiving help.

After pondering, he gave up on finding someone to care for Elizabeth tomorrow. Connie had doctor appointments and Tyrone was going with her. The babysitter was unavailable. He even let Chelle call Tina to see if she could help out. Unfortunately for the girls, Tina couldn't take off the entire day since a couple of the other secretaries had already requested time off. Johnny had run out of choices.

Chelle and Elizabeth were doing their homework at the table.

"I need you to stay at home with Elizabeth tomorrow."

"Daddy, no. I have preps for my midterms."

Johnny felt badly about putting his daughter in such an awkward situation, but he didn't feel there were any other alternatives.

"I have to go to school tomorrow," Chelle reiterated with tears surfacing.

Johnny sighed and rubbed his forehead. The stress was mounting. Chelle was his last resort, and that wasn't panning out.

"What now?"

Elizabeth was quiet. She felt like Johnny and Chelle were both upset because of her. She began to cry.

"Why are you crying, Elizabeth?" her father asked.

"Because you and Chelle are mad at me."

Instinctively, Chelle jumped to her sister's defense. "Don't cry. I'm not mad at you. You didn't do anything wrong. Finish your homework."

"Yeah, Elizabeth, don't cry," Johnny consoled from afar.

Chelle felt awful about making her sister cry.

"Daddy, I'll stay home with her."

Johnny felt worse.

"No, Chelle, you go to school. I will take her to work with me."

Elizabeth's eyelids widened. Her father's job was always made out to be a big deal in the family. For a little girl like Elizabeth, going to work with her father was like going to the White House to meet the president. It was an honor. She dried her tears and perked up.

Johnny didn't know how he was going to do it, but he had to do whatever was required. Taking care of the kids alone wasn't easy. He was doing the best he could without the help of his partner.

The three got through the evening without any fanfare. Early the next morning Johnny dropped Elizabeth off at his office. Thankfully Sonja had agreed to watch the little girl.

Johnny headed to the school to meet with Ms. Bartel. He had never been to a parent-teacher conference for any of the kids. Karen faithfully went to each conference and reported the findings back to him. He didn't know what to expect. His kids were intelligent, well mannered, and quite exceptional in school. He assumed the teacher would go over Elizabeth's grades, attendance, and conduct, and at the end, hand him a few of her completed assignments. He planned to be in and out in fifteen minutes or less.

"I don't think we've ever met, Mr. Clark," Ms. Bartel said shaking his hand. "I've always dealt with your wife. Thank you for coming today."

Johnny was humbled and kept the greeting light.

"I would have called sooner but decided to wait since the

conferences were coming up anyway."

"Called me sooner about what?"

Ms. Bartel placed a scoring chart in front of Johnny. She took a pencil and drew attention to several numbers.

"As you can see, Elizabeth's grades have dropped dramatically over the past month."

The numbers were clear, but he had difficulty digesting them.

"She is quite an active and engaging student. Recently she has been withdrawn and very emotional."

Johnny sat back in the chair. He didn't know what to say. Everything was falling apart. It was hitting him on every side. Nothing seemed like status quo.

"Elizabeth has been an excellent student. This change is totally unexpected."

"Huh." Johnny sighed. "Unexpected for you? What about for me?"

"I can imagine, Mr. Clark. I didn't feel alarmed until I began to see the change in her behavior. Do you have any idea what could be causing this change?"

"Yes," Johnny eked out. "We are dealing with a crisis at home."

The teacher patiently waited.

"My wife is back in the hospital with cancer."

"I didn't know." The school had a policy which suggested parents inform the school of any significant events in the student's life that might have an impact on their school performance. She flipped through her file to see if there was a note somewhere she'd overlooked. She found none. "I can't find the note in her file."

Outside of Karen, Chelle was Johnny's eyes and ears for school business. He was unaware of the policy and had not informed anyone about Karen's condition. If Chelle hadn't informed the school, then it hadn't been done. "My apologies. I didn't think to send a note or tell anybody at the school."

Johnny felt a loss of control. Unknowingly, he was letting so many important items fall through the cracks. He was letting his children down at a time when they needed to depend on him, now more than ever.

"Elizabeth is very close to her mom. I guess she's having a hard time with her illness." Johnny was disturbed. "I guess we're all having a rough time."

"I'm sorry to hear about Mrs. Clark. My thoughts are with your entire family."

'Thank you."

"Now, about Elizabeth. I would like to immediately set her up with the school psychologist. She may need an outlet to discuss her feelings. We need to get on top of this," Ms. Bartel firmly suggested to the distraught father.

Johnny nodded in agreement.

"I only need your signed consent."

"You got it. Whatever I need to do for my little girl, I'll do it."

He felt guilty and dejected for being in tune with his daughter. It bothered him that he hadn't noticed. He was stretched between paying the bills, running the house, working, keeping the girls alive, and visiting Karen at the hospital. There was no room for anything else. Johnny hadn't stepped foot in Floods in over a month and couldn't recall the last time he'd responded to Annette's messages. Only the important areas of his life received attention. There wasn't room for extra.

He couldn't fathom being a single parent. There was no way he could raise the kids without Karen. Johnny knew it and he needed to tell her too.

Chapter 30

The term *overwhelmed* was becoming an understatement for Johnny. Work, home, and hospital had become his full time schedule with none seemingly under control, especially the past few days. Napping at the hospital was routine.

In between nods, he'd grown accustomed to someone checking Karen's vital signs every six to eight hours. This last check was being done directly by Dr. Costas.

"What is going on with Karen?" Johnny asked worried about the way she sounded. Her breathing was shallow and her temperature hovering around a hundred and two. "Why isn't she getting any better? Why is she sleeping so much?"

Dr. Costas asked Johnny to step into the hallway. Once they'd gotten out Karen's presence, she said, "I can't explain what's happening with Karen. Her vital signs are weak, and I can't tell you why. She's in a coma, but at least she's breathing on her own."

"Is it from the cancer?"

"No, I don't think so."

"If you don't know, then who does?"

"What I mean is that the cancer should not be causing this much deterioration in her body. We've completed the treatments. Her body should be much stronger than what we're witnessing. She suffered from malnutrition and dehydration a week ago. However, I'm confident we convinced her into letting us administer the IV fluids in plenty of time to ward off any related setbacks."

"So why is she in a coma?"

Dr. Costas shrugged her shoulders, at a loss for words.

"I'm sorry, but I just don't have an answer for you. For an

unknown reason, she isn't progressing. There's no medical explanation for it."

Johnny scratched his head in utter frustration. "If you don't know what's wrong with her, then how can you treat her?"

"We're doing the best we can. We'll keep her on the fluids, meds, and oxygen until we see some kind of change." Dr. Costas seemed a little uneasy. "Johnny, there is something else we need to discuss."

"What?"

"In the event Karen isn't able to continue breathing on her own," Dr. Costas said and then hesitated before giving the final blow, "do you want her put on life support?"

It felt like a trick question to Johnny. Karen had never discussed a living will, even though they'd been through her life-threatening illnesses in the past. There was no good answer. If Karen couldn't breathe on her own and needed the machine, that wasn't going to be good. If she couldn't breathe on her own and he chose not to put her on a respiratory machine, that wasn't going to be good either. It was a no-win dilemma, one that Johnny wasn't eager to rush into.

He always had options and never ran away from making a tough call. Johnny prided himself on being able to get the job done under the most adverse conditions. He rubbed his palms together. He didn't have the answer for this problem and had no idea where to find it.

"I don't know what to tell you." He felt like sticking his head in the sand and letting the matter pass.

"She's not doing well right now. Before her condition gets worse, I'm going to need an answer."

"You'll have to give me some time to make a decision."

Dr. Costas needed an answer, but felt it was inappropriate to apply more pressure on Johnny than she already had.

The doctor left and Johnny found himself alone and scared. He didn't know what to do. He schlepped into the room, sat, and let the sound of calm usher him into a light sleep. Johnny wasn't tired, but the sleep felt good. It gave him a few moments of desperate escape from this bad dream. If only he could sleep away the problem and wake up with it all behind him. Johnny felt a surge of despair rising within. He'd never admit it was crippling. He was too strong for that.

He was awakened by the nurse's routine check. He slowly opened his eyelids. The short, two hour nap was the most uninterrupted sleep he'd gotten in weeks. Once he was able to focus, Tyrone and Connie came into view.

"Hey, chief," Tyrone greeted.

Connie chimed in too. She rolled her wheelchair around the bed to get closer to him, careful not to bump Karen's bed. She gently took his hand and said, "How's she doing?"

Johnny was visibly disturbed with Karen being in a coma. His words didn't flow as freely.

"Not good, Connie. The doctor came in earlier and asked me if I wanted to put her on a life support system if it comes to that."

Johnny wasn't crying, but he was choked up. Connie sensed his pain and consoled him by rubbing his hand.

"Hang in there, Johnny, no matter what it looks like. You have to keep the faith."

"I'm trying, Connie. It's a lot easier said than done."

Tyrone stood behind Connie's chair and placed his hands on her shoulders in support. He could imagine how hurt she was about Karen's condition, since they were so close.

Connie patted Tyrone's hand. "Honey, can you roll me back? I don't want to hit the bed."

"My goodness, it looks like a party up in here."

Everyone in the room turned around to see Tina standing in the doorway.

"Surprise, surprise, I didn't realize you were coming out here today," Connie said.

Johnny didn't have the same warm disposition for Tina

that Connie had. She was the last person he wanted to see at a tense time like this.

Tyrone didn't think Tina had seen Johnny hurl a chilling stare at her. But he had seen it and took the gesture as a sign that Johnny probably needed to step away and take a break.

"Hey, Johnny, why don't we go grab a cup of coffee?"

"I don't know, man. I should probably be around, just in case something—I don't know what—happens."

"Come on, man. You could use a break."

"Yeah, go on, Johnny. I'll be here with Karen. Go on with Tyrone. You need some time," Connie said.

Johnny conceded and took the couple up on their offer.

The two men headed to the cafeteria in virtual silence. Tyrone knew Johnny didn't need advice. A shoulder to lean on and a listening ear would suffice.

The two women left in the room weren't nearly as quiet.

Tina took a chair between the bed and Connie's wheelchair. "How long have you been here?" Tina asked.

"Not long before you came in." Connie lowered her voice. There was the possibility Karen could hear the conversations around her while she was in the coma. Connie wheeled her chair toward the door as Tina followed her lead.

Once the women relocated into the hallway, Tina asked Connie, "Any news?"

"Apparently the doctor hasn't seen sufficient improvement. They're hoping she can continue breathing on her own, without life support. Johnny is pretty upset, and I feel sorry for him."

"Humph. I don't feel sorry for him. Some of it's probably his fault anyway. He's done enough dirt to drive anybody to the grave," Tina stated.

Neither woman saw the men coming around the corner until they were well within range to hear the conversation.

"Tina, how can you say something like that? This is not the time or place for you to be talking about Johnny like that.

We need to be supportive," Connie replied.

"Please. How supportive has he been to her? Karen might have to pretend he's the ideal husband, but not me. I don't have to live with him. I can say exactly how I feel about the jerk."

"Jerk--" Johnny chuckled. The humor in his voice didn't last long. "Girl, you got some nerve bringing your venom in here. I guess it's not enough for you to be miserable at home alone. You feel it necessary to come over here and make everybody else miserable too." Johnny was getting louder and angrier with each word. "You need to go. My wife is sick and you show up with this crap. Get out of here."

"Calm down, partner," Tyrone said. "Take it easy."

"Yes, Johnny, try to calm down. This much aggravation can't be good for you," Connie insisted.

"You're right. I don't know how I let this witch get to me."

"What? No, you didn't call me a witch, especially when you're the one with the bag of tricks."

"Please stop." Connie was determined to maintain some peace and quiet in the hallway. She knew how irritating excessive noise could be for people who were sick. "We are here to give Karen support. This is not about your differences. If anything, the two of you need to be in prayer together."

"Girl, please. There you go. You're always trying to shove prayer down my throat. It doesn't work for everybody," Tina said.

"Yes, it does work—for anybody," Connie replied.

"Why hasn't it worked for you?"

Tyrone had been quiet while everyone else talked back and forth until Tina crossed the line. He didn't tolerate anyone saying anything about Connie in his presence.

"Whoa, wait a minute, Tina. You need to contain yourself. You're letting your mouth get way out of line."

Tyrone was sensitive to how people interpreted his wife's demeanor. She appeared passive, and some unwisely used it as an opportunity to push her around. He was quick to protect her whenever necessary.

"That's okay, honey." She sat on the edge of her wheelchair. This time she chose to speak up for herself. "Listen, Tina, let me tell you something."

Tyrone was stunned to see Connie stand up to Tina. As he glanced at Tina, she had a puzzled look but seemed to be listening for a change.

"I know you are angry and bitter because your husband left you once you got sick. I'm sorry about that. I can only imagine how you feel. I've told you time and time again that it wasn't your fault you got cancer, but it's not our fault either."

"Connie, you're the last person to preach to me about cancer. You don't even acknowledge your own condition. How can you possibly understand how I feel?"

"Tina, that's..." Tyrone jumped in. He had heard enough.

Connie patted Tyrone's hand, letting him know that she was fine with Tina's outburst. Connie grinned with her lips tight, seeming unfazed.

"Tina, I do know what you went through with the cancer. I could be angry and bitter, just like you. I choose not to be. I have decided to focus on the good in my life and block out the negativity. It's what keeps me alive. Because I don't walk around with my head hanging down and acting mad with the world, you think that I'm living with my head in the sand about the brain tumor."

Tina wanted to respond, but Connie didn't allow her to interrupt.

"I know exactly what the doctors have said about the tumor. I just choose not to claim it as my tumor. I know they don't expect me to live, but that doesn't stop me from living and believing. Every day I'm alive is a good day for me, no matter how bad I feel. I am too grateful to waste my time with a bunch of negativity."

Tina was speechless.

"Now don't get me wrong; I am appreciative of doctors for their help. But they don't determine how long I live or even how I'm going to die. I can choose life or death. Some people in my situation spend so much precious time focusing on dying that they don't do any living. I don't have the luxury of worrying about tomorrow. Every day has to count, because I don't want to die knowing I spent my time just trying to stay alive."

Tears streamed down Tina's face from a combination of shame, guilt, and hurt. Connie was the friend she had so often viewed as the weak duckling who needed protecting. Through her teary vision, Tina saw a strong, soft-spoken woman who let her actions speak. Tina admired few people and saw most as hypocritical. She respected the fact that Connie didn't just talk about living right. She actually practiced it. Tina felt odd. It was as if the armor surrounding her heart had been penetrated and the hurt exposed.

"With my faith in God, I choose to live every day I'm alive as though it is my last, and I'm okay with that."

Tyrone hugged Connie as she eased back in her chair. Her hope was that things would start to look up for both of her friends.

Chapter 31

Johnny walked into the kitchen carrying bags of groceries. He set them down on the counter and pulled out the honey-roasted chickens, plastic containers stuffed with corn, rice pilaf, and green beans. The girls were light eaters, but Johnny got two small chickens anyway.

"You girls hungry?"

The kitchen had become Chelle and Elizabeth's nightly study area. "A little," Chelle answered without disrupting her schoolwork.

He proceeded to pull the paper plates from the cabinet. Johnny had never realized the benefit of using disposable eating utensils. Convenience wasn't an issue when Karen was home running the household. Johnny and the rest of the family had taken their meals and the daily cleaning for granted.

"Anybody feed the dog yet?"

The girls froze, knowing the outrage that could follow. Karen wasn't there to rescue them. They knew blaming the other was not going to help this time. Without denial, both girls dropped their pencils and hopped to their feet.

"Wait, wait," Johnny told the girls in a strong voice.

Both girls halted in bewilderment.

"Don't worry about the dog. I'll feed him from now on. Since Mommy's gone, each of us has extra assignments. And the two of you have plenty to do between the chores you're already doing and your schoolwork. Sit back down and do your work. I'll go out and feed Mindy."

The girls sat and went right back to their homework. After Johnny went outside, Chelle told Elizabeth, "I'm glad we don't have to feed that dog anymore."

Elizabeth said, "Me too," and returned to her math work.

Erick fumbled with his keys outside the front door. He hadn't been home since Christmas. The thought of being thousands of miles away with his mom in the hospital was too much to bear. He had used the remaining balance on his credit card to get a ticket. Coming home took a great deal of courage. He wasn't looking forward to facing his father, based on their last conversation.

Erick finally got the door opened and carted his duffel bag and backpack inside the foyer. There wasn't any activity in the front room. He headed for the kitchen and family room area. The chatter got louder as he approached the room. His steps got faster. He felt a special bond with his younger sisters and had missed them.

When he hit the doorway, Elizabeth caught a glimpse. For a moment she wasn't sure if it was him, but quickly concluded it was. "Erick," she screamed and leapt from the seat, running toward him.

The screeching yell startled Chelle. It took a second for her to get her bearings. Once she did, she too rushed him.

They hugged one another in unison.

Johnny heard the scream and came rushing in the back door to see what was going on. He was shocked to see John Erick standing in the kitchen. The sight of him didn't draw the same excitement as it had from the girls. He loved his son, but his stubborn side often diluted his outward display of affection. Johnny was still feeling the sting from comments Erick had made in their last conversation.

"Hey, Dad."

Erick did have a streak of his father's stubbornness. It was tempered with his mother's willingness to concede. The main reason he came home was to be with his family and offer support to his mom. He was determined that nothing was going to interfere, especially not an ongoing fight with his dad.

He tore himself from the girls and humbly approached his father. Erick knew that if there was to be a reconciliation, he had to initiate. "I apologize for how I spoke to you."

Erick didn't take back what he had told his dad on the phone. He apologized for how and when he had said it. Afterward he extended his hand for his father to shake. Erick wasn't sure where his dad's mind was on the matter. He didn't know whether he'd accept the apology or not.

Johnny stared at his son and processed his apology. For a moment he did nothing. Then he reached out and grabbed his son, with tears mounting.

"I'm glad you're home, son." Johnny patted Erick on his back. Johnny had barely been holding it together at home. With Chelle's help, he'd gotten by. But too much was falling through the cracks, like Elizabeth's emotional welfare.

John Erick had no idea how much his father admired him. Perhaps it was because his son was one of the few people in Johnny's circle who would stand up to him. Johnny's outpouring was confirmation of the joy he felt in having his son home at this critical time. He couldn't find words to verbalize the moment.

The hug was sufficient for Erick. It was more than he'd ever received in the past and more than he could ever hope to get.

"I'm glad you came home too, Erick. I miss you a lot when you're gone. Are you going to stay here?" Elizabeth beamed.

Johnny was glad to see her happy. Of the two girls, she was having the most difficulty with her mother's illness. Her grades were slowly climbing back up, primarily resulting from the school counseling.

"I can use your help around here," Johnny told his son.

The girls adored their big brother. He was protective, while at the same time affectionate with them. Johnny took care of them, but there was nothing like any extra dose of doting. Erick was a welcome sight.

Chapter 32

The hypothetical scenarios had become an agonizing reality. Johnny didn't hesitate to put her on life-support when Karen had actually stopped breathing last week. He wanted her to stay alive any way possible, even if it was by assisted means.

The rising and falling of the breathing machine created a rhythmic hum. *Tzzzzzt, tzzzzzt* blended with a series of beeps.

Weeks ago, the unfamiliar setting and nagging noises would have made it impossible for Johnny to get any sleep in Karen's hospital room. His tolerance coupled with frequent lengthy days and overnight stays had increased as her condition worsened, but Johnny hadn't come close to getting a good night's sleep. His trench coat barely shielded his upper body from the cold draft. He clutched the garment like a toasty wool blanket unable to fully relax.

Beep, beep, the IV alarmed. Within a few minutes the nurse came in to change the bottle. She tried to be quiet, seeing the large man crunched into the high-backed chair shoved into the corner.

It didn't matter. Johnny heard her enter the room as his eyelids flew open. He grunted during his stretch.

"Oh, Mr. Clark, I didn't mean to wake you up."

"You didn't. I wasn't really asleep, just napping here and there." In the middle of his sentence, Johnny covered his mouth. He got a whiff of the foul breath seeping across his lips. His shirt was wrinkled, his mouth dry, and his feet sweaty. He could only hope the nurse didn't smell his less than desirable aroma. He immediately jerked his arms down and pinned them to his sides.

"Perhaps you should go home and get some rest. We'll

call you if anything changes. You won't do Mrs. Clark any good if you let yourself get run down."

Karen's condition was continuing to deteriorate. As long as she was unstable, the nights seemed endless for Johnny and her medical team.

He didn't know what to do. Johnny hadn't always come through for Karen, but this time he wanted to be there for her, whichever way her condition went. If she woke up, he wanted to be the first face she laid eyes on. If she didn't wake up, he knew the anguish of not being at her bedside would eat him alive.

"I'll wait to see if someone else shows up before I run home. How are her vital signs? Any improvement?"

The nurse shook her head in disappointment. "There has been no change. She's weak but holding on."

He couldn't have pictured this scenario several months ago. Wrinkled shirt, tart breath, hair stubbles, funky feet, and a drooled chin were a far cry from the impeccably dressed, clean-shaven, proud man standing at the entrance of Floods.

"On second thought, I will run home." So, he left.

*　　*　　*

The nurses paid close attention to Karen, watching for any dramatic change in her condition that might warrant contacting the doctor.

It was eleven-thirty on a Thursday night, and Dr. Costas happened to be awake when her phone vibrated on top of the desk before falling to the floor. She fumbled to get it. By the time she did, the vibrating had stopped.

It was the hospital. She dialed the number back. "This is Dr. Costas. I got a call from the hospital."

"Oh yes, Doctor. Mrs. Clark's vital signs have deteriorated dramatically. Her pulse and blood pressure are both low. Her fever is also spiking."

"Is she on fluids?"

"Yes, she is. We also put her on an ice pad to help get the fever down. It topped off at a hundred and five over an hour ago. It was at 104.8 when we checked fifteen minutes ago."

"Doesn't sound promising."

"We've done everything we can."

"I guess we wait and hope she makes it through the night. Is anyone from her family there?"

"No, Mr. Clark left several hours ago. I think he's coming back, though. He's been staying here every night. If you want me to, I can call him. I just thought it would be best to call you first."

"You were right to call me," Dr. Costas conceded. "I will contact her family. I was hoping it wouldn't come to this, but here we are. Can you give me the phone number in her file?"

"Sure thing, Doctor. Hold on while I get the number."

Dr. Costas was careful not to cross ethical lines. However, she and Karen did connect on more than a purely patient-doctor level. Dr. Costas was grieved to know Karen could very well be approaching the final phase of her battle with breast cancer.

"I have the number for you."

Dr. Costas scribbled the number onto a notepad. "Keep me posted on her condition."

The doctor stood in her office, slow to make the unavoidable call.

Johnny had taken a hot shower when he got in from the hospital around nine P.M. Exhausted, he had stretched out across the bed to catch some of the Pistons and Sixers game, intending to eat the sandwich Chelle had made for him.

The ringing cordless phone lying next to Johnny's head sounded like an alarm clock. He woke up with the TV playing and his sandwich untouched. He unconsciously grabbed the phone just to stop the testy noise.

He answered with an edge in his tone.

"Johnny, this is Dr. Costas."

Johnny popped up in the bed.

"Is something wrong?" His heart was pounding. He had asked the question, but wasn't ready for the answer.

"I got a call from the hospital. Karen has a fever near a hundred and five, and her other vital signs aren't looking too good."

"And?"

"She's taken a severe turn for the worse and is in critical condition. Karen might not make it through the night."

"What else can you do? There has to be something you haven't tried," he cried out.

"We have done everything we can medically do to turn her prognosis around. Nothing we've tried has gotten the results I was hoping for. I'm sorry, Johnny. I feel awful having to give you this news. I was hopeful that she would overcome this last bout. Really, I am truly sorry."

"I'm going to the hospital. Will you be there?" he asked.

"I won't go unless her condition takes the final turn for the worse," Dr. Costas answered. "At that time, we will need to make some decisions."

"Like what?"

"Remember when we discussed whether or not you want to terminate the life support and let her expire naturally?"

"I'm not ready to make that decision."

"I realize how difficult this is for you."

Thoughts were swirling and he couldn't catch hold. "I need more time to think about it. I can't give up on her. I don't care what it looks like." Johnny's voice was building momentum.

"Try to keep calm. You're going to need to be as rational as possible in the upcoming hours."

He wasn't able to respond.

"I wish we could do more. If you need to get in touch with

me, have the hospital call me, no matter what time of night."

Johnny clicked off the cordless phone. He slid over to the side of the bed and planted both feet on the floor. His head hung down, with his eyes tightly shut. Drops fell onto the floor. There weren't any boo-hooing wails coming from his room, just a continuous stream of tears. He didn't know what to do first. He thought about informing the kids, then decided against it. The thought of telling the children their mother was dying tore him apart. The tears intensified. Johnny felt grave turmoil. He tried to get himself together. He wiped away the tears and dug deep inside to find enough strength to get off the bed and make some necessary decisions. He allowed himself a brief moment to grieve and think. Finally he was able to make it to his feet.

This was one of the few times he felt the loneliness of being an only child with both parents deceased. It was a similarity he and Karen shared. Despite a limited extended family, the Clarks hadn't felt an overwhelming void in the past. Tonight was different. The first person who came to mind was Tyrone, a friend who had proven to be dependable. That's exactly what Johnny felt he needed.

Tyrone and Connie were already in bed. When the phone rang, Tyrone rolled over to grab it. Instead, he knocked the phone onto the floor.

Johnny called out but nobody replied.

Tyrone fumbled for the phone with one hand, searching for the tabletop lamp switch with the other.

He called out again in a deeper tone.

Finally, Tyrone heard Johnny. He squinted to bring the clock into focus. Midnight. Tyrone knew this was important. He sat up in the bed, braced to hear whatever news Johnny was about to lay on him. "What's up, buddy?"

Connie woke up too.

Johnny had decided before calling Tyrone that he would hold it together. It was the manly thing to do. At least that was what his rational mind said, but his heart didn't agree. He wanted to find the words. They wouldn't roll off his tongue.

Tyrone sensed Johnny was troubled. "Is there a change with Karen?"

"Yes," he solemnly admitted, as if he were releasing the weight of a heavy secret. "Her doctor called me a few minutes ago and told me she wasn't doing so good." Every word he spoke was slow and life draining. "They don't expect her to make it through the night."

"Oh, no, Johnny. Man, I don't know what to say."

"What, what?" Connie asked, tugging on his arm.

"Karen's not doing well."

"Is there anything we can do?" Connie asked Tyrone loud enough for Johnny to hear.

"Yeah, what can we do to help you?"

"I'm going to the hospital. I was wondering if you could meet me there? I don't feel up to going out there by myself."

"Consider it done. I'm on my way right now. I'll see you there."

"Tyrone..." Johnny paused to find the words that would adequately convey his appreciation. "Uh, thanks, partner. You're all right with me." The lump in Johnny's throat moved up and squashed his vocal cords. He couldn't talk.

"I get what you're trying to say. See you in a few minutes." Tyrone ended the call and sprang to his feet. "Connie, I'm meeting Johnny at the hospital. Doesn't look good for Karen. He's taking it hard. I want to be there for him. Do you mind if I go?"

"Of course not. I expect you to go." Connie kissed Tyrone on the cheek to seal her approval. "And I'm going too."

"Do you think you should? What about getting your rest? You need to conserve your energy." He rubbed her head and kissed her forehead.

"You know Karen would be there for me. I'm going and that's that, Mr. Sims."

Tyrone adored his wife. When she firmly spoke her mind, he was not one to change it.

"Let's throw something on and get out of here, young lady."

Tyrone's support gave Johnny enough boost to get off the bed and make his way toward the hospital. The severity of the moment was plain. He was glad to have Tyrone meeting him at the hospital, but he required something more. He was trying to rally every ounce of hope from any willing source.

I should tell the pastor, he thought. He picked up the phone and then reconsidered. No, it was too late to call. Johnny remembered the pastor telling him to call anytime. *Maybe I should.* He went back and forth on what to do. He didn't feel close enough to the pastor to call him in the middle of the night. What if something happened to Karen? He had to get somebody at the hospital who could pray.

He was trying to sort mixed feelings. One part of him wanted to believe Karen would defy the doctor's prognosis and live. The other part felt like he should have someone there who could pray for her one last time, if necessary.

Whichever way it went, prayer couldn't hurt. He wanted whatever spiritual strength he could muster. He tucked pride in his back pocket and proceeded to dial the pastor's phone number.

"Reverend Lane."

"Yes, Johnny." The pastor was gifted with a sharp ability to recognize voices with ease.

"You asked me to call if Karen's condition changed."

"Yes."

"Well, she's taken a turn for the worse. The doctors don't expect her to live through the night."

"Are you at the hospital?"

"Not yet, but I'm on my way," Johnny confirmed.

"Would you mind if I met you out there?"

"No, I wouldn't mind at all." Johnny was happy the pastor

had offered without having to be asked.

"Is there anything else I can do to help?"

"I was also wondering if there was any possible way that older lady could come with you."

"Which older lady?"

"The one who prayed for Karen at the hospital. I can't remember her name."

"You mean Mother Walker or as we call her, Big Mama?"

"Yes, her." Johnny hadn't appreciated the oil and praying mumbo jumbo she did in the hospital. But there was no doubt she knew God in some fashion. Anyone who could offer a prayer was a welcome sight in ICU room number three.

Johnny carefully made his way to the stairway, trying to avoid turning on the lights. It was late, and he didn't want to wake the kids.

"Dad," sounded Erick's raspy voice as he stood in the doorway. "Are you heading out?"

"Yes, I am, son. I'm going to check on your mom."

Johnny wasn't expecting his children to be up. Erick had no idea how dire his mother's condition was, and Johnny wasn't prepared to share the latest news with him, not yet. If there was any possible hope of Karen getting better, he would cling to it.

"Do you want me to go with you?" Since his dad frequently spent nights at the hospital, this late night run didn't seem abnormal. It was not an indication that anything was wrong.

"No, Erick. If you could, I need you to stay here with the girls."

"You got it." Erick wiped across his tired eyelids, watching his father descend down the stairs and out of sight.

Chapter 33

Johnny arrived at the hospital before anyone else. The intensive care unit was hushed except for the minor movement around the nurses' station. Karen's condition had weakened. Johnny didn't know what to expect. He entered the room gingerly. The room was dark, barring the light above the head of her bed.

Stark sounds of noisy life sustaining machines had taken over. *Tzzzzzt, tzzzzzt* blended with a series of recurring beeps saturated the ICU room.

Recent years had been peppered with many countless ups and downs in the marriage. Yet, Johnny vividly recalled how full of life Karen was. It was excruciating seeing her lifeless body lying with a machine breathing for her. Johnny hadn't foreseen the relationship ending like this. He had contemplated when and how to leave Karen numerous times, wanting to escape the clutches of her dependency. But never had her dying been an option.

Salisbury steak, mashed potatoes, and apple sauce was the lunch Johnny remembered being served the day he met Karen while standing in the high school cafeteria line. He was captivated by her beauty the moment he'd laid eyes on her. Her wit sealed his interest.

With time came changes. Their financial pressures eased. Johnny's career soared and so did the animal magnetism they shared. The couple grew apart with his focus on the business end and hers on the religious side. With both squared off in their corners, finding common ground became difficult over the years.

"Karen--" Johnny gently took her hand. "I don't know if you can hear me. If you can, you have to know that I love you.

I'm so sorry about Isabelle and the other women. I'm through with that. Please believe me. I never meant to hurt you. I just got caught up. Please forgive me. I want us to work things out. I didn't realize how much you mean to me." He forced the words out with his voice cracking at times. "You can't leave me, Karen. I need you. Please help us, God." He laid his head on her leg and allowed his mind to drift away to an easier place.

Johnny was out of his comfort zone. He couldn't order up a team to fix the problem, demand results from an assistant, or simply write a check to cover the damage. The closest he could get to a SWAT team was the group of friends and family that he was able to conjure up for support and prayer. He wiped the tears from his eyes and continued holding his wife's hand. He would have given anything to be able to slip into a restful sleep, far away from this moment. He tried but grief wouldn't let him taste a pinch of peace.

A few minutes later, Tyrone wheeled Connie in.

Johnny was glad to see the couple. All three understood the purpose for being there, and no small talk arose.

Connie immediately rolled over to Johnny and patted his shoulder.

"How are you holding up?"

"I..." he began and went silent. He covered his mouth. Not another thought could find its way out. He broke down and wept openly.

Tyrone was taken aback. He had never seen Johnny so torn apart and vulnerable. It wasn't like him. The Johnny he knew was someone who didn't show signs of weakness, let alone break down emotionally.

Tears swelled in Connie's eyes to see Johnny so broken.

"It's going to be all right, Johnny. We'll be here with you for as long as you need us."

"Thank you," he choked out, "for being here." His lips quivered and Johnny wrung his hands. His wailing moans cast a somber feeling in the room.

Reverend Lane, Big Mama, her friend and several others entered the grief-riddled room. They were the ones who provided emergency prayer for situations such as this.

Big Mama quickly adjusted the tone in the room. "Good morning."

Hellos were quietly returned from the bunch in the group. Johnny felt a bit awkward about the last run-in with her. He avoided direct eye contact.

"Johnny, I want to thank you for letting me come here. It's a blessing to me," Big Mama said.

It was just like her to put folks at ease, even if they had mistreated her in the past. Living without regrets and bottled hostility was her motto.

"No, Ms. Walker, I want to thank you for coming." He gave a deep sigh, which was the residual lump from his earlier crying episode. He felt badly enough for losing control in front of Tyrone and Connie and much worse for doing it in front of strangers.

The church mother grabbed him by the shoulder. "We're family. Please call me Big Mama."

Johnny wasn't able to suppress his feelings. His moans continued. "Please pray for her," he eked out.

"Don't you fret. We'll believe God for Karen's healing."

The encouragement brought Johnny a morsel of hope. He used to say, "I'm not into that touchy feely crap. Leave the religious stuff for the poor slobs who don't have anything else going for them. I prefer to put my faith in my hard work and a few lucky breaks." With Karen nearing the end, Johnny was receptive to prayer, since his professional success, financial stature, and social prestige offered no help.

"I don't know why this happened to Karen. She is such a good person. It's not fair. There's a whole lot of mean people out there who don't have a sick day in their entire lives."

"I can't say why one gets sick and another doesn't. What I

do know is things all things work together for good." Big Mama wanted to give him a ray of hope without giving him a false sense that every question could be answered. "It just doesn't seem right to me. She goes to church. She believes in God, and it hasn't done any good." "Johnny, it might not look like it, but believing in God has done Karen a world of good. I know," Connie added passionately.

He was careful about the words he chose for Connie. He considered her situation to be fragile. He was hurting. But the last thing he wanted was to say something hurtful to Connie and Tyrone.

"I'm sorry, but I just don't see how you can say that. I don't think I could keep up as much hope as you do if I had to go through what you've gone through. I honestly don't know how you do it. It's been hard enough for me with Karen's cancer. How do you do it?"

"I made up my mind a long time ago that I wouldn't go up and down with my emotions. I am at peace with my circumstances." She grabbed Tyrone's hand, knowing that it wasn't quite as settling for him. "Don't be confused. I want to be healed, and I know God is able to heal me. I also know He didn't promise me a hundred years of perfect health. So, if my days on this earth aren't as long as I think it should be, God is still God. I'm at peace with that."

"How can you be at peace? I mean, what if you don't get better?" Johnny implored.

"Whichever way it goes, I'm okay with it."

"You sound like it doesn't matter whether you live or die."

"It does matter, but not in the way you think."

Johnny appeared puzzled to Connie.

"What matters to me is that God's will be done in my life."

"So why would it be God's will for you to die? I thought Big Mama said that everything God did was supposed to be good. I can't understand..."

Connie chuckled. "You know how I get my peace?"

"No," Johnny admitted, but he was curious to know the answer. A bit of peace was exactly what he was hoping to get.

"I choose to feel truly blessed just as I am. The difference with us is that people like you throw away tough days searching for the easy ones. It's like you're digging through a table of clearance clothes, picking out the few good pieces, and throwing most of them away because they're not to your taste. To someone with no clothes, they're all good. So it is with my life. I don't know what tomorrow is bringing. That's why every day I'm alive is a good day, no matter how I feel and no matter what happens in it."

It was impossible for Johnny to debate such a heartfelt expression whether he accepted her religious convictions or not. He did maintain his belief that there was a tinge of denial in Connie.

"I just don't get it, Connie; I'm sorry. How can you feel blessed when you can't even walk on your own?"

"I'm not walking on my own, Johnny, but I'm alive for a reason—for a purpose." She affectionately rubbed Tyrone's hand. "God could have let me die years ago, but He didn't. I'm alive. So every moment I can spend with Tyrone and the people I love is a blessing. It soothes whatever pain I suffer." She cleared her throat. "Some expect to live forever. I just so happen to be one that doesn't."

Connie's passionate words brought tears to Tyrone's eyes. No one readily responded. One of the sickest in the room had brought in the most light.

"Okay, okay with this mushy stuff. Hey, chief, how about a cup of coffee?"

"Nah, I'd better hang around here."

"Johnny, go on and get some coffee. You just told Big Mama how tired you were. Go on. We'll be here with Karen," Connie said.

Reluctantly, Johnny gave in. "I could use a little break."

Big Mama wasted no time humming one of her favorite gospel songs, "God Is," while Connie prayed softly with the other warriors.

The men aimlessly found their way to the hospital cafe.

"How you holding up, partner?"

"I'm hanging in there, man, but to be honest, I don't know how. Honest to goodness, I really don't know how."

"I know it gets rough, but brother, the most you can do is hang in there."

"It's kind of funny. I've spent the last four years figuring out how to get rid of this woman." He grimaced and sighed. "Now the thought of her leaving me is too much."

"Don't even think like that. Have faith, man. You have to go the distance. How you think I feel when I look at Connie's frail body? I want to scream, but what can I do besides love and support her. So that's what I do."

"But it's not at all what I thought it was going to be like."

"What?"

"Me and Karen, with her being sick this way." He shook his head in despair. "I just don't want her to go out like this. I wish there was something else I could do for her." He wiped the tears from his eyes. "I want to save her, man."

Tyrone patted Johnny on his shoulder.

"Don't be so hard on yourself. It's no joke watching somebody you love suffer. The bottom line is that there is only so much you can do. You are only human. You can't be her savior." His gaze dropped thinking about his wife. "If nothing else, Connie has drilled that into my head. Most you can do is believe and pray. That's it. The rest is out of your control."

Tyrone fumbled in his pocket for a cigarette. It was a habit he had begun when Connie got sick several years ago. He never smoked around her, which limited his puffing opportunities. He wanted to quit but found himself clinging to it during stressful times. This was one of those times. "Let's take a walk outside."

Chapter 34

The prayer team had their hands locked in a semicircle near Karen's bed when Johnny and Tyrone entered the room. Big Mama was leading the prayer while others joined.

"Yes, Lord," came from one.

"Have mercy, Father. We ask you to pour out your healing blood," prayed another.

Each person took the lead at some point in the round-robin session.

Not knowing what else to do, Johnny broke the link between Big Mama and her friend to join the circle. Big Mama squeezed his hand in acknowledgment and continued praying. The group wound down to close after an hour h.

Big Mama wrapped her hands around Johnny's and said, "Hold on, son. You can expect challenges. Everyday won't be sunny. But even when it's cloudy, don't lose faith. God will never leave you, nor forsake you—that is, if you let Him." She continually rubbed his hand with gentle compassion. "Hold on to the Lord."

He shook his head. "I don't know how." He bit his lip, and his body trembled from holding back the sorrow bubbling up inside. He couldn't move forward without some peace from God or somebody. Ten years ago, he hadn't cared whether God existed. Through Karen's suffering, it had come to this.

Big Mama discerned that Johnny was ready to accept the Lord as his guide and savior. He needed the deep, penetrating comfort only God could give. She thought about the years Karen had probably prayed for her husband to take this step. Big Mama marveled at how cancer, the thing Karen loathed the most, was the element being used to turn Johnny's heart toward God. The church mother never grew tired of seeing how God would take something bad and turn it for good. Her heart was overjoyed, as it always was when someone wanted to know more about God and His love. She would say, "The angels in heaven are surely singing today, because another one of God's children has found their way home."

The rest of the room was silently praying. This was the moment of truth for Johnny.

"Your first step to knowing God is to repent. Do you know what that is?"

"Kind of."

"It means you have to ask God to forgive your sins. Once you come to the Lord and ask for forgiveness, He doesn't hold the old mess you've done over your head. He lets you start off fresh and clean. Praise be to God."

It was hard for Johnny to believe some of his past could be wiped away so easily. He recalled how difficult it had been for Karen to let go of Isabelle. "How can God forgive me so easily when I don't forgive other people?"

"That's the old Johnny. The new Johnny will learn how to repent for his mistakes. You'll learn to love folks even when they do you wrong. Forgiveness isn't always easy, but if God can forgive us, who are we not to forgive somebody else?"

Many nodded in affirmation.

"If you're ready to invite the Lord into your heart and accept the gift of salvation, we can do it right now."

The urge to say yes loomed mightily as Johnny wrestled with confusion. He didn't know what to believe, except that Karen was in desperate need of a miracle, something he didn't possess the power to grant her. If there was a God with the power to heal, then shouldn't he give Him a try?

"How about it, son? Are you ready to get some peace in your life," Big Mama asked.

Johnny toyed with the notion and finally made a decision. *What the heck?* "Sure, what do I have to do?"

"It's simple. Just repeat after me. Please forgive me for my sins."

Johnny recited the words but wasn't certain if he was sincerely able to make huge changes in his life. But if this would help Karen, he had no choice.

"Yes, I accept Jesus Christ as my personal savior."

"Then if you believe in you heart and confess with your mouth that Jesus is Lord, you are saved."

"I do."

"Then welcome to the Lord's family." She hugged him.

"What else?" he asked, eager to get this done.

"That's it."

"Just repent and ask God into my heart?" Johnny didn't know what to expect. Fire and brimstone, chariots of angels? He did feel some sort of release. He didn't know if it was guilt, stress, or emotional relief. "So I'm different now?" It wasn't logical. There had to be more to his supposed transformation. Couldn't be this easy.

"Yes, but not every change will come overnight. It a slow growth process that comes from prayer, reading the Bible, trusting, believing, and a desire to change your ways. But no matter what you go through from here on, the Lord promises to be with you if you let Him. The Lord is here," she said laying her hand in the center of his chest. "How much you rely on Him is up to you."

Johnny didn't know how to respond. So he didn't.

After a brief moment of praise, daylight slipped into the room as the crowd thinned out.

"I guess we're going to head out. God bless you, brother," Reverend Lane said.

"I'm staying here to fast and pray." Big Mama locked her fingers together. "I aim to stay until I've heard from the Lord, and some answers only come from fasting and praying."

"Well, Mother, I'll pick you up later today."

"Pastor, if it's all the same to you, I'd rather call when I'm ready, because I don't know how long it's going to be. It might be a while."

Johnny couldn't imagine someone committing so much time to help a someone else. He was practically living at the hospital, but it was expected of him. He was the husband.

"You're going to stay here?" he asked.

"Oh, pardon me, Johnny. My apologies for not respecting you and asking you first." She reached for his hand. "Is it okay with you if I stay?"

"Yes, please. It's definitely okay with me. Thank you for being here. I know Karen would want you here."

"I'm going to stay for a while, too," Connie told Tyrone.

"Don't you think that might be too much? You've been up all night. Don't you think staying might tire you out? We have to think about your health too."

"Tyrone, what good is my health if I can't be here when the people in my life need me? You know how I feel about Karen and Johnny. They're more than friends. They're family. They need me, and I'm going to be here. I'm not going home, babe."

Tyrone wasn't pleased with Connie's decision but didn't hesitate to respect it. As much as he wanted to shelter her, Connie was determined to live life to the fullest, unhindered by her condition. It was something he'd accepted early into her diagnosis.

'The boss has spoken," Tyrone joked. 'That's that." He kissed Connie on the forehead and she returned the affection.

"Do you mind if I have a few minutes alone with Karen?" Johnny asked.

No one hesitated to give him the time he requested. They shuffled into the hallway.

The room emptied out. Johnny and Karen remained. He stood above the bed looking down at her. His mind could have gone down any number of disparaging paths, but he chose to stick with his small flicker of hope. He pulled a chair close to the bed with one hand and grabbed Karen's with the other.

"Karen," he whispered into her ear, "I don't know if you can hear me. I don't even know if you want to hear me, but I'm here with you. I'm even thinking about God. Can you believe that? What a surprise, huh?" He squeezed her hand tighter. "I love you, Karen, and I need you. The kids need you. I want you to pull through this. You can do it. I know you can. You have to wake up, because I want another chance to work out this marriage. I love you. God, please let her live. I want to be a better husband. Karen, please forgive me."

Johnny realized there was a long list of items he needed Karen to forgive. He was hoping his failures would be buried in the past and be unable to jeopardize his optimistic outlook.

He continued pouring out his heart to Karen and then rested his head on her leg. After nearly an hour, he stood to his feet and schlepped toward the door. Big Mama, Connie, and Tyrone were the remaining warriors left standing in the hallway. Each saw Johnny open the door, but no one rushed in. They wanted to move at his pace.

"You okay, chief?"

"Yes, I am. I feel like it's going to be all right now."

Big Mama nodded her head. "It sure is."

"You can come back if you want."

"I'm going to head home, if you don't mind," Tyrone said. "I want to grab a few hours of sleep and then go to work."

"Hey, no, that's fine, man."

"If you need anything, I mean anything, give me a call or tell Connie. She knows how to get in touch with me at all times."

"I appreciate you. I couldn't handle this without you," Johnny uttered.

"You're family."

The two men clasped hands and each pulled the other into his bosom for their secret fraternity handshake, patting each other on the back with their other hand.

Big Mama resumed prayer.

Before Connie wheeled in, Tyrone kissed her. "Connie, honey, promise me you won't overdo it."

"I promise." She hugged him, and he left. As she watched him walk away, Connie thanked God for giving her such a fulfilling life with the man of her dreams. She turned the chair around and faced the door. With each turn of the wheel, she reflected on both her journey and blessings.

Chapter 35

Johnny had faithfully sat by Karen's bedside through the past two nights as each lingered into the next morning. Just before daybreak on Saturday, the walls began closing in on him. He had stepped out briefly for a walk and fresh air.

Rays of light shining through the window punctured the darkness. Big Mama was sitting in the corner chair reading Psalms 91 from her Bible while Connie prayed silently.

By the grace of God, Karen was hanging on.

A nurse entered the room, conscious not to distract those present. She took Karen's pulse, then placed the thermometer censor on her limp finger.

"How's she doing?" Connie asked.

"Amazingly, her vitals are much stronger. Her fever has dropped from a hundred and five to a hundred. Her pulse is up to seventy-three beats a minute, and blood pressure is stable."

"Praise the Lord." Connie quickly shouted.

"The two of you have been here most of the night, right?"

"Yes, we've been here praying since late Thursday, or I guess you could say really early Friday morning."

"Boy, that is some sacrifice to stay here so long. How wonderful of you. Mrs. Clark is very fortunate to have such a supportive circle of friends and family." She pushed a few buttons on the IV machine.

"We're glad to be here. Long as God gives us the strength we're staying here and praying for our sister." Big Mama planned to be around until.

"Well, whatever it is you're doing, keep it up." The nurse completed her examination and left the room.

Several minutes later, Tina stormed into the room.

"What is going on here?" Her voice was condescending and sharp but not loud.

"Shhhhhh," Connie insisted.

"What is going on?" Tina demanded.

Connie took the lock off her wheelchair and turned it around to face the door. She beckoned for Tina to follow her into the hallway.

"What is wrong with you bursting into this room?"

"When I called the hospital earlier, they wouldn't tell me anything about Karen's condition except that her family members had gathered here. Everyone, that is, except me." Tina balled her fists tightly and gritted her teeth. " What is going on?"

"Karen took a turn for the worse."

Tina had to steady herself after hearing the news. "Why wasn't I told to get out here?"

Each time Connie attempted to reply, Tina flung another question at her.

"When did you get here?"

Connie finally got a chance to squeeze in a reply. "Since Johnny called me early yesterday morning."

"Are you kidding me?" Tina shouted.

"Johnny, humph, of course I'm not surprised he left me out. But Connie, what about you? Why didn't you call me? Had I known what was going on, I'd have been here."

"Tina, I couldn't call you to come out here."

"Why not? She's my friend too, you know."

"You're right. But truthfully, this isn't about our feelings. Right now, Johnny and their children need our support. The doctors were expecting Karen to die. There's no way he could have you here. He had plenty of worries on his mind as it was without drama with you. Remember what happened the last time that the two of you were in the room together. He didn't need that this weekend; no one did."

Tina had to concede that what Connie was saying made

sense, although it didn't bring much ease to her unrest.

"Still, you could have called me just to let me know."

"You're right. I apologize for not thinking to call you. All I've had on my mind is Karen."

Tina calmed, softened the bass in her tone, and relaxed her confrontational stance.

"I understand. It's okay. How's she doing, anyway?"

"She's showing signs of progress, thank the Lord."

"How long do you plan to be here?"

"Mother Walker plans to fast and pray for as long as she needs to. I can't fast right now, but I plan to pray with her for as long as I'm able."

"Well, I can't stay the whole day with you, but I can be here a few hours." Connie didn't feel right with Tina at the hospital. She was expecting Johnny to return at any minute from his run home. The last thing he needed was to have Tina hanging around.

"Tina, I don't feel that it would be good for you to stay here. Johnny will be back here any minute."

"I came way out here to be with Karen. Why do I have to leave?"

"Because this is about Karen. Everybody else, including the two of us, has to take a backseat. That man needs to be able to spend this time with his wife in peace. Even if you don't think much of Johnny, you owe at least that much respect to Karen. Don't you agree?"

Whether or not she liked it, Tina wanted to honor her friendship with Karen. She'd back off and show Johnny some respect. She felt awful about not being able to stay with the group. Her sharp tongue had given her power in the past. At this moment, what she got was overwhelming alienation.

"I hope nothing happens to her. I would feel so terrible for not being here." She hung her head. "Will you call me if her condition changes, good or bad?"

Connie took Tina's hand and gave a half grin.

"I promise to call you."

Tina slung her trench coat over her arm and walked toward the bank of elevators. It took everything in her not to cry.

*   *   *

Johnny returned shortly to find Big Mama and Connie sitting at Karen's side.

"Any change?"

"Her temperature is down to a hundred, and the other vital signs are good."

"Great," he echoed. "By the way, I think I saw Tina pulling out the parking lot."

"You probably did. She just left."

"She was here? I thought that was her."

"Don't worry, Johnny; she thought it best not to stay around. You know how the two of you can get at times. You don't need that, and she knew it."

"Tina definitely has some issues. I can't deny that. But I know she cares about Karen. She could have stayed."

Connie's eyebrow arched.

"Trust me, I don't have enough energy to go toe-to-toe with Tina. If you talk with her again, let her know it's no problem."

"Are you sure?"

He nodded in affirmation. "Somebody has to take the first step. Might as well be me."

"That's shocking."

"It's no secret. We don't get along, and that's the way it's been. That's not the way it has to be."

"Good for you. I'm glad to hear it. I know Karen will be happy too. You're a good guy. I'll let Tina know. I'm sure she'll want to come back out here."

Big Mama continued reading Psalm 91, while listening. She was pleased to know Johnny was taking his repentance seriously and willing to seek forgiveness from those he'd wronged. It was a huge step toward spiritual development, and it appeared he was on track.

The morning hours ticked by. The nurse checked Karen's vitals every couple of hours. She continued showing progress, pieces at a time.

Johnny was watching the TV and holding Karen's hand when he felt a tightening. He didn't pay any attention. When the tightening turned into a mild squeeze, his heart jumped.

"Karen, Karen," he whispered, "can you hear me?"

Her hand squeezed his. Johnny sat up with zeal and concentration. He also had the undivided attention of Big Mama and Connie.

"Is she waking up?" Connie asked Johnny.

"I don't know. I think so. It feels like she's squeezing my hand."

Connie rolled close to the bed and grabbed Karen's other hand. Big Mama turned up the heat on her prayer. The room was instantly converted to a cheering forum.

"Karen, come on, baby, wake up," Johnny said. One eye flickered and peeped open. "Come on. You can do it."

She forced her eyelids open with the morsel of energy residing in her body. The light kept them partially closed, but they were wide enough for her to see Johnny and for him to see her.

"You're awake. Thank God." Johnny wept openly. "It's good to see you."

Connie gave a sigh of relief and wiped her eyes. Big Mama praised the Lord.

Karen couldn't talk with the tube in her mouth. Her gaze roamed frantically. The long sleep left her disoriented.

Johnny rang the nurse's button to inform the staff.

In a matter of minutes, several people rushed in from the

nurses' station. They'd prepared for Karen to pass away and were poised to make the appropriate code blue emergency call.

When the nurses entered, they stood in astonishment. Fully prepped to revive Karen's stopped heart, they were quite surprised.

"She's awake!"

"Yes, she is," Johnny acknowledged with pride.

The nurses checked her vital signs and did a quick exam.

"Boy, this is a miracle. There is no other way to describe this. I'd better get Dr. Costas on the phone."

Karen was pointing to the tube.

"You want that out, don't you?" the nurse asked Karen.

Karen nodded yes.

"Let me call Dr. Costas to see what she wants to do."

Joy and happiness consumed every nook and cranny of the room. Johnny couldn't express enough how grateful he was to Connie and Big Mama. Several hours after she woke up and began regaining her orientation, Connie and Big Mama left in order to give Johnny and Karen time alone. Their work was done for now, although neither intended to cease praying for the couple.

Johnny stayed put. He watched an entourage of staff parading in and out of the room throughout the afternoon.

"Well, Mrs. Clark, we haven't gotten approval to remove the tube yet. But we do need to draw some blood and take another look at you."

Johnny stepped into the hallway while the medical team worked with Karen. He was eager to share the good news with their kids. He pulled out his cell phone and anxiously dialed.

"Erick, I have good news. Your mom has made a turn for the better."

"She has! Oh, wow," he sang out with glee.

"She woke up. She's alert and the doctors say she's doing good," Johnny said.

"That's great."

"Yes, thank God."

"Can I talk to her?"

"Not yet. The breathing tube isn't out. She might not be able to talk for a day or two. But she's doing much better."

"Do you want us to come to the hospital?"

"Well, I'm certain she's anxious to see you kids, but why don't you wait? The doctor said she'll be tired for a while. I think we should give her a day."

"Okay, Dad. Do you want to tell the girls about Mom?"

"You can go ahead and tell them, son."

"They're going to ask when can they see her. What should I tell them?"

"Tell them they can come out tomorrow. I want to get back into the room with your mom. I'll see you when I get in. It might be a little late, so grab some money from the desk drawer and you guys get something to eat."

"Will do, Dad. See you later."

Johnny was preparing to disconnect the call when he remembered something else.

"Erick." He yelled, wanting to catch him.

"Yeah, I'm here."

"Don't let Elizabeth eat too many sweets. She gets a little hyper in the evenings, and I want her to sleep tonight."

"Sure thing, Dad. I gotcha covered."

Johnny broached Karen's room relieved. Perhaps his dire straits were turning around.

Chapter 36

Karen was sleeping soundly. Johnny decided to go home and get some rest. Being awake most of the past few days left his body drained.

He crept along the driveway, allowing the garage door to open fully. One of the other two cars was missing. Johnny figured the kids were out. He slowly made his way from the car to the back stairs, bypassing any stops along the way. Once he sat down, he knew his body wouldn't have enough strength to get back up. He carefully climbed the stairs, feeling every aching muscle.

Johnny walked into the bedroom. He immediately peeled off his shirt and tossed it onto the couch with the other heap of unhung clothes. The room was in chaos. It needed to be cleaned, but such tasks had been low on his priority list for months. His strategy was to just get by.

He considered getting into the whirlpool before going to sleep. He took his socks off and rubbed his feet. A short shower would have to do. Afterwards, he expressed a sigh of relief with a renewed zeal. He hadn't eaten and contemplated grabbing a snack from downstairs.

There was a knock on his bedroom door.

"Come in."

Erick eased the door open with the girls standing behind him. "Are you decent?"

"Yeah, come on in."

Elizabeth was glad to see her father. She had clung to the rest of her family during her mother's absence and, in doing so, strengthened their bonds.

"Daddy," Chelle cut into the conversation, "I'm so glad to hear about Mom. Erick told us she's awake and wants to see us tomorrow."

"Sure does. I know she'll feel even better once she sees you."

"I'll be glad when tomorrow gets here," Elizabeth added.

"In the meantime, young lady, you need to finish your chores and get ready for bed." He kissed her on the forehead.

Johnny had made noticeable strides with Elizabeth. He had worked on expressing more affection with his children since the counselor pointed out the need. It wasn't a gesture that naturally flowed for him. It required conscious effort on his part.

"Don't forget our upcoming meeting with your counselor, and you need to be rested. Erick, can you hang back for a minute? I want to talk with you about something."

"No problem, Dad."

Even though Johnny had shielded them from the severity of Karen's illness, what they did know had been a doozy. The girls left the room skipping, and he couldn't be more content.

After Big Mama led him to the Lord, he'd began self-evaluating more and more. Life was too short, he gleaned. Johnny uncovered areas he didn't like and felt an inkling to tear down walls and defenses he'd crafted in his life. It might take some time, but he had to make it right, It was a promise to himself. The initial step was making amends with his son.

"Son, I appreciate your coming home and helping us out." Johnny slid his hands into his pockets. It was hard for him to humbly lay it out. He had the desire to freely open up, but a significant part of the old prideful, domineering Johnny lingered. It would take commitment, work, and time before he could make the changes he desired.

"It's cool, Dad. Really, I wanted to come home." Being his father's son, Erick slid his hands into his pockets too. He shrugged his shoulders, not sure how to react. Hearing his father express gratitude was not a scenario with which he was familiar. "I had to come home."

"And I needed you." Johnny removed his hands from his pockets and extended them toward his son.

Erick saw the tears rolling down his father's cheeks. The unfamiliar sight touched him. He hugged his dad. Adult or not, he longed for a hug from his father. He admired his dad's strength as much as he despised his dad's overbearing ways.

"You helped me get through a rough spot. I couldn't have done it without you." He pushed Erick out to arm's length so he could talk with direct contact. "I apologize to you for the things I said over the phone." Johnny held his head back to temper the flow of tears.

Erick shook his head out of awkwardness. This long-awaited moment with his dad found him unprepared.

"It's cool, Dad."

"No, it's not. Son, I haven't always done right by you and your mother."

Erick continued to shake his head, not knowing how to receive this emotional outpouring.

"I've made mistakes. I hope you believe me when I tell you that I never meant to hurt you or your mother. I love you all, and I want the chance to prove it to you."

"It's cool, honestly. I know you love me." Erick looked away. "And I want to apologize to you for what I said."

"Nah," Johnny said flicking his hand in the air. "You don't owe me an apology. I am so proud of you for sticking up for your mom and for your sisters. You are a man, and I respect you. I can't be prouder."

Erick wanted to break down. Finally, his dad saw him as a capable man and not a juvenile boy. "That means a lot to me coming from you." More than his father would ever realize.

"What about school?"

"I don't know yet. I can probably get an extension on a couple of classes. Either way, I'll probably take calculus over."

"Can you make up any classes in summer school?"

"I'll just have to see. Right now I'm going to hang around

here. I know you need me to be here, and I'll stay out of school as long as I have to. This is more important than any school."

"But I don't want you burdened with taking care of us. You've already done too much. It's time for you to go back to school. That's what your mom and I want for you. Your future is important to us." Johnny gave Erick a firm pat on the back. "You've done your part here. It's time for you to go back to school."

"I'll think about it," Erick replied.

"That's a start." Johnny draped his arm over his son's shoulder. "Let's grab a bite to eat."

Chapter 37

Nearly four days had passed since Johnny got the news of Karen's impending demise. By some miracle she had escaped her brush with death. He glided into her room as if on the wings of an eagle. She had moved from ICU and back into a normal room for the first time in weeks. She was sitting up in the bed with three pillows propped behind her head when he walked in. He was elated about her remarkable strides toward a full recovery.

"How are you feeling?"

"Tired." She scrunched her face and swallowed slowly. Her throat remained sore from having the breathing tube inserted for the past week. She constantly swallowed small sips of water. She saw the bright bouquet of flowers in his hand. Her eyelids widened and her eyebrows arched.

Flowers in hand, he wrapped his arms around her like an extra-large shirt on a small body, careful not to grip too tightly. He didn't want to cause any pain to her rejuvenating limbs.

Karen was limp in his arms. She was slow warming up to his newfound affection.

Johnny sensed her reluctance and pulled back. He set the flowers on her meal tray.

Lilacs and gardenias drew her close. She breathed in the sweet fragrance and soaked in the nectar for a few moments.

Johnny took a seat near her bed.

"Where are the kids?" she asked in a muffled voice.

"I had errands to run Erick's bringing them after school."

"You look tired."

He stretched his arms into the air. "I don't know why. I slept like a baby last night, for the first time in a while." He extended his long legs. "When I woke up, it was almost noon."

"Noon?"

A late start was odd for Johnny. Up and out of the house before six was his routine. It ensured his ability to get to the office well before the primary production line started up at seven.

Karen saw her husband sitting in the chair and wondered who was this strange man. She'd left a controlling husband and a load of emotional baggage at home. Idiosyncrasies and all, she knew the old Johnny. She didn't know if it was worth getting to know a different one. Her doctor's entrance interrupted Karen's assessment of the man in the chair.

Dr. Costas was elated to see the turnaround in Karen's condition. She couldn't explain how Karen had emerged from the coma. It didn't stop the doctor from taking pride in acknowledging her patient's miraculous recovery.

Karen's speech was strained. "Better."

Dr. Costas patted her legs, which had become her consistent comforting gesture. She flipped through the chart, pleased to see the vital signs in normal ranges. She placed her thumb on Karen's pulse and heartbeat to verify for herself.

"Nice strong pulse and strong heartbeat. Any aches?"

Karen sipped her water and shook her head no.

"Any discomforts?"

"My throat."

"That will go away in a few days." Dr. Costas crammed the stethoscope into her oversize pocket. "How's your appetite?"

"Umm," Karen muttered, and rocked her hand back and forth, implying it was so-so.

"That's what I expect. You've been on liquids for months with a nasty tube down your throat for a week. It's going to take time for you to handle a normal diet with solid food. In the meantime, we will keep you on the liquids."

"For how long?" Karen whispered.

"You're tired of the needles, I bet."

Karen nodded.

"Understood." Dr. Costas sighed. "To be quite honest, I'm not sure. We need to leave it in until you regain some strength and an appetite."

Karen frowned, and Dr. Costas detected the discontent.

"We are treading in unfamiliar territory here. I can't medically explain why your health deteriorated so rapidly landing you in a comatose state. I have even less scientific rationale as to why you came out of the coma."

"This was a miracle, right?" Karen uttered.

Dr. Costas folded one arm and sluggishly rubbed her forehead with the other. She'd built her profession on making statistically and medically sound diagnoses. To admit her patient's recovery was outside the bounds had Dr. Costas in unchartered territory. Yet she had to acknowledge something other than the medicine and her expertise had revived Karen. She threw her hands up and pinched her lips.

"I can't say it was a miracle, but I will say your will to live, or her faith as you call it, was a major factor."

Johnny didn't expect the doctor to admit Karen's recovery was more a result of prayer than medical treatment. What she had said was plenty. He snickered having been doubtful too, before desperation drove him to consider the possibility.

"Dr. Costas, when can I take her home?"

"Depends on how quickly she regains her strength. We'll work on the appetite for starters. If she gets enough strength to go to the bathroom on her own, then I'll have the catheter removed. I suspect if all goes well, it could be a week or so."

It wasn't as soon as Johnny would have liked. At least it was a goal to shoot for, which was more than he'd had in weeks.

"I hate to say this, but the coma was secondary. We have to deal with the primary issue."

"Which is?" Johnny wondered, sitting tall.

"The cancer. After Karen gets settled at home, we'll need

to follow up with more tests. I'm hoping we got it all with this last round of treatment. Once I get the pathology report, I'll know whether or not we'll have to do chemo."

"Are you saying I could still be sick?" Fear washed over Karen.

Dr. Costas didn't want to be the grim reaper in any way. "I'm saying we aren't out the woods yet. We need to monitor the situation and be prepared for anything. I don't want to alarm you, but I also don't want you to become too relaxed with your health and diet. We have to take this one day at a time and go from there. All right?" her elevated voice rang out.

Johnny grabbed Karen's hand.

"Don't worry; we'll be fine. It will work out. I know it will," Jonny said.

"That's good," Dr. Costas interjected. "We can use as much positive energy as possible. Anything that can help us get you to where you need to be, I want to consider. Do you have any other questions for me?"

Johnny peered at Karen, who was shaking her head no.

"I don't think so, Dr. Costas. Not right now."

"Well, I'll be here if you do. Take care of yourself, Karen. I'll see you on my rounds tomorrow. "

"Thanks for everything, Dr. Costas," Johnny told her.

Dr. Costas waved on her way out.

Johnny wasn't sure how Karen was really feeling about the not so good news. He wanted to find a way to encourage her in spite of it. He sat on the side of the bed so that she wouldn't have to strain her voice.

"Karen, I don't want you to worry about what the doctor said. She's only doing her job, but she doesn't have the final say. Just like you came through the coma, even when the doctors didn't believe you would, you can get past the cancer."

"Johnny, I heard you praying for me when I was in the coma."

"You did. What else did you hear?" Johnny wondered, not sure if the revelation was a good or bad thing.

"Nothing else, I don't think. I can't remember anything else."

"Did you hear Big Mama or Connie? They stayed in this room and prayed for you from Thursday night into Saturday morning," Johnny told her.

"Connie too?"

"Can you believe it? She refused to leave until you showed improvement. Tyrone couldn't talk her into going home."

"I guess I'm not really surprised. That's how she is. She's just a real friend."

"I don't know how she did it. You can see how weak she is," Johnny interjected.

Karen sipped from the cup of water and shook her head.

"Connie and Tyrone have been good to us. We owe them a lot." Johnny reflected on the amount of support the couple had given him. He couldn't have survived without them.

"Ms. Emma too. I have to thank her," Karen noted.

"Don't worry about it. I'll thank her at church on Sunday."

"Church? You! Sunday?" Karen was shocked to hear Johnny talk about church—and it wasn't a holiday.

"Yes, me. I'm planning on going to church. I can do that, can't I?" he teased.

"Of course you can. It's just that...well, you know, church and religion haven't been your thing."

"You're right, but my back was against the wall. I had nowhere to go except to the people from the church. I'm not ready to preach or anything," he joked, "but I'm ready to see what God is about. Big Mama helped me with some of that."

"It's hard to be in her presence and not be interested in the Lord. And she was here the whole time?"

"Most certainly was. The pastor and some of the other church members came out Thursday night. There was some serious praying going on in this room. And you didn't hear any of that praying or anything?"

"Nope. All I remember is hearing you." She took a tiny sip of water and let it slide down her throat.

"I had no idea you could hear me."

"Johnny, you helped me pull through. When I heard you crying and asking the Lord to let me live, it made me want to live. I figured if you could trust God for my healing, then I could too." She sipped the water. "I could easily have let go, but I didn't because I heard your voice. I heard you say you love me, that I mattered to you." Her eyelids watered a little. "Do you know how long I've wanted to hear that?"

Johnny took his wife into his arms and held on, wanting to protect her from now on. It felt good to be connected and not arguing.

The children entered the room before she could respond. Karen figured what she had to say could wait until later.

Their two girls greeted her instantly. Elizabeth wasted no time in executing her normal routine. She hurried to Karen's bedside and gave her mom a hug.

Karen swallowed hard and opened her arms wide for her babies.

"Hey, Mom." Erick was able to squeeze into the pileup his sisters had formed around their mom long enough to give her a peck on the forehead. He plopped down on the chair next to his dad with a short greeting and gently removed the designer shades from his face.

Johnny scanned the room. He was content with his entire family in one place, well and happy. None of his professional, financial, or social accomplishments could bring him more fulfillment than this priceless moment. This was what living well meant.

"Mom and Dad, I've decided to head back to California for the summer quarter?"

Chewing on a piece of ice, she shook her head to indicate no.

"Yep, I'm going to make up a few classes and maybe even take an extra one."

"It's a great idea," Johnny stated. "You've been a huge help to me, to us," he said spreading his hands out. "Time for you to get on with your life and let me handle these ladies. It's time, son."

Chapter 38

Johnny attempted reaching Isabelle Jones two months ago. He'd left no more than a grunt and a hello on the message service. It was enough for her to recognize his voice. They hadn't spoken in years, but she'd contemplated calling him back for weeks. It was a door she was reluctant to open, but Johnny's magnetism had potency. She didn't know what to expect. What would they talk about?

Curiosity got the best of her. She dialed the number from her caller ID. She aborted the call, only to revisit the notion several seconds later. Eventually, anticipation won. *Why not. Wouldn't hurt to say hi.*

* * *

Johnny had been out of the office for over a week. When he walked into the office Tuesday, Sonja was thrilled to see him. She jumped up and shook his hand.

"Mr. Clark, I am so glad your wife is getting better. That must be a tremendous relief. I've been praying for her and for your entire family."

"I appreciate your prayers, Sonja. Prayer is what got us through."

"Oh, I almost forgot." Sonja went around to the other side of her desk and pulled a three-foot card from underneath it. "This is from the team."

Johnny opened the card with names and well wishes crammed in each space. He was visibly touched and dared not verbalize his gratitude.

Sonja read his expression on face and grabbed his hand.

Johnny went into his office, sat down in the big-backed leather chair, soaking up the moment. He gradually worked through the stack of presorted mail on his desk. It would take some time to bounce back to a normal routine. His world had been turned upside down. That didn't stop any action around Tenner Automotive. Johnny was treated like a valued asset to the company and had shown his gratitude by devoting countless hours and untiring efforts toward his job. He turned back and forth in the seat twirling a pen. During his absence, the place hadn't missed a beat.

"Sonja, what key items need my immediate attention?" he inquired through the intercom.

"The production manager in Tennessee has to speak with you as soon as you get a chance."

"Well, let's start there. Can you get me the last production report and then get him on the line please? I also need you to set up a meeting with my entire management staff."

"Some are in Tennessee this week."

"Get them on a conference call."

"Will do, sir. I'll get right on it."

Johnny was back in the saddle, but somehow it seemed different. Work was his comfort zone, and even that was going to take some adjustment. It wasn't so exciting to be back in control and running the show. The rest away from the office had done him good.

Sonja knocked on Johnny's door.

"Come in."

She opened the door and took a few steps into the room. "Mr. Clark, I checked everyone's schedule, and the only time that works for everyone is five-thirty this afternoon. So I'll go ahead and get that confirmed?"

"Um..." Johnny responded while flipping through his day planner. "Wait. That's going to be too late in the day." He knew it would conflict with the time he had scheduled to meet with Elizabeth's counselor. Erick hadn't left. Their mom was showing tremendous progress, but Johnny knew the girls needed his assurance and support. He fully intended to do his part.

"Too late?" Sonja responded.

Johnny was a driven boss. There were times when he had conducted meetings after nine P.M. He did whatever it took to get the job done, and expected everyone in his group to have the same dedication.

"Yes, that's too late. Shoot for this afternoon. Otherwise it will have to wait until tomorrow."

"I'll see what I can do, Mr. Clark."

Johnny continued with the stack Sonja had placed on his desk. From the corner of his view, he saw his phone light up without ringing. Then it dawned on him. He'd forwarded his calls to Sonja.

"Mr. Clark's office," Sonja said. There was silence on the line. "Hello, Mr. Clark's office. Can I help you?" Sonja raised her voice the second time in case there was a poor connection and the person had difficulty hearing her.

"Yes, uh, hi," the soft voice said. "Is Mr. Clark in?"

"Let me check. Please, ma'am, who might I say is calling?"

"Um, tell him it's a friend."

"Can I give him a name, please, ma'am?"

"That's okay. Thank you. Bye."

Sonja found the woman's timidity odd. She didn't bother relaying the partial message to Johnny. There was plenty of real work to worry about with him back in the office.

Her intercom beeped and Johnny's voice came across.

"Sonja, I forgot that my phone is forwarded to yours."

"You're right, Mr. Clark. You just missed a call."

"Anything important?"

"No, I don't think so. They didn't leave a message."

"Good. I have plenty of calls to return as it is, without adding new ones. If you don't mind, Sonja, I'm going to leave the forwarding on while I catchup. Otherwise, it might get too hectic for me."

"No problem, Mr. Clark. I will take care of it."

"Oh, Sonja, any calls from the hospital or from my family, I want them put through immediately, please."

"Absolutely, Mr. Clark."

Johnny's stack of backlogged tasks wasn't shrinking. He was keen not to overload himself. The most important tasks would get done. The rest would be shoved to the back burner. Killing himself to get the job done wasn't as alluring as it once was. Karen's brush with death forced him to redefine his priorities. Maybe not completely, but for sure he was seeing his circumstance more realistically than before.

Chapter 39

Bedcovers were snuggled tightly around Karen's body, as she slept in her bed at home.

Johnny nestled next to his wife. He propped himself up resting on his fist and stared at Karen as she slept, admiring her beauty. A few stubbles managed to grow back on her head after the radiation therapy. *What a difference a day made*, he thought.

It had been less than three months ago when he couldn't appreciate much beauty in the marriage, let alone in Karen. Every time Johnny thought about the recent chain of events he became nostalgic. Cancer, the very element which broaden the wedge between them, was the same tool that drew them back to the marriage.

Karen began stirring. Her sight slowly came into focus. She positioned her hands over them like a visor. The light coming through the blinds was modest, but was too much for her. She peered around the room in a daze, not able to get her bearings. The slight confusion was short-lived once her eyes focused on Johnny.

"Good morning," he greeted. "Did you sleep well?"

"I think so. What time is it?"

Clocks were conveniently located on both sides of the bed, but he chose to lean over and read the one on her side.

"A few minutes after six."

"Umm." She stretched and moaned. "I've been sleeping for that long?"

Last night had been once in several years when the family had collectively sat down at the table to for dinner together. They laughed, talked, and shed a few tears. Karen tired out around eight o'clock and went to bed. She'd been asleep ever since.

"It's going to take some time to get your strength back." He gently glided his hand along her arm. "Don't rush yourself. There's no hurry."

Karen didn't jerk her arm away from Johnny's touch, but she did tense up. The simple gesture told Johnny she didn't want him too close, not yet.

"Does that bother you, my touching you?"

Karen didn't want to start an argument so soon out the hospital. Johnny had been right. She didn't have energy. She searched for sugarcoated words which would get him to back off without opening the old floodgates of bickering.

Johnny detected her reluctance to be truthful and set the tone whereby she could open up. He didn't want to squander an opportunity to fix their relationship and communication.

"It's okay to tell me how you feel. I'm sure you're thinking about how I normally act. I promise not to fly off the handle."

Karen's lips didn't move, but her scowl spoke volumes.

"Really, Karen. I mean it. I love you, and I want to make this work. We can do this, if it's what you want. You have to want it too, Karen; I can't do it by myself."

She nodded with a half grin. "I don't know what I want."

"Let's start over?"

"I don't think it's that easy. There's a lot of water under the bridge." Karen sat up with Johnny's assistance. "Being in the hospital made me think about my life, my marriage, our kids, and you. I realized how much time has been wasted pretending we have it together; that I have it together. I'm wasting time. I'm not going back to what we had."

Johnny hung his head, dreading what might come from Karen's mouth next.

"I've apologized to you for my past mistakes, and I am truly sorry about things that happened. But there's nothing I can do about the past other than learn from it and not make the same mistakes."

"I know you've apologized, and I accept it. But there is so much more to this. Forgiving is easy to do when you love somebody, but putting everything behind us will take some time. You broke my trust, Johnny. The women, the lies—it all hurts. Even when you knew how much damage Isabelle had done, it didn't seem like you cared."

"What can I say, Karen? I'm sorry about the women. And I do care. I realize it's no excuse, but I don't know what to do half the time. We keep doing the same thing over and over. I always reach out to you after you get sick. You're fine with me for the first couple of months. Right after the honeymoon period is over, you stop wanting me sexually. But you don't want a divorce. That doesn't work for me any more. We have to decide if we're staying together or not. I want to be with you, but I need you to want me too."

"I'm not saying it's totally your fault, but there's a lot to get over."

"I don't expect you to forget everything that's happened. Shoot, I can't even forget, as much as I'd like to. No matter how I might want to, Karen, I can't promise we won't have challenges in the future. That's part of living. What I can promise you is that I will be one hundred percent committed to this marriage and I will do whatever I have to for it to work. That's my commitment to you. What I'm asking is for us both let go of the past, so we can build a future." He put his hand on top of hers and looked directly into her gaze. "What I am saying to you, Karen, is that you either have to forgive me or let me go."

Karen couldn't discount his tone of sincerity. The biggest part of her wanted the relationship to work. She was just more apprehensive than Johnny was to jump back into the marriage with both feet. One thing she did know was that he was right about letting go of the past. If she couldn't remember anything else from her lengthy conversations with Ms. Emma, forgiveness stood out. She couldn't recall exactly how many times Ms. Emma had quoted Psalm 103, but parts of the chapter were embedded in her mind. She thought about the parts where it said that God's mercy and love enabled him to forgive sins, to not stay angry forever, and to not punish people to the extent that their shortcomings deserved. For Karen, Ms. Emma had been clear that forgiving also meant forgetting and letting go.

"I'm not eager to walk out on nineteen years of marriage either. Believe it or not, I do love you. Just give me some time to figure out what I want. Can you do that?"

"That's good enough for me." He gave her a loose hug, afraid to squeeze too tightly. "I want this to work for us, and I believe it can. If God can help you with everything that was going on in the hospital, then I know there's hope for this marriage. I honestly believe we can do this." He kissed her cheek and slid back to his side of the bed.

The mere concept of God crossing Johnny's lips was a miracle to Karen. Here was a man who had lived on his own terms, accountable to no one, not even God. It encouraged Karen's heart to know Johnny was making some effort. It had been a major area of contention in the past. It was the one thing she'd held over him. Reflecting on their marriage, Karen had to admit, she had played an active role in their struggles.

"Johnny," she said humbly, "I can't blame you for every bad thing that has happened to us, just like I can't take full credit for the good times. We have both done our fair share of damage. What you did seems more wrong." Karen buried her face in her hand and sighed. Blaming Johnny had been easier than accepting her own faults. Perhaps it was time to come clean. "Truth is, I know it has taken both of us to tear down this marriage. I used religion to make you feel less than a man. I've judged you and used religion to justify it. That was wrong, and I am sorry. I didn't mean to do it. After a while, it made me feel good to have something you didn't. I am truly sorry."

Johnny hung his head again. "And I used my career to make you feel like you weren't contributing. Neither one was right." He gulped.

"That's not all," she interrupted. "I kept throwing Isabelle in your face. I wanted to remind you over and over about your mistake. I wanted you to feel badly and to hurt like me. I wanted to punish you by not having sex with you; at least that's how it started. Then I ended up losing interest for real."

Karen leaned toward Johnny. The two embraced, with both giving emotional sniffles.

"I agree. It's been rough. I get it, but I'm here," he said jabbing his index finger downward. "We're legally married."

Karen wiped her eyes with a tissue that Johnny handed her. She was apprehensive about Johnny's abrupt change in attitude and with the marriage. It was too good to be true. Had God finally answered her prayers? To see the compassion and concern in her husband after years of distance was overwhelming. Karen wanted to soak in Johnny's interest, but her wounded trust in him didn't allow her to be completely vulnerable. Words and empty promises masked in lies would no longer sway her emotions.

"Where do we go from here?" he asked.

Karen shrugged her shoulders. "I'm not sure, maybe we can get some counseling?"

Johnny cut her off. "Hey, whoa, hang on. Counseling?"

"Yes, counseling," she replied with a spirit of boldness. "What, you don't want to go?"

He swung his body around, folded one knee on the bed, and let the other hang over the side. He held her hand.

"I'm willing to go," he said.

Her eyebrows rose. Johnny had consistently opposed counseling and letting someone know his personal business. He never had a problem with her going alone, if it was going to help her. He hadn't seen the need for himself.

"You can believe me when I tell you I will do whatever I

have to do to make this work. I mean it. I've had plenty of time to think about changes."

Karen reluctantly basked in the moment not sure how excited to get. "Johnny, it's seven-thirty. You're late for work."

He didn't leap to his feet or show any anxiety.

"I'm not late. I don't have any meetings this morning. Besides, I am right where I need to be." He grunted. "I'm not going to let my job kill me. Tenner Automotive will click on whether I'm there or not. There's more to life than work and money."

Karen squinted and giggled. "Johnny Clark, what is going on with you? Are you for real? This seems like a big change in a short time," Karen said briefly stroking his hand.

"You know I'm not into the religious mumbo jumbo, but I'm not lying. I'm motivated. As a matter of fact, I've never felt better in my life."

Taking a risk, Karen decided to open up a little. "You're not the only one who has to make changes. I had to look at my life too. I thought it would be better to quit everything, life, you, the kids, the cancer, my faith, everything. Now I realize quitting wasn't really what I wanted. I'm tired of pretending and worrying, but I definitely want to live."

"I want you to live too, that I'm sure of." Johnny rubbed her hands. "It won't be easy, but we can make this marriage work."

She squeezed his hand in return as he continued. "With counseling, time, and faith in the Lord, I think so too."

Chapter 40

Tyrone was the chef behind the grill. Steaks, chicken, burgers, salmon, and ribs lined the double-decker racks. The aroma from the barbecued meats wrapped around the house in a cloud of smoke. It was like an invisible arrow, pointing visitors to the deck.

The summer heat soothed Connie's skin. It was one of the simple pleasures she could appreciate with little physical effort. One by one, the gang poured onto the deck to partake in the Labor Day barbecue.

The Clarks were the first to arrive.

"What's up?" Tyrone greeted.

Karen handed Tyrone a bowl of potato salad to add to the table of delicacies.

"Where are the kids? I know Connie was looking forward to seeing them."

"Their youth group from church had a swimming party. Anything to do with water, they're in it." Karen got close to Tyrone and whispered, "How is Connie doing?"

"Not good. That's why she wanted everyone over for this cookout."

"Ah, Tyrone, I'm sorry." Karen stood silent for a moment, "You have our support."

Karen put on a brave face and approached Connie. "Don't you look summery with your straw hat. You go, girl."

"This old thing," Connie said snickering. "I'm glad you could make it. Look at your little Afro. It looks good on you."

Karen smoothed her short hair, acknowledging Connie's compliment. "My stubbles are finally growing out since I'm off chemo. I'm sticking with the natural look this time. I'm giving up on wigs."

"Well, it looks good on you. Hey, where are my girls?"

"They went to a swimming party with the church group. You know how those girls are about water. I can't keep them out the pool. They send their love."

Tina strolled into the fold, wearing a slenderizing linen dress and carrying a bowl of fruit salad. She found a spot to place it on the serving table. Johnny was at the table fixing plates for him and Karen. Tina took off her shades.

"What's going on?" he asked.

"Not much. I've been meaning to ask you about Karen. Is she really doing as well as she's been telling me?"

"Far as I know, everything is looking great. She's back in remission."

"Good, good. I wasn't sure if she was hiding the truth."

"No, she's doing well. I've been to the doctor with her. So it's true."

"Great."

"Let me take this food to Karen," he said.

"I can tell she hasn't missed any meals. Who's cooking at home, you?"

"Ha, ha, ha, funny. You know Karen's cooking. How else could we eat?"

Tina allowed a slight grin to surface. Too much more and Johnny might get the wrong idea.

"Later," Johnny told her, and walked off.

Tina fixed her plate. Karen had told her changes were happening in their marriage. Tina preferred to make her own evaluation. She hadn't seen Johnny at Floods recently. And each time she'd spoken to him over the past few months, he'd surprised her. She'd even been welcomed to their house while he was home. It was a nearly impossible feat, but could she be watching a leopard change his spots in plain view? Maybe there was hope for men yet.

An abundance of food and company kept the deck filled well into the evening. Slowly the guests trickled out, leaving

Tyrone, Connie, and their three closest friends.

"Why don't we go inside before the mosquitos flare up out here?" Tyrone suggested.

The gang moved the party from the deck to the sunroom. Tyrone made sure Connie was comfortable. Laughter filled the air. It brought Connie satisfaction seeing Tina and Johnny in the same room, let alone civilly participating in the same conversation.

"Listen up," Tyrone shouted. "Connie has something to say."

"What's up, Connie?" Tina was learning to exercise more tact but was by no means a diplomat.

"I'm dying, Tina."

"Yeah, right," Tina interjected. "Everybody's dying."

"I mean I'm expected to die soon." At times, her speech slurred.

Tina gasped and quickly shifted to a serious mode. She restated the word as if it would somehow make more sense if she heard it again. "Dying? Don't say that. What happened to your faith, Connie? You have to believe you're going to get better, just like Karen and I did. You can do it too."

"No, Tina. This is my time."

"How can you say that? How do you know?"

"Tina, I know because the pain is too much to bear."

"Can't you get back on the meds? That will take away the pain."

"It's not that simple. I got tired of taking medicine a long time ago. How would you like to take pills all day long, and the best you can hope for is a few good hours in a week? Life is not worth dragging on like this. No, Tina, this is the kind of pain only death can ease. I feel it in my soul."

"You can't give up like this."

"I'm not giving up. I'm resting in the peace that God has given me. When I got diagnosed, I asked God for strength and understanding on what to do. I prayed an entire year for healing. Then, suddenly one day I knew in my spirit my time was near. I knew my body would not recover from this tumor. God has given me two years to prepare for this. It's my time, and I'm at peace with it."

"I thought you believed in healing."

"I do, but getting healed in my physical body isn't for me, not this time."

"Forgive me, Connie, but it's not as easy for me. It hurts to see you this way. You're too young to be in this condition."

"No, I'm not, Tina. Everybody has to die."

"Right, when we're old. I don't get why God would let someone as kind as you die so young. I'm sorry, but it doesn't make sense."

"It's not about our age Tina. It's about how we've used the time God has blessed us with. It really doesn't matter how long I live, so long as I'm guaranteed a place in heaven when I leave. Do you have the same guarantee?"

Tina stammered.

"It's never too late to accept Christ so long as you're alive and breathing, but don't wait too long. I definitely know tomorrow isn't promised to anyone."

Tina threw her hands in the air.

Connie figured Tina wasn't ready to accept salvation or her condition. But she wanted to comfort Tina. "Besides, if God can let His only son, Jesus, be crucified at thirty-three, then clearly it's not in the plan for everyone to get old." Connie squeezed Tina's hand. "He has a plan for my life and nothing that's happening with me is a shock to God, and it's certainly not out of His control. The bottom line is when I accepted Christ into my heart, I also agreed to yield to His divine will and purpose for my life, from start to finish."

"You'll never get me to agree. You don't deserve to die," Tina pleaded.

"But it's my time. I've fulfilled my purpose."

"And what was that?"

"I kept the faith. Through my medical ups and downs, I have not wavered in my faith in God. Whether I got healed or not, God is still God in my life. I know He loves me and has never left me, even now."

"Ok, everyone has to die," Tina conceded, "but why does it have to be like this?"

"Because I'm not above getting sick. I'm not the only one who's ever been sick and passed on. Life goes on."

Tina wanted to understand what Connie was saying, but it hurt too much. She shook her head in denial.

"Tina, you've known me for a long time. Don't let these last few years be the only memory you have of me. We've had good times. Let that stand for something."

Connie let go of her hand and Tina made her way to one of the sofas.

"You don't even have children."

"I've lived a full life. I have no regrets. Look at all of you. You are my legacy," she said laying both hands on her chest near her heart. "I love each of you. I feel blessed for that, let alone all the other wonderful things God has done for me."

The evening had been tense. Connie's circle of loved ones were in denial. She had done what she could to prepare them for her final days, but now that her death was imminent, they weren't ready. Each wanted to cling to a little more time and a few more memories. Connie wanted to help each of them through this trying time, but she knew they had to find the way to their own acceptance. She turned to Karen. "You keep trusting in the Lord. He's going to keep you well."

It was Tina's turn. Connie passionately told her, "Girl, I love you."

Tina was shaken. She mouthed the words, I love you.

"I know your toughness is just for protection. I know how vulnerable you are inside. You are going to mess around and let God get hold of you, and that's going to be the end of that." Tina smiled past the tears.

"Johnny, you're all right with me. You have been a good friend to my Tyrone. I want to thank you. From time to time, can you please check in on him?"

He nodded in affirmation.

As much as each person in the room wanted to change the subject, Connie was determined to let this moment of sharing be a positive and unhurried time. She was content.

Tyrone agonized. Maintaining his staunch demeanor was nearly impossible. "Can I get coffee for anyone?" he inquired.

Tina jumped up and said, "Tyrone, let me get it."

"I appreciate that. In the meantime, I will get out a deck of cards. Any takers?"

Johnny and Karen leaped at the opportunity to change the tone of the evening. Tina declined. She was feeling sorry for Connie and for herself.

"Okay, that leaves the two of you, me and Connie. That's four. We can play spades." He dumped the cards out the box onto the tabletop. "Oh," Tyrone uttered. "I forgot, Connie can't see very well." He wrenched his hands. "She won't be able to read the cards." He gathered the cards together and was planning to put them away.

"No, Tyrone, don't put the cards away." Connie grabbed his arm. "Get Tina. The four of you can play. I can sit back and listen."

"You sure, honey?"

"Positive. Besides, I'm tired now. It won't be long before I have to go rest anyway."

"I don't feel like playing," Tina said.

"What, are you scared I'm going to beat you?" Johnny asked.

"Please, that's the least of my worries."

"Prove it, " Tyrone insisted wanting to lighten the mood. "Men against the women."

Tina sighed. "Fine, I'll play, but you're winning anything here. We're going to beat you bad, right, girl?" She gave Karen a high-five to seal the challenge.

Connie appreciated the people closest to her. It had been nearly four years since they'd sat together and had fun without Johnny and Tina hurling bitter words at one another. Bantering and jokes were tossed around the table and the warmth drenched the friends. Laughter reigned during hand after hand of cards being dealt. Connie relaxed. Everything was well with her loved ones.

Chapter 41

Connie experienced a rough night with strained breathing and hollow snores. Each breath sounded like her last.

It didn't take Tyrone long to wake up. He'd been sleeping lightly for the past two weeks, ever since the doctors said there was nothing else medically they could do for Connie. It was in God's hand.

"Connie, babe, wake up." Tyrone nudged her.

Her body was trembling in a seizure-like fashion. She gradually opened her eyelids, only for her gaze to rapidly scan the room without fixating on any item.

The doctor had explained to Tyrone that Connie might have a series of seizures and possibly strokes. He knew any one of them could be severe enough to kill her.

"Connie, Connie." He gently held her.

The trembling slowed, as her eyelids opened wide enough to see Tyrone.

The recent growth in her tumor severely impacted her rational abilities. When she did speak, half of it didn't make sense. He bent down so she wouldn't have to strain.

"Can you hear me?"

"Yesss," she slurred.

"I need to get you to the hospital."

"Nooo--"

"Please Connie." Tyrone agonized with teary, bloodshot eyes. "Let me take you to the hospital. I know we agreed to let you stay at home. But Connie, please forgive me. I don't think I can. It's much harder than I thought it would be."

Connie had spent the past year preparing him for this moment when she would be at this final crossroad in her life. Yet she knew Tyrone needed her now more than ever before to help him stand strong during her transition. She took his hand and placed it across her cheek.

"Sweetheart, I don't want to be in a hospital." Her words slurred, but she force them out hoping Tyrone understood. "They can't do anything for me. We know that. It would make me happy to be here at home with you. Remember, honey, that's what we talked about."

The boatload of conversations and preparation they'd discussed meant nothing. Tyrone quickly realized thinking and talking about being strong in the midst of a loved one's death was dramatically different when the time actually came. He simply wasn't ready.

"Okay, okay, I know. I'm going to get it together. Just give me a minute."

Connie stroked his face. None of her pain and suffering compared to the agony she felt knowing how brokenhearted Tyrone was. She wanted to console him. She prayed for God to give her soundness of mind to express her feelings.

"My darling, my wonderful husband, my hero, I don't want you to be sad."

Tyrone wiped the drool from her lips as she continued.

"If you're sad, I'm going to be sad. I don't want this to be your last memory of me," she explained.

Nothing else mattered so long as she was alive. But he felt selfish and guilty for wanting Connie to stay around, even if it meant having her lingering in a compromised quality of life. He considered stealing away for a few minutes to call her doctor and visiting nurse, but with a heavy heart decided against it. Having people poking and prodding Connie in the final moments was against her wishes.

Tyrone had promised to let her die peacefully at home. He dug deep within searching for strength required to honor a nearly impossible promise. With every shred of compassion and love resonating in his body, he resolved to keep his promise to the woman he adored, no matter how difficult. He held her hand as Connie drew her last breath.

Tyrone couldn't let go of her hand right away. He was numb. He laid his head on her belly and clung to what solace there was. She was finally able to rest after a heart-wrenching night of suffering and seizures. The constant pain was finally gone.

He was overcome with a sense of helplessness as close to fifteen minutes ticked by. Tyrone sat on the side of the bed gazing at his wife of eight years. He gently stroked her face, feeling the warmth lingering in her body.

Despite her immobilization, weight fluctuation, and hair loss, he always saw her as the same vibrant, mesmerizing, and humble-spirited woman he'd met in the beginning. Perhaps that was what he loved about her most. She never lost her radiant spirit even when her body and mind began to fail. He thought about the countless occasions when she could have opted to be a bitter and mean-spirited woman in light of her battle. He was certain she'd never considered it an option. To Tyrone, she was like a walking testimony and it had made him a better man.

He sat on the edge of the bed for a little while longer, desperately clinging to the futile moment. He finally felt it was time to call the visiting nurse and have her come over. Tyrone was glad the nurse had explained the process to him weeks ago, even though he hadn't been eager to hear it at the time. He was thankful the nurse would make the necessary calls to Connie's doctor, coroner, and the undertaker. Mostly, he was glad she would tidy his wife's body. Regardless of how strong Tyrone wanted to be, he knew that holding Connie's body again would be too much for him to bear.

While Tyrone was waiting for the nurse to arrive, he remembered Connie had prepared information for the nurse ahead of time. He stood and took the long, grueling walk to the desk drawer and pulled out the folder of items Connie had left. His face lit up seeing the note stuck inside.

My darling, dearest Tyrone,

I love you. I am leaving this note because I know it might be difficult for you right now. I don't want you to be sad, but I know you probably will be for a little while. But don't stay sad too long. There's no need for tears. We had a beautiful marriage. I am so blessed to have been with you these past eight years. I truly have no regrets. I am grateful to you for taking care of me while I was sick. I know you'd never say it, but you sacrificed so much for me, and I can never thank you enough. Even if you hadn't told me a million times how much you love me, I would have known it based on how you treated me and everything you did for me. You are a good man and an even better husband. So, sweetheart, in time I want you to get on with your life. Don't sit around moping about me. I'm at peace, and that's what I want for you.

Mr. Tyrone Sims, you're truly my soul mate, and I'll love you for another lifetime if it's in any way possible.

Your loving wife,

Mrs. Connie Renée Sims

He pressed the note tightly to his chest. If he could just press it hard enough, her note would leap from the page and be permanently engraved on his heart. He flipped through the other pages in the folder and found a list for the nurse and another for him. He froze for a brief moment not eager to take the next step and finally let out a deep sigh. It was just like Connie to leave him a list of things to do so he wouldn't have to figure out what to do on his own. He choked up thinking about what he was going to do without his beloved wife.

He sat at the desk, folded his arms, laid his head down, and wept. He cried two years' worth of heartache.

After nearly ten minutes, he opened the folder containing

his to-do list. The items read:

> *Tyrone, if any of this is too difficult for you to handle right now, let Johnny and Karen know. I've already spoken to them, and they're going to help you do · whatever needs to be done. You won't be alone.*

1. *Call the nurse. She'll make the calls for you, including the one to Dr. Moseley (their phone numbers are on the next page).*
2. *Call Johnny and Karen, because I don't want you to be alone. Give them my love.*
3. *Call Tina next, because she'll have a fit if she has to find out any other way. Tell her I love her too.*
4. *Whenever you feel up to it, call my cousin Dee. She'll contact the rest of my family for you.*
5. *Perhaps Karen can call my sorority sister Dorothy. Once somebody gets in touch with her, she will let the rest of my sorority know. You know that whatever help you need, my sorors will be there for you.*
6. *See if Karen can call Pastor Lane to let him know.*
7. *When Karen arrives, give her the instructions on page four. She agreed to coordinate the funeral with my cousins, Bonnie and Dee, so you won't have to.*
8. *Don't forget to say a prayer. You're going to need God to help you get beyond this. Selfishly, I must admit that I'm the fortunate one. It would have been so hard for me if you had gone first. I'm not as strong as you are. I couldn't have imagined living without you. Still, I want you to be okay, and you will be.*
9. *After the nurse gets there, I want you to get something to eat. Then I want you to get dressed and get out the house for a while. Go for a walk, a drive, or anything which will help you deal with this moment. Push yourself if you have to, but please go out. It won't do*

you any good to just sit there moping.

I'm eternally grateful for your love and friendship. I might not have lived as long as other people, but I sure did live well. Every day with you was a dream. Be at peace my hunk of a man.

Goodbye my love, and I look forward to seeing you again. With all my love. -- C

Tears mounted as he remembered his wife. He laid his list on top of the folder and went to the phone to call the Clarks. It was three-thirty in the morning, but he dialed the number without hesitation. Johnny and Karen were family. They'd understand.

The phone rang and neither rolled over immediately to pick it up.

"You have reached the Clarks. To leave a message for Johnny, press one, for Karen press two..." was the only voice Tyrone heard.

Johnny was roused, but not in time to get the call before it went into voice mail.

Of the calls on his list, this was the one Tyrone needed to make but dreaded. He tapped the reset button on his phone and then pressed redial.

Johnny glanced at the clock when the phone rang again. He figured either someone was crazy for calling so early or it was urgent. He grabbed the phone with a tinge of sharpness and stirred up an audible greeting.

"Hey, partner."

'Tyrone--" Johnny popped up in the bed, ready to hear undesired news.

"Yeah, buddy," Tyrone said, rubbing his hand across his face, "it's me." He paused before sharing the news.

Johnny waited patiently.

"She's gone."

Johnny flung both feet onto the floor. "I'm sorry, man. What can I do to help?"

"Nothing right now. I have a list of calls Connie left for me to make." He chuckled. "Man, can you believe she left me a honey-do list?" He put every effort forward to squeak out a little humor.

Both men laughed.

Tyrone couldn't forget how often they'd joked about the list of items Connie had given him. Each list started off with the heading *Honey, can you*...It wasn't long before Tyrone's laughter morphed into crying.

"I can't believe she's gone, Johnny. Connie hung in there longer than many thought she would, she's gone now. What am I going to do without her?"

"It's going to be hard but you'll get through this."

Karen awakened and listened in without disrupting the conversation. She figured Tyrone had to lament with Johnny more than he needed to hear from her. She rubbed Johnny's arm to let him know she was awake and listening.

"It's harder than I thought, partner. Even though she was sick for two years, I wasn't ready for her to go."

"I don't think you can ever be ready for something like that."

"I guess not. I remember how often she was suffering in pain and there wasn't any relief. That was brutal for her and for me to watch. I tell you, man, it was tough with Connie being too sick to function independently, but too coherent to be hospitalized. Being in limbo was a killer."

"I hear you man." Johnny hadn't been in the exact situation as Tyrone but came close enough during Karen's ordeal to understood the swirling emotions Tyrone was dealing with.

"Many nights I thought it would be better for her to pass and be done with the suffering rather than stay here with constant pain and sleepless nights. I even thought a part of me would be relieved when she either got better or died." He contemplated the notion in momentary silence. "I was wrong. I would rather have had her with me, sick as she was, than to be without her now."

Johnny provided a listening ear, with a few agreements tossed in to let Tyrone know he was there. His friend wasn't looking for advice. Tyrone just needed a place to empty out the grief in his heart.

"I should have done more for her."

"No, you can't say that. You did everything humanly possible for Connie, and she knew it. You went farther and longer than most could have."

"Yeah, but there were times when I was drained trying to take care of her, keeping up with work and everything else. I'm not going to lie, man. It was hard."

"I know the feeling."

"Yeah, well, I feel terrible about it," Tyrone stated.

"Don't. It's like you told me months ago, we're human. There's only so much we can do."

The doorbell sounded, followed by a banging knock that could be heard faintly in the bedroom. Tyrone stood up.

"Hey, Johnny, that's the visiting nurse or coroner at the door. I have to answer it."

"All right. Karen and I will be over in a little bit."

"No need. It's too early in the morning for you and Karen to be coming out."

Johnny ignored his comment and reconfirmed, "We'll see you within the hour."

"Okay, chief. Thanks. Your support means a lot to me."

The doorbell rang again. This time Tyrone hustled to the door yelling, "I'm on my way. Just a minute."

Chapter 42

A frigid Michigan wind whisked over the collage of orange, brown, and yellow leaves which dangled from the supporting limbs. Some couldn't withstand the pressure and detached from their life source, fluttering to their demise. Those that endured were a vibrant display of beauty.

It was Karen's favorite time of the year. The leaves had always caught her attention, but they didn't have much other meaning before. She had begun to see life in its simplicity following her relapse of cancer in the spring. She sat on the park bench reading a book the marriage counselor recommended. It was nippy out, but the brisk air felt tranquil. She was glad to be alive.

She looked up from the book and gazed into the distance. She often reminisced about her friend. Certain smells, songs, or places would prompt a memory without warning. She took the knuckle of her index finger and brushed away the tears forming. It had been barely two months since Connie passed. Adjusting to her being gone, someone who had been a sister, would take time. The best Karen could hope for was to reach a point where she could reflect on memories of Connie without falling apart. She picked up her book and continued reading.

"Oh, my goodness." Suddenly Karen sprung from the bench, anxiously grabbing her belongings. It dawned on her that their new housekeeper was scheduled for two o'clock.

It didn't take long zooming to 712 Morning Glory Circle. The housekeeper stood in the driveway, as Karen anticipated. She pulled in and hopped out. "I apologize for being late. I lost track of time."

"No problem. I've only been here a few minutes."

"Good. Come on in, Leslie, and I'll show you around."

"By the way, you were right. This is the only house in the area with the tall black wrought iron fence. That made it easy to find. Your directions were perfect."

Karen waited for the garage door to open, revealing a few boxes and a workbench. "Come on. I'll take you in this way."

"A three and a half car garage—nice."

"It was nice when we had three cars. We sold one."

"Must be nice to have this much space."

Karen grinned. "Actually, this house is too big. That's why we're moving to a smaller house in Southfield."

"I can't imagine giving up this big beautiful place."

"Huh, don't get me wrong. This house has been wonderful for my family, but it really is more house than we need. My husband and I decided less is more. Less house, less upkeep, and less expenses. That means less stress and less work."

"I wish you could convince my husband to do the same for us. It seems like the more we work and accumulate, the more he wants. He's never satisfied," Leslie stated.

"Trust me, we've been there. We dug ourselves into a big hole. Thank God we finally woke up and changed."

"Well, maybe my husband needs to get a dose of whatever it was that caused you and your husband to change."

Karen smirked and told Leslie, "No," shaking her head. "I don't think he wants to go through what we've gone through." Karen gave Leslie a peaceful and cheerful look. "Just pray that you and your husband will have God's wisdom. There are some lessons you'd rather not have to learn the hard way, like we did. Come on, let me show you around."

Getting to this mindset had been very costly, financially, spiritually, physically, and emotionally, but Karen didn't feel led to share her journey with Leslie, at least not yet.

*　　*　　*

Johnny transferred a mountain of work to his assistant. His goal was to get down to one late night a week and reduce travel to the point where he'd be away from home a max of five nights per month. He'd learned how much of a difference his presence made with the girls. He was also learning how fulfilling it was being an involved father.

"Excuse me," Sonja interrupted. "Mr. Richter on line one."

"I'll take it. Please close my door?" Johnny pressed line one, not expecting a call from the CEO. "Al, what's cooking?"

"What's cooking are your second and third quarter numbers. I don't know how you did it. Your production levels were twenty percent over plan with a thirty-five percent increase in quality levels. Congratulations, big guy."

"Thanks, but it wasn't totally my doing. I have an entire staff of people who made it happen, like Deon and DeWayne."

"There's no doubt you have a solid team, and that's also to your credit. John, the bottom line is that you got the job done with limited resources. You continue to be the kind of leader Tenner Automotive needs. In light of your numbers, I have some exciting news. I preferred telling you in person, but there's no way I can get out of this meeting in New York with the Wall Street analysts. But please let me thank you for your efforts and be the first to congratulate you in your new role as chief officer of manufacturing."

"Chief? Are you talking about a promotion?"

"I sure am. I'm taking the entire production operation off my plate and handing it over to you. You've proven that you can handle this level of responsibility."

"I don't know what to say."

"The title comes with a two hundred thousand dollar annual salary increase with ten thousand additional shares of stock. The stock is currently trading around forty dollars a share. Hopefully it will still be worth something after I finish throwing my two cents in with the analyst." Al chuckled.

Johnny took a deep breath. He was in awe. Less than a year ago he'd have jumped at the money, power, recognition, and responsibility. That was when getting ahead meant everything. Instead, Johnny reflected on the problems he and Karen had battled. Through sickness and marital disputes, money hadn't bought him any extra happiness or Karen any more health. He shook his head, acknowledging the peace he was now enjoying hadn't cost a dime. He had reevaluated what was truly important. Johnny wasn't quick to accept. A few factors had to be considered, like the resulting workload. Besides, he was winding down at work, not gearing up.

"So what do you say?"

"I certainly wasn't expecting a promotion. This is quite a shock. Thank you. This is huge. Uhm, I'll need some time before accepting the role. You okay with that."

"Of course, and I can address any questions you have when I get back in the office Monday. Have Tammy put you on my schedule, and we'll talk then. I want to move quickly on this. I want you transitioned into the new position in plenty of time to get our projections together for next year."

"Will do. Thanks again, and have a safe trip back."

"You've earned it. I'll see you Monday."

Johnny hit the button that released the speakerphone. He sat back, twirled his pen, and pondered the promotion. He was in an awkward position. He couldn't ignore the impact on his family if he took the offer. But turning down a promotion would be damaging to his career, especially the coveted chief officer roles. He knew several peers who declined promotions and ended up blackballed and labeled as a non-team player. In each case the men were slowly phased out of their jobs and the company. After being with Tenner Automotive for over eighteen years, he didn't want to look for another job. There might be an alternative. He called Karen to share the news.

Karen was giving Leslie a tour of the house and going over what she wanted cleaned before the realtor put the house on the market. She heard the phone.

"Excuse me." She grabbed the cordless phone from the kitchen to find Johnny on the other end. "Hey, I'm showing the cleaning lady around."

"Oh, I forgot she was coming. Don't forget to ask if she can clean for us after we move to Southfield."

"Oh, trust me, I won't forget. So how's your day going?"

"Al called me a few minutes ago. He offered me a promotion to chief officer with an extra two hundred thousand, plus stock valued around four hundred thousand dollars."

"Really?"

"Yep, how's that for a surprise?"

"What did you tell him?"

"I haven't told him anything yet. I want to think it over and talk with you first."

"How do you feel about it?"

"To tell you the truth, it sounds perfect. The catch is that it requires more work and responsibility than I want on my plate. These past few months have been a dream for me. I'm done with living at the office."

"So are you thinking about turning it down?"

"I don't know." He rubbed his head. "That might be hard to do. Maybe I can use about seventy-five percent of the salary increase to hire a few more assistants. With the extra help, I can keep my workload at a reasonable level. And I'll still end up with a nice raise plus two additional staff members without impacting my operating budget."

"That sounds pretty good, right?" Karen replied.

"It sounds better and better the more I think about it. After everything is said and done, I'll still end up with at least four thousand more a month. That's not bad," he said filled with pride.

"We could use the extra money," Karen said.

"You go that right. With the money we're saving each month by getting rid of the car and downsizing into a smaller house, we should be in good shape. When I think about it, this is a real blessing."

"You're right. What about the stock options?"

"Shoot, I'm not crazy. The stock is mine. I want to retire early, and it will go a long way toward helping the cause."

"This is great news."

"I think so. I have to present my plan to Al, and we'll see what happens." Johnny aimlessly pushed a pen across the top of his desk. "By the way, I'm packing up early this afternoon. I'd like to meet with Tyrone this evening, if it's okay."

"Sure and give him my love. Are you going to Floods?" Karen briefly reflected on other times she'd gotten sick. Johnny would drop his shenanigans and rush to her side. Each time she accepted him. Shortly after the crisis was over he'd return to his watering hole, Floods, and pick up a few stray women. Four years, round and round they went with the scenario like their dog chasing his tail.

"Oh, no. I've paid my dues at Floods. It's time to move on. We might catch a game of pool somewhere."

"Go ahead. I'll be fine. Tina's coming by later to tell me about this guy she's seeing. She's finally getting serious with someone since her divorce. Can you believe it?"

Johnny chuckled and said, "That ought to keep you busy. Tell her I said to go easy on the guy."

Karen snickered. She prepared to disconnect. "I almost forgot. The counseling session needs to be changed from next Tuesday to Wednesday at five-thirty P.M. so that my appointment with Dr. Costas can take the Tuesday slot. Will those times work for you?"

Without checking his schedule Johnny quickly answered, "I'll make them work. Go ahead and confirm both."

"You sure?"

"Definitely." Their past flashed before him. He and Karen got close during her illnesses. He was supportive and she was receptive. After the battle was over, intimacy was great. But it wasn't long before she would lose sexual interest and eventually cut him off. He would plead with her, each time less and less, before heading to Floods and finding a few comforting female friends. Johnny promised himself he was done with the draining cycle. This time was different. "Our family comes before my job. I can get another job. I can't get another you."

Karen beamed profusely. "Ah, you're making me blush." She was more than satisfied having experienced a renewed chemistry between them which had previously vanished. It was refreshing being in sync. She was soaring high like a butterfly that had finally gotten some wind under its wings. "Have fun with Tyrone, and I'll see you later."

An aroma of passion and interest drenched Johnny. It was less of what Karen said and more of how she spoke to him, with respect and trust. Her warmth was reassuring and the relationship benefited. They'd appreciated more intimacy in the last four months than in the past four years. He didn't know a lot about having God in his life, but from what he could tell, it was already better than what he had before.

"I love you, Karen," he uttered without hesitation.

"I love you more."

Reading Guide

Now that you have read **No Regrets,** consider the following.

1. What are the red flags/warning signs associated with a marriage headed for disaster? What signs did the Clarks have? What could Karen or Johnny have done sooner?
2. Tina and Connie differed on what Karen should do. Tina said leave Johnny. Connie said work it out. Do you agree with either? What's your advice?
3. Close friends share secrets, including marriage "stuff." Is there anything that should be kept in strict confidence, not to be shared outside the relationship with even close friends and family? Did Karen overshare with Tina?
4. How do you shield children from issues occurring with their parents? How do you keep them from feeling like they have to take sides? What could Karen have done to improve the relationship with Johnny and John Erick?
5. Can a married woman like Karen seek marital advice from a single person like Tina?
6. How and when do you forgive a loved one for hurting you? Is there a time when enough is enough? Are there conditions where you can't/won't forgive? Can you forgive without forgetting? Should Karen forgive Johnny for seeing another woman?
7. Is Karen an innocent victim? How did she contribute to the marital breakdown?
8. How do you get God involved with a troubled marriage or tough financial times?
9. How do you handle a close friend who cares for you but envies you and is quick to share hurtful information?
10. Can mates be compatible if they don't have the same edu-

cational, professional, or religious aspirations? How did Karen's religion and Johnny's career impact their union?

11. How much did the Clark's financial problems add to their marital strife? What could the Clarks have changed?

12. If a person is mean, nasty, whiny, or clingy during their illness, how tolerant should the caregiver or friend be? Is there a limit? Did Karen push Johnny to a limit?

13. What was it about Big Mama that enabled her to befriend Johnny in the hospital, even after he was so rude?

14. Was Connie in denial or acting in faith about her illness?

15. Can men like Tyrone and Johnny change? Do you think Tyrone will remarry?

16. How do you check for breast cancer? Karen had cancer in her early 30s, yet mammograms aren't recommended until 40 or 50. How early should you have one if there's no family history of breast cancer?

17. What does the dusty Bible metaphor on page 1 represent?

Acknowledgements

Thank you Lord for this book idea and for the literary gift you've entrusted to me. I thank you for surrounding me with so many supportive, helpful, and encouraging people. I know for sure that none of us show up in this world on our own. We are all linked to somebody, and many times the support from others is the only way to realize some accomplishments. God blessed me with a host of people who've each played a special role in helping me to get my books into the hands of my dedicated readers. I am honored and humbled by each of you.

Thanks to my hubby, moms (Fannie & Jeri), my girls (TJ & Azha), nieces, nephews, siblings, godchildren, and fathers who have gone on to glory. I'm grateful for my Tennin, Haley, Moorman, Glass, Thomas, Rome families, my extended circle, friends, colleagues, sister-friends, spiritual parents, sorority sisters, sisters and brothers in Christ, and a countless number of those in the literary arena: booksellers, media contacts, and vendors. I extend a heartfelt shout out to my cousin Kimberla Roby just for being special to me, Audrey Williams for proofreading, and to iMarketing PR/Good Book Promoters for the cover design.

Last, but most certainly not least, I acknowledge you, my cherished readers. My writing is for you, and I wish the best for each of you. I pray you come to know the purpose for which you were created and every aspect of your calling will be fulfilled to the glory of God. May you be blessed abundantly as you use your talents and gifts. You're special, and there's no one on earth exactly like you. Be encouraged and motivated.

Author's Note

Dear Readers:

Thank you for reading **No Regrets.** I hope you enjoyed the story. While it is meant to entertain and encourage, I hope the topic also enlightens you about breast cancer. There is a war against all forms of cancer, and we have the power to dramatically improve our ability to win by equipping ourselves with knowledge and increased awareness. Visit your local library, health care provider, other trusted sources and online sites for more information. Preventive care and early detection makes a difference.

I look forward to you reading my other books, joining my mailing list, dropping me a note, or posting an online review for *No Regrets*. You can also reach me by visiting my web site, liking my Author Patricia Haley fan page or friending me on Facebook at Patricia Haley-Glass.

As always, thank you for the support. Keep reading, and be blessed.

www.patriciahaley.com

Made in the USA
Monee, IL
05 October 2020